DELICIOUS and SUSPICIOUS

Riley Adams

BERKLEY PRIME CRIME, NEW YORK

THE BERKLEY PUBLISHING GROUP
Published by the Penguin Group
Penguin Group (USA) Inc.
375 Hudson Street, New York, New York 10014, USA
Penguin Group (Canada), 90 Eglinton Avenue East, Suite 700, Toronto, Ontario M4P 2Y3, Canada
(a division of Pearson Penguin Canada Inc.)
Penguin Books Ltd., 80 Strand, London WC2R 0RL, England
Penguin Group Ireland, 25 St. Stephen's Green, Dublin 2, Ireland (a division of Penguin Books Ltd.)
Penguin Group (Australia), 250 Camberwell Road, Camberwell, Victoria 3124, Australia
(a division of Pearson Australia Group Pty. Ltd.)
Penguin Books India Pvt. Ltd., 11 Community Centre, Panchsheel Park, New Delhi—110 017, India
Penguin Group (NZ), 67 Apollo Drive, Rosedale, North Shore 0632, New Zealand
(a division of Pearson New Zealand Ltd.)
Penguin Books (South Africa) (Pty.) Ltd., 24 Sturdee Avenue, Rosebank, Johannesburg 2196,
South Africa

Penguin Books Ltd., Registered Offices: 80 Strand, London WC2R 0RL, England

This is a work of fiction. Names, characters, places, and incidents either are the product of the author's imagination or are used fictitiously, and any resemblance to actual persons, living or dead, business establishments, events, or locales is entirely coincidental. The publisher does not have any control over and does not assume any responsibility for author or third-party websites or their content.

PUBLISHER'S NOTE: The recipes contained in this book are to be followed exactly as written. The publisher is not responsible for your specific health or allergy needs that may require medical supervision. The publisher is not responsible for any adverse reactions to the recipes contained in this book.

DELICIOUS AND SUSPICIOUS

A Berkley Prime Crime Book / published by arrangement with the author

PRINTING HISTORY
Berkley Prime Crime mass-market edition / July 2010

Copyright © 2010 by Penguin Group (USA) Inc.
Cover illustration by Hugh Syme.
Cover design by Annette Fiore Defex.
Interior text design by Laura K. Corless.

ISBN: 978-0-425-23553-9

BERKLEY® PRIME CRIME
Berkley Prime Crime Books are published by The Berkley Publishing Group,
a division of Penguin Group (USA) Inc.,
375 Hudson Street, New York, New York 10014.
BERKLEY® PRIME CRIME and the PRIME CRIME logo are trademarks of Penguin Group
(USA) Inc.

PRINTED IN THE UNITED STATES OF AMERICA

10 9 8 7 6 5 4 3 2

Murder in Memphis

Lulu felt queasy. She was not a fan of scenes and there had been far too many over the past twenty-four hours.

Tony thumped his fist on the door. "Rebecca!" he bellowed. "Rebecca! I want to talk to you."

Tony tried the door, but of course it was locked. He thumped loudly on her door again.

"You don't think," asked Lulu, "she killed herself, do you?"

"With poison? No way. If she'd planned it, she'd want to be found tucked in her bed, looking like Sleeping Beauty. Besides, being banned from Aunt Pat's wouldn't have made her suicidal, you know."

"When you put it that way, it does sound a little silly."

Ten minutes later Tony was back with the manager and one of the hotel's security men. The manager inserted a master key and opened the door a crack. "Miss Adrian?" He waited, listening hard, but hearing no response. He pushed the door open farther. "Miss Adrian?"

He stepped into the room, then backed up a step. The security man pushed them back into the hall, but Lulu was able to see a sprawled figure on the floor of the room. Rebecca Adrian—quite obviously dead.

◇◇◇◇◇◇◇

For my family, with love.

Acknowledgments

Special thanks to Ann and John Haire for their warm hospitality, helpful information, and for so generously introducing me to their hometown of Memphis.

My appreciation and thanks to my editor, Emily Beth Rapoport, for her enthusiasm and hard work.

My sincere thanks to my agent, Ellen Pepus, for her thoughtful professional advice.

Thanks to Tom and Dottie Craig for all their help during my visit to Memphis.

To Henry and Beth Spann for being careful first readers.

Thanks to Mary and Jed Peterson and Douglas and Jennings Boone for all their support.

Thanks for the encouragement and inspiration from the online community of writers.

And last but not least, to my husband, Coleman, and children Riley and Elizabeth Ruth for their constant encouragement and love.

Chapter

1

Memphis, Tennessee, is a little bit of heaven in the springtime. The azalea bushes burst with blooms, magnolias perfume the air, and daffodils nod sassily in the breeze. Children scamper right down the middle of the street, with their scolding mamas hustling after them. Folks pull leashes from the closet and take Buddy and Princess for a little stroll.

The barbeque business goes into full swing. It's never out of season, mind you. But in the springtime, it's God's gift. Order your barbeque to go and eat it in W.C. Handy Park on Beale Street. Listen to some live blues music, realize how good you have it to be in Memphis in the spring, and hand out a couple dollars to the street musicians who are serenading you.

And right there on Beale Street, you can find the reigning queen of the barbequing art, Lulu Taylor. She's not back in the kitchen anymore, of course. You'll find her holding court in the dining room, cutting up with some customers, and buttering up others.

◇◇◇◇◇◇◇◇◇◇

"Get a load of this," breathed Ben to his wife Sara. He steered her to the heavy wooden door of the back-room office of Aunt Pat's. Sara peeped around the door. "Mother's really flipped her wig this time."

Ben's mother, Lulu, perched behind the desk and beamed out at empty space like it was her dearest friend. She brandished, oddly enough for the office, a pair of tongs.

"Friends," she said earnestly. "Great barbeque is made with great tools. Your tongs and spatula need to be nice and long so you won't burn yourself." She sadly shook her head at the empty air again, "I'd hate for my friends to burn themselves." At that moment, the entire effect was destroyed when the hairpin she'd carefully stuck in the hair piled up on top of her head fell out. Her white hair cascaded down. "Shoot!"

Sara walked in the office. A slow smile spread over her good-natured, freckled face. "Having a wardrobe malfunction, Lulu? And by the way . . . what exactly are you doing?"

"I'm practicing for my new Food Network show, naturally. This qualifies as more of a coiffure malfunction, I think." She wound the hair up onto the top of her head again. "I'm going to have to figure out something to do with this hair of mine. Got to be ready for my close-up, you know."

Ben fingered his mustache as he absorbed the notion of a close-up. The mustache was a recent addition to his features—a new hairstyle to make the most of his few remaining follicles. Unfortunately, the styling necessary to give the illusion of hair on top of his head resulted in a helmetlike effect. Ben had fancied that the mustache might make him look like Tom Selleck. He had sadly come to terms with the reality of looking a lot more like Captain Kangaroo.

Ben said, "But, Mama, this *isn't* Food Network coming. Don't you remember? It's that *other* cable food channel."

Lulu said, "Shoot! I keep forgetting. The Cooking Channel is the name of it, that's right. Ben, we have to be *careful*. We've got to act like the Cooking Channel is the only cable station out there! 'Cause you know they feel bad having to compete against Food Network . . . they've only been around for a little over a year now, and they're small potatoes next to them."

"Besides, as far as I'm aware, we have a Cooking Channel *scout* coming here today. And the scout is *scouting* for the best barbeque in Memphis." He turned to his wife. "Sara, have you heard anything about a TV show? Why am I always kept in the dark?"

"Smarty-pants," said Lulu. "I haven't got the show yet, no. But with Paula Deen such a success, they might want someone like me on contract." She stretched out her fingers and looked at them, critically. "I need big diamonds."

"Pardon?"

"My wardrobe malfunction is the complete and total lack of diamonds. Paula's just dripping with them, you know. Even keeps them on when she's squishing up ground beef."

"You *have* big diamonds? Why the heck am I slaving every day over a fiery pit, then, if we're so loaded?"

Lulu leveled a quelling look at her son. "I don't have them yet, no. But with a major contract, I could buy myself some. Or maybe," she added vaguely, "the wardrobe department provides them. Just to use during the shows, of course."

Ben mouthed, "She's lost it" to Sara. He was going to have to break it to Lulu that the Cooking Channel wardrobe department likely didn't include Harry Winston jewelry.

"I think you'd have better luck buying yourself some diamonds, Mother."

"And I should do that *how*?"

"You guess every puzzle on *Wheel of Fortune*. Maybe you should go on the program and win yourself some big money."

"California is on the other side of the country, Ben. I can't just pop over there, buy some vowels, and win big money. Plus, there's a lot of dumb luck involved, too. That's a big wheel to spin. I could hit 'lose a turn' or 'bankrupt' every time. I might not even have the power to spin it all the way around." But Ben's suggestion had clearly given Lulu ideas. Already her mental wheels spun as she tried to calculate how she might get to California.

Her ruminations were interrupted by her younger son, Seb's, arrival in the office. "All right—out, out," he said, motioning to the office door. "I've got to get to work. Time for me to cook the books. Just kidding," he added in response to Ben's menacing look. "You take care of the pork. I'll crunch the numbers."

"Hey, Seb, how about that hunting trip we keep talking about?" asked Ben. "Haven't you gotten the hunting bug yet?"

Seb sighed. He knew the kind of bugs he associated with hunting. Mosquitoes and chiggers.

Ben continued, "You've been telling me for the last couple of weeks you're ready to go. I want to throw the Labs in the truck and head out into the country." He looked wistful. "Subdue nature for a little while."

Seb grinned. "Just your Labradors get to go subdue nature? What about your other dog?"

A cloud passed over Ben's face. Lulu hid a smile.

"What's her name? Yvette?"

Ben mumbled something. Sara moved over and put a supportive arm around him.

"What was that? Oh, right. Babette. I'm sure Babette

would love to hunt something with you. Might want to take off her jewelry first, of course. And her princess sweater."

"You know that's Coco's dog!"

"I see . . . blame it on your little girl! But *we* know who found the dog and laid down the money. And I don't think it was a nine-year-old."

Ben glowered. "If you don't want to go hunting, just say so."

"All in good time, brother," said Seb. This hunting trip was going to be put off as long as possible. He'd spent enough time in New York to lose interest in the sweaty, remote, silent activity that hunting in the South entailed. The door chime sounded again, and Seb craned his neck around the office door. "Who is *that*?" Lulu peeped around the door, too. Seb did a double take and seemed to peer closer at the visitor, but by that time, Lulu's mind was spinning.

"That" was a sophisticated blonde dressed in casual clothes that probably cost a whole lot more than Lulu's dressy stuff. "Got to be the Cooking Channel scout," Lulu hissed. She scurried to the mirror. "I *knew* I should have worn my power suit today!"

"Power suit?" murmured Sara.

"From her former life as a day trader. Didn't you know?" asked Ben, straight-faced.

His twins Coco and Ella Beth rushed into the small office. "What's going on?" demanded Ella Beth. "Where did everybody go?"

"You *do* realize," said Coco, who was nine going on twenty-one, "that the dining room is chock-full of people?"

"Don't be sassy," said Sara crossly. But Coco's pronouncement had the desired effect.

"Well?" bellowed Lulu. "What's keeping everybody?

We better jump into action and start dealing out the lunch specials." Lulu peered around the door. "Oh Lord, the dining room's completely full of hungry customers. What's she going to think about the service?"

Sara propelled her toward the door. "Not a thing. She's going to think this barbeque is so darn tasty that the whole town is beating down our door to get in here and eat some. And she'll be right."

Ben raced to the kitchen to work his magic on the barbeque, Sara grabbed an order pad and pencil and tied an apron around her waist, and Lulu headed to the dining room for a visit with their guests.

The smell of the seasoned pork cooking in the pit and the sweet aroma of the baked beans permeating the restaurant was enough to make your mouth water.

The customers felt more like guests to Lulu, maybe because they came so often they were now all friends to her.

Coco was right; the dining room was jam-packed, even the barstools. Lulu walked in to a chorus of greetings, her small frame belying the fact that she had eaten barbeque every single day of her adult life. Lulu motioned to the hostess that she would be greeting this particular guest.

The sophisticated blonde finally took off her large sunglasses and looked around the dim restaurant. A muscular man with a shock of black hair and a warm smile, lugging a bag of camera equipment, stood beside her. "Welcome to Aunt Pat's!" said Lulu. "Are you dining in or taking out?"

A perfunctory smile spread across the woman's pretty face, although it didn't reach her violet eyes. "Dining in. But not really dining, just sitting." She glanced around. "It looks busy, though."

"Oh, it'll settle down in a minute. There should be a table opening up soon."

"I can wait," she said, and she sat down on the worn wooden bench near the door.

Lulu peered closely at the woman. "Are you, by any chance, the Cooking Channel scout?"

"Very perceptive of you," she said dryly and smoothed out invisible wrinkles in her slacks. "I'm Rebecca Adrian, Cooking Channel. I suppose I stand out."

"Of course not," said Lulu. "But we've been expecting you, you know." She gave her a sweet smile. "Besides, honey, the camera man is a dead giveaway."

"Oh. Right."

"I have the perfect place for you to sit down, Miss Adrian. Right over with some of my friends. I think you might enjoy their company."

"I'm not going to eat today, Mrs. Taylor. I'm here to get some ideas for presenting the story, and Tony will do a light and sound check. But I'll have a seat, sure. Talking to customers might help me find an angle."

Tony, the camera man, smiled to see hard-nosed Rebecca Adrian being led off by Lulu Taylor. She wasn't known for her ability to act on suggestions. This story might be more fun than he'd thought it would be. His big face split into a smile as the hostess offered him a barbeque plate, gratis. This was his kind of assignment.

In fact, Lulu was in the mood for a little something herself. Sara, who seemed to have a waitress's second sense about these things, raised her eyebrows inquiringly. "Ribs and some beans?" she asked as she passed by.

"Please."

Rebecca Adrian coolly summed up Lulu Taylor as she followed the woman across the crowded restaurant. She saw white hair tucked in a demure bun, a gentle smile, and a flower-print cotton dress.

Many a hapless person had been lulled into thinking Lulu was a sweet little old lady. Nothing could be further from the truth. Nice, yes. Sweet, no. And the "little" part had only happened in the last ten years when she shrank down from her substantial height like the melting witch in *The Wizard of Oz*.

Unfortunately for her, Rebecca Adrian was one of those less-perceptive types who would make the fatal mistake of underestimating Lulu.

Rebecca's gaze swept quickly across the restaurant, taking in the large booths topped with red and white checkered tablecloths. The restaurant must be ancient, she thought. She squinted at the old brick walls—what she could see of them, anyway. They were jam-packed with photographs of smiling faces, school pennants, and what appeared to be autographed menus.

"Mind if we join you for lunch today?" Lulu asked her regular customer, Susan Meredith.

"Oh Lord, *please* take a seat," said Susan, scooting over. "I felt bad about hogging the whole booth for myself. There weren't this many people when I came in." A wry look spread across her pretty face. "If only I could funnel this many folks into the gallery."

Lulu looked startled. "Now, I thought you were having some luck with business lately, honey. You said they were beating a path to your door."

"I wish they were beating a path to the cash register, though. They might be coming in, but they're not spending enough time in there to do any buying."

Lulu gave Susan's offhand remark the same grave consideration she gave to most things. "Maybe you should have an open house night. Not like a regular show. I could cater it for you . . . barbeque, slaw, and beans?"

"Don't forget the sweet tea."

"Oh, we do have some great tea. Have to, since the corn bread muffins are so spicy."

"But delicious."

"Are you absorbing this great propaganda?" Lulu elbowed Rebecca Adrian, who looked startled. Since the conversation had had nothing to do with her, she'd tuned it out. In fact, she was secretly annoyed. Usually she was treated more as a visiting rock star and flattered and spoiled by owners. And here was Lulu Taylor doing a marketing analysis for this tunic-wearing, hippie customer.

Lulu's attention swung back to Rebecca. Lulu spoke, widening her clear, gray blue eyes. "You must know so many people. Right? In the industry, I mean."

Rebecca smirked. This was more like her usual experience. "Sure. I'm out a lot. I run into the same people all the time."

"Not just food people? Oh, it's hard to find the right words sometimes." Lulu paused as if collecting thoughts that were flying off like bits of dandelion. "Not just restaurant owners and chefs?"

Rebecca was losing patience. "No. I have tons of contacts in New York." Rebecca dropped names of all the different people she knew in New York. She wasn't even dropping them—more like smacking her audience upside the head with them. Lulu, thought Susan, actually seemed to be attentively listening to her drivel.

Rebecca blathered on, "You see, I never know where the next story will come from. So I know traders, socialites, magazine editors, gallery owners . . ." She stopped at Lulu's frantically wagging finger.

"Perfect. Just perfect," said Lulu, pushing up from the booth and rushing away.

Demented, thought Rebecca.

Lulu grabbed Sara's arm, pulling her toward the booth.

She took Sara's pad and pencil from her and motioned for her to sit down. "This is your next big story." Rebecca blinked at her. "Sara is," said Lulu impatiently, "my daughter-in-law."

"She sets the waitressing world on fire?" asked Rebecca in a dry voice.

"*Because*," said Lulu, narrowing her eyes at Rebecca, "she's the best artist you've ever seen. And she needs some contacts in the art world. I'm sure you won't mind helping her out, seeing as how you have so many New York contacts." Lulu swept off regally, taking orders at the next table.

Sara's broad face flushed at the unexpected interview, but nobody could blame her for being slow on the uptake. She slid into the booth across from Rebecca.

Rebecca summed her up with a glance and found Sara completely lacking in star quality. It was true that Sara wasn't exactly model thin, although her weight looked good on her bigger frame. Like her friend Susan, Sara had cultivated an offbeat look, with curly, strawberry-blond hair that swung below her shoulders.

Sitting with friends had its advantages. It was a good thing because Sara wasn't sure exactly what to say after Lulu's pronouncement. Susan Meredith jumped in. "I could display some of your things in Southern Accents tomorrow for Miss Adrian to see. I've been trying," she said pointedly, "to get her to do a show for ages."

A bored expression wafted over Rebecca Adrian's face. She opened her mouth to issue a cutting evasion when a croaky, deep voice from behind her chimed in. The voice was so resonant, she jumped and clamped her mouth shut again.

"Who is that little woman?" The voice belonged to Big Ben, an Aunt Pat's regular, who was deaf as a post. "What's going on?"

Another loud, old voice said, "She's that food scout from the TV network. Sara wants the woman to get her contacts for her art."

"A food scout? You tellin' me that tee-tiny thing *eats*?" His choking guffaw hinted at a dire need for CPR. "Well, she's a fool if she doesn't help out," Big Ben barked. "The woman would be lucky to discover Sara." Big Ben had an unfortunate habit of bellowing out private observations. He was usually hushed quickly. No one moved to hush him this time.

Rebecca Adrian's face took on a petulant look. "All right," she said grudgingly, "I'll drop by your gallery tomorrow."

"It's right down the street on Second," said Susan, sliding out of the booth. "I'd better run, then. It takes a lot to set up a show in a day."

Lulu tapped Sara on the shoulder. "We've got you covered with waitressing. Dina came in because she saw the Cooking Channel's *Foodmobile* truck at a parking meter, and now we've got her working. Don't you think you'd better run help Susan?"

Sara gave Lulu a hug and ran to the office to get her keys. "Well, now that that's all settled," drawled Lulu, "you can start asking me a little bit about Aunt Pat's. For your story."

Rebecca leaned over and fished in her designer handbag for a pad and pencil. "So," she said, flicking her blond hair back over her shoulders, "this is a family-run operation, right? It's you, your son Ben, and your daughter-in-law?"

"Mercy, there's more of us than that!" Lulu twinkled winningly at Rebecca. "There's Sara's nephew, Derrick. He's the one that's lurking by the door who can't take his eyes off of you."

Rebecca swiftly glanced over. She flicked her hair again.

"Then there are the twins, Ella Beth and Coco. Or Cordelia, as she wants to be known, since she's such a grown-up nine now."

"They're your . . . ?"

"Granddaughters. They work here every day after school, sweeping, wiping tables, and setting out silverware."

"The silverware," said Rebecca. "You know, I don't think I've ever gone to a barbeque restaurant that sets the table. Usually you use plastic forks."

Lulu looked faintly shocked. "No, we couldn't allow that to happen. Aunt Pat wouldn't want her guests to eat with plastic cutlery. It wouldn't be seemly."

"Certainly would save a lot of washing up," muttered Rebecca. And why the hell did they use paper towel rolls on the tables instead of cloth napkins if the sainted Aunt Pat was so particular?

Rebecca made some notes.

"So we've got your son Ben, grandchildren, and in-laws here. Oh, and the dogs I saw on the porch on the way in. Anybody else?"

Lulu would give Rebecca the benefit of the doubt—maybe sounding like a snippy little name-dropping snob was only because she was shy. Or something. "Actually, yes, Miss Adrian, there is one more—my other son, Seb. He's recently come here from New York to help us out."

Rebecca stopped writing and temporarily looked confused. "Seb?"

"Sebastian. But we all call him Seb."

"Big guy? Dark, curly hair?" asked Rebecca.

"Oh, you saw him when you were coming in? Yes, that's him. He's handling all our accounting right now. New York kind of burned him out, I think. Besides, so many people were getting laid off in his company that he was sure he'd be on the chopping block next. So of course we took him in. 'Home is the place where, when you have to go there, they have to take you in' and all that."

Rebecca looked over sharply at Lulu. Was she aware she was quoting Frost? Was she a lot sharper than Rebecca thought?

Lulu smiled benignly.

"Tell me a little about Aunt Pat," said Rebecca. "I'm assuming there was at some point an Aunt Pat?" asked Rebecca, stifling a yawn with the back of her hand.

Lulu's eyes grew reminiscent as she looked into the past. "Aunt Pat was the dear woman who raised me. You see, I grew up at this restaurant," she said, smoothing a hand across the checkered tablecloth. "I'd sit on a tall stool in the kitchen and tell her about my school day as she mixed together the dry rub or made the corn muffins. Later on, she let me help her in the kitchen and taught me about food and flavor. Her love for food was there in every succulent bite of barbeque. Aunt Pat's was always full of heavenly smells and conversation. She gave me a love for cooking and a love for this restaurant. And later on, when she passed away, she willed it to me."

Rebecca, who rarely listened enough for follow-up questions, was already moving on. But Lulu had a point to make.

"You see," said Lulu. "the entire restaurant is one big family."

Well, zip-a-dee-doo-dah, thought Rebecca Adrian. Exactly the kind of sap she avoided. She wanted a little dirt, a little conflict. Some vivid local color.

A torrent of local color abruptly slid into the booth next to Rebecca and Lulu. "Look no farther, Miss Lulu, it's the hallelujah chorus come to sing the praises of Aunt Pat's. Amen!"

Now this was more like it, thought Rebecca. Five oddball Southerners to liven up the story and coo on cue over the barbeque. Perfect. She smiled at them and held up her pad. "Could you give me your names? For the story."

Lulu broke in. "We call them the Graces, because they're docents at Graceland. They're the finest group of regulars anywhere in the world," she added warmly.

"Because you've got the finest *ribs* in the world!" said one of the Graces stoutly. She beamed at Rebecca Adrian. "I'm Flo."

"Cherry."

"Peggy Sue."

"Jeanne."

"Evelyn."

They sounded like Mouseketeers, thought Rebecca. And the one named Cherry wore a motorcycle helmet with a picture of Elvis on it. No one seemed to find that fact at all odd, or suggested that she remove it. Lulu, now overly sensitive to any slights from Rebecca (either real or perceived) registered her puzzled stare. "Isn't that a fine-looking helmet, Miss Adrian?"

There was a warning tone in Lulu's voice, so Rebecca nodded slowly in agreement. Cherry beamed. "Thanks. It makes me feel like Elvis is my guardian angel keeping me out of trouble."

"Out of trouble?" hooted Evelyn. "I'd like to see that. Maybe he's keeping you *safe*. You couldn't stay out of trouble if your very life depended on it."

Cherry leaned forward over the table and talked as though Rebecca eagerly hung on her every word. "At first I only wore it when I rode my motorcycle. Then, after my riding mower bucked me off that time, I put it on to cut the grass. Then I got to thinking how many people get hurt in car crashes, so I thought maybe wearing it in the car would be a good idea."

"And," said Rebecca with a tight smile, "in the barbeque restaurant?"

"There's a threat of tornadoes!" said Cherry triumphantly. "A helmet is perfect to prevent head injuries during tornadoes."

Cherry provided far more local color than Rebecca had counted on.

"Pooh," snorted Lulu. "I don't believe a word. There's not a cloud in the sky."

"Just the same," said Cherry, "there's a threat." She patted her Elvis helmet, complacent in the knowledge that she was well prepared for any exigency.

Rebecca tried to find her way back to her story. "So you come here . . . how frequently?"

"Once a week," said Evelyn. And she was, thought Rebecca, possibly the only one with any fashion sense. She looked at Evelyn's Hermes scarf with approval. "On Thursdays, we always come here for ribs after we give tours at Graceland."

"But today is Monday."

"Today," said Peggy Sue, "is an exception to the rule."

Rebecca frowned. "I went to Graceland six or seven years ago, and I don't remember any docents there at all. I remember a sling-around-your-neck audio tour guide and some staff who kind of kept an eye on everything."

Cherry beamed. "That's just it! They didn't have anybody there at all who was a docent. That's why the Graces are so incredible. We made Graceland *history*."

Rebecca attempted a look of interest, which fell completely short into the boundaries of bored disbelief.

"You see," said Evelyn briskly, "we were all huge Elvis fans. Huge. So we were, separately, mind you, going each and every day to Graceland."

Rebecca looked a little queasy. "To Graceland. Every

day. I guess the lines must not have been as bad as when I went."

Cherry shook her head. "No, that just shows how devoted we were! We waited every day in the line for a ticket, and then waited forty-five minutes for the shuttle to take us for the tour."

"After months of doing this, we still felt like we belonged there. It was *home* to us. We started making friends with each other and coming here for a bite to eat of 'the best barbeque in town,'" Cherry said animatedly, with full-on air quotes. She continued on in the same breath, "Even though Aunt Pat's isn't even close to Graceland."

"And the Graceland people were making friends with us, too," added Jeanne. "They'd cut up with us and laugh. But we were always serious and respectful at Graceland. It's really a quiet place, you know. It's one of the most peaceful places I know."

"So then the staff asked us if we'd like to be official docents. We don't get paid and we don't give tours, but we direct people in the right direction and make sure they don't touch Elvis's things or try to walk into the rooms under the ropes or anything like that. So we're the first *official docents* for Graceland." Cherry beamed.

"And very decent docents," said plump Peggy Sue, smugly. "I was so happy today to be in the pool room. You know, I think that's my very favorite place to go. I feel like I'm enveloped in this big Elvis tent. It's divine."

"That's the room that's covered with folds of fabric?" asked Rebecca.

"The very same one! And it's so much calmer than the TV room—too much yellow in there." Peggy Sue immediately looked regretful at her revelation as though Rebecca might end up sharing her opinion on the Cooking Channel.

Rebecca was bored again. She was now more interested

in finding out how she might get the conversation back over to barbeque and remind her cameraman that he was supposed to be working, not scarfing down barbeque.

"You're going to take her back in the kitchen, aren't you?" asked Evelyn. She turned to Rebecca. "You'll feel right at home in the Aunt Pat's kitchen. There's not any kind of an industrial feel to it at all."

"It looks," interrupted Cherry eagerly, "like you're at your grandma's kitchen and watching her cook something up just for you."

Flo nodded. "Every pot and pan has some family history backing it up."

Lulu looked pleased. "Y'all are so sweet to say that! That's exactly the way I want the kitchen to feel. Because if that's the feeling *in* the kitchen, the food coming *out* of it is going to be just as comforting and loving. It's the heart of the restaurant. And there's a little bit of my heart there, too. I swear I feel closer to Aunt Pat in that room than anywhere else. Maybe she's our guardian angel here at the restaurant."

Rebecca craned her neck to locate Tony.

Cherry wasn't ready for Rebecca to go yet. Not until she'd impressed some more important Aunt Pat's information on her. She tapped her on the arm to get her attention. "See over there? No, *there*. That picture? That's a picture of the Graces from five years ago. And *that* picture?" She gestured to another spot on the crowded wall. The old brick was barely visible underneath a massive collection of color and black-and-white photos and memorabilia from years back. "That's us nine or ten months later. That's *another* way this restaurant is like my meemaw's house. Walls that are jam-packed with pictures. It gives you a sense of history, like you're connecting to a real family."

"You *are* connecting to a family," said Lulu warmly.

"You're right up there with baby pictures of my grand-daughters, toddler pictures of Ben and Seb, and even pictures of me when I was little."

And apparently, thought Rebecca, when you go up on the wall, you never come down. The wall was full of pictures, and she couldn't see an empty spot anywhere. Very busy looking, thought Rebecca, whose tastes ran to the Spartan look.

"You forgot to tell the best part," Flo said reproachfully to Cherry. "Remember?"

Cherry slapped a manicured hand on the table. "I *am* losing it." She pointed to the very center of the wall. "One of the King's guitars. *Signed.*"

Rebecca was impressed, despite herself. "You're smart to put it in a case. It must be valuable."

"Lulu and Aunt Pat *knew* Elvis," said Jeanne in an awe-struck voice. The ladies looked at Lulu wonderingly.

"Well, not to hang out with. But if he was in Memphis, he was at Aunt Pat's."

Ben strode out of the kitchen and saw Seb sitting in the office. "Why're you hiding out in the office, Seb? I thought you were a middle-of-the-action kind of guy. It's not *every* day we have Cooking Channel camped out at the restaurant."

Seb looked briefly annoyed, then gave a short laugh and said, "Oh, you know. That hippie gallery owner, Susan something—is out in the dining room. Mother's got a bee in her bonnet about fixing me up with her. It drives me right up the wall."

Ben picked up his tongs and said, "Well, I know it gripes you, but I'd appreciate it if you could go out there anyway. *Not* to flirt with Susan," he added as Seb opened his mouth to protest, "but to schmooze with the Cooking Channel folks. You're the Taylor clan's best schmoozer."

Seb stood up. He knew an indirect order when he heard one. And he wasn't exactly in the position to say no. The last thing he wanted was to slink back to New York with his tail between his legs. Without a job, he wouldn't be able to pay rent. And the debt collectors would be thrilled at having another crack at making him pay up.

Lulu and the Graces bantered back and forth while food came and went and people came over to say hi. Everyone appeared to know them. Then Rebecca's cell phone, which looked capable of doing everything short of baking bread, rang, and she abruptly slid out of the booth and hurried off to chat.

Everyone she'd been sitting with gaped in surprise at her rudeness. Tony, Rebecca's cameraman, noticed their reaction to her abrupt departure. He took a last bite of his red beans and rice and walked across to the vinyl booth. He wore an apologetic grin. His handsome face and Mediterranean coloring spurred the Graces to forget their shock and dive into their pocketbooks for their lipsticks. Cherry sized Tony up with an expression that Lulu recognized as indicative of future flirtation. "That," Tony said emphatically, "was some good barbeque. I'm not the official scout, but yours was the best barbeque plate I've ever eaten."

Lulu beamed at him. "I'm so glad you enjoyed it, hon." Then she caught sight of Seb poking his head out from the office door and glancing around the restaurant. Lulu motioned him over. He hesitated, and Lulu frowned and waved him over again. "Don't be shy, Seb!" she called.

Seb reddened. "For heaven's sake!" said Lulu. "You're not usually so bashful. You can at least say hi to Tony here.

And Tony, let me introduce you to some of my friends. . . .
Tony here is the cameraman for the Cooking Channel."
Seb shook his hand and then Lulu introduced Tony to the
Graces.

"You should be meeting Miss Adrian, too, but she's
gone off for a little stroll."

Jeanne, one of the Graces, said, "Well, at least she's trying to be thoughtful. It can be really rude when people talk
on their cell phones."

Flo snorted. "You are way too sweet, Jeanne. That
woman just doesn't want us to listen in on her calls."

Tony laughed, "You got it, Flo. Rebecca *always* walks
off to make calls. Sometimes I think she's placing bets
with her bookie."

Seb gave an uncomfortable chuckle. "Well, hate to say
it, but I've gotta run. See you later, Mother. It's nice to meet
you, Tony." Lulu frowned, irked that he hadn't even met
the food scout. The least he could do was to stay and visit
for a while.

Rebecca finished her conversation and walked up to the
booth. Lulu noticed that she wore a pair of stilettos to compensate for the fact that she was clearly less than five feet
tall. "Have you got what you need?" she asked Tony. Then
she gave a short laugh. "I mean for the story. I can see that
you're set as far as pigging out goes."

Tony ignored her. "I think we're good. Let's head out."
He shouldered his bag and walked toward the door.

"What," breathed Cherry, "a beautiful man. Reminds
me of you know who." And she patted her Elvis helmet, in
case anyone had any doubt whom she referred to.

Rebecca gave a quick roll of her eyes. "We're going to
go. It looks like the dinner crowd is coming in full force.
I'll be here tomorrow," she said to Lulu.

Flo grabbed Rebecca's arm, startling her. "I know what

we should do! Let's go out with Rebecca and Tony. We could show them some Memphis nightlife."

Tony, who had returned to the booth since Rebecca seemed to be waylaid, looked hopeful at this idea. When they'd arrived in town last night, he'd noticed Beale Street throbbing with energy. "I don't care about the nightlife," Rebecca said. "It's not part of my story."

Tony said, "Beck, they're not talking about the story. They're inviting us to have fun." Partying on Beale with locals sounded to Tony like an excellent way to accomplish having fun.

She pursed her lips, considering. "Well . . . I wouldn't mind getting some ideas for the piece. But I don't feel like going out anywhere. How about over at the Peabody? It has a bar."

Flo lit up. "Sure! I love those ducks. What time is it? She glanced at her watch. If we leave now, we can watch the duckmaster put the ducks up."

Rebecca groaned. "Oh no. Not the duck people." She rolled her eyes at Tony, who looked confused. "You were out doing Memphis location shots this morning, so you didn't see the ducks. By the way, did you get some good stuff for the location shots?"

"Sure, lots of footage. And some great shots of the pyramid," said Tony.

Cherry said, "Oooh. You know, I think that's one of my favorite things in Memphis. I love lookin' at it, with the sun going down and glinting on all that steel."

"A pyramid. In Memphis." Rebecca winced. "That's not going to work, Tony. I'm doing a quirky story."

"Pyramids aren't quirky?" Tony asked.

"I mean quirky-oddball, quirky-colorful. Southern eccentric," said Rebecca.

"Pyramids aren't eccentric?"

"Okay, never mind. We'll edit the tape later. Back to what I was saying. While you were out this morning shooting pyramids, at . . ."

She looked questioningly at Flo, and Flo supplied, "Eleven o'clock in the morning."

Rebecca nodded. "You explain it to him, please."

"At eleven o' clock, they roll out a red carpet from the elevator at the Peabody, and out from the elevator waddle the cutest ducks ever. They spend all day splashing and swimming in the fountain at the Peabody, then at five o'clock the duckmaster calls them and sort of directs them with his cane, and they waddle back into the elevator and go up to the Royal Duck Palace on the roof."

Tony looked charmed. "The Royal Duck Palace?"

"Well, honey, they have their own suite up there! With sun decks and a fountain and their very own miniature Peabody coop."

All the talk of duck palaces and duckmasters irritated Rebecca. "And *hordes* of people line up with cameras and push and shove to see the ducks. And they play Sousa." She heaved a rather tortured sigh. "But I definitely need a drink. Let's head out."

Sara's nephew, Derrick, who'd been trying to look cool and listen in on the conversation at the same time, asked, "Is it okay if I come along too, Flo?"

Flo called Lulu over. Since Sara was out helping Susan with the show, and Ben had his hands full of dry rub, Lulu would have to stand in for the parental oversight.

"To a bar? What are you thinking, young man?"

"It's just the Peabody." Derrick shrugged. "I thought I'd go see the ducks and hang out with the Graces for a while."

Flo said, "If he wants to come along, I'll keep an eye on him, Lulu."

Lulu figured Derrick was happy to be anywhere but

home. He'd shown every indication of being completely miserable since moving to Memphis from Chicago and seemed determined to infect everybody else with his suffering. Lulu got it—he'd rather be with his mom, Sara's sister, in Chicago. Too bad his mom didn't agree with him.

"Okay," Lulu said. "But only for a little while. Then you can still drive over to the church and make it to Youth Group."

This time Derrick didn't make the face he usually made whenever Youth Group was invoked. Although his manners weren't well developed, he had an unerring instinct for getting his way. In his estimation, a blatant show of cooperation would engender more goodwill than his customary churlishness.

"Sounds like a plan, Lulu. Thanks, Flo," Derrick added meekly.

Flo looked over at Big Ben, Buddy, and Morty, the three old regulars who were still trying to listen in on their conversation—Big Ben quite obviously, since he had his hand cupped around his ear. "Want to come along?" she hollered at him.

"Do what?"

"Want to come along to the Peabody bar with the ladies? We're going to hang out with Miss Adrian and Tony for a while."

Big Ben gave his rasping chuckle again. Buddy answered for them all, "No thanks, honey. Y'all go ahead and have fun though." As he and Big Ben watched them go, Buddy said, "I think our days of hanging out in hotel bars are done, don't you?"

Morty smiled. He looked for all the world like a black version of Mr. Clean—even down to the earring. Except that Morty always had a twinkle in his eye. And now a dreamy, contemplative look stole over his features that meant he was going to tell a tall tale. "Remember back in the day? We really did some traveling with the band, man. And a pretty lady in every hotel bar in every town we played."

Buddy snorted. "Traveling? We stayed mostly in Memphis, remember? And when we *did* travel, the dumps we stayed in didn't have bars. And I sure don't remember any pretty ladies."

"Emmaline. I remember Emmaline with her pretty braid." Lulu rushed by, and Morty pushed up from the table. "Think I'll go tell Lulu about Emmaline. She always likes my stories." He wandered off toward the counter at the back of the restaurant.

Buddy sighed. "Thinking about the old days and being young makes me want to sing the blues."

"But we always sing the blues, Buddy," boomed Big Ben.

"Maybe that's why we're usually happy."

Big Ben changed the subject. Or maybe he couldn't actually hear the subject. He barked, "So whatcha going to do now, Buddy? Got any plans?"

"Well, it's almost five o'clock now. I'm thinking about sitting on my front porch and waving at cars for a while."

"That so?" Big Ben considered this, rubbing his jaw thoughtfully with a big hand. "That might be enjoyable. Better than my plan, anyhow. Mind some company?"

"Feel free," said Buddy.

"Might there be a beverage of some kind offered?" Big Ben looked hopeful.

"I do have a Domaine Vincent Dauvissat Chablis Les Preuses in my possession right now. For a special occasion."

Big Ben's eyes widened.

"Which waving at cars, unfortunately, doesn't qualify as."

Big Ben nodded slowly. He could understand that. "Sweet tea, though?"

"Let's grab a gallon to go, since we're here. There's no way my sweet tea can compare with Aunt Pat's."

Cherry left the restaurant a few minutes behind the other Graces. She was just climbing onto her motor-cycle when the storklike figure of fellow regular Mildred Cameron approached. Cherry always felt very sophis-ticated in her jazzy, bright, tight clothes, jangly bangles, and Elvis helmet. She had a soft spot for spinster Mildred, who wore clothes that hung on her gangling frame like they were draped on a clothes hanger.

"Hey there, Mildred! How's tricks?"

Mildred beamed at the friendly greeting. "Good!" She glanced at her watch, which slid like a bracelet on her skinny wrist. "You're done eating already?"

Cherry laughed. "We did things a little different today. Ate early, now we're going to see the ducks at the Peabody. That Cooking Channel scout is here, remember?"

"Oh, I forgot. What's she like?"

Cherry considered the question. "Tee-tiny, like a little blond doll. And she has this perfect cupid-bow mouth. She seems kind of mean, though. But she sounds like she knows ever-so-many people in New York. She told the Graces all about the movie stars she knew and the places she went. She's going to look at Sara's art tomorrow morning at Su-san's gallery. She might connect her with some big shots in the city that she knows."

Mildred splayed her fingers across her face. "Oh! Do you think . . ." she stopped and caught her breath. "Do you think she knows any publishers in New York? Could she find me a publisher for my book?" She looked for all the world like the Scarecrow asking the Wizard of Oz for a brain.

"I don't see why not. To hear *her* talk, she knows everybody there is to know up there."

Mildred swung abruptly around and walked back into the parking lot.

"Hey!" called Cherry. "Didn't you forget to eat?"

"I'll come back tomorrow," said Mildred. "I've got a manuscript to prepare!"

Dreaming was romance writer Mildred Cameron's stock-in-trade. In fact, she'd been dreaming for so long that now she moved and felt and acted like she was stuck in the dream all the time.

Dreaminess aside, though, she was a determined cuss. And patient. Who else would spend forty years on the same romance novel, just to get it perfect?

Mildred may not be as innocuous as everybody thought. Maybe she wasn't only a pleasantly eccentric oddball, but something a little more indefinable. And now that she was about to turn over her romance into the capable hands of Rebecca Adrian, she daydreamed of book signings.

Sara Taylor pushed open the squeaky screen door to the restaurant. "Time to go home, girls," she called. She was taking a quick break from helping set up the show around the corner, and she decided to stick her head in to take the twins home. She was preoccupied with her own thoughts and didn't notice the face Ella Beth made.

But Lulu did. "Sara, if you want, I can drop Ella Beth off at home a little later."

Sara gave an absentminded "okay" and hurried off to the car with Coco in tow.

Ella Beth could stay all day and all night at the restaurant. She'd sit with the Labs on the screened porch and do her homework before the crowds came at the end of the day to hear the music. She'd set out new rolls of paper towels on the tables every afternoon before the rush hit. All the regulars loved her and called her "their girl" and made her feel just as pretty as Coco. And they likely made Coco feel just as smart as Ella Beth.

"It's been an exciting day, hasn't it, sugar?" asked Lulu as she wiped off tables.

Ella Beth shrugged. "I guess so."

Lulu shot her a searching look for the less-than-enthusiastic reply. "What's wrong, sweetie? Not a fan of the TV scout?"

Ella Beth shrugged. "Coco thought she was really cool. She kept talking about Miss Adrian's fancy clothes."

Lulu hid a smile. "Sounds like you really weren't taken in, though."

"I like things the way they are, Granny Lulu. I never want Aunt Pat's to change. Uncle Seb said stuff like we're going to get all these tourists and start selling tee shirts, salt and pepper shakers, and those stupid bells." Ella Beth sounded affronted.

Lulu frowned. "Well, I'd have to give the okay on that. Seeing as how it's my restaurant. And I certainly don't recall approving Aunt Pat kitsch. I think Aunt Pat would be rolling around in her grave if she thought her likeness was on somebody's tee shirt."

"And . . . well, I just didn't like her. She reminded me of my teacher from last year. She was pretty and seemed real nice at first, but she was the meanest teacher ever. She'd bite your head off if you even asked her a question."

"You don't think she's the real deal."

"Nope. Just a phony." An idea popped in Ella Beth's head. Maybe she could find out more about Miss Adrian.

Some detective work would be fun. And everybody expected to see her lurking around anyway, so they wouldn't suspect a thing.

"Well," said Lulu, considering the phony label, "she does have those colored contact lenses in. Nobody has violet eyes but Liz Taylor."

Flo would have agreed one hundred percent with Ella Beth. Rebecca Adrian was definitely a phony. Worse than that, she was sneaky. She'd pretended to be great friends with the Graces while Tony kept a watchful eye on her and shook his head from time to time.

The evening was just fine to begin with. The Peabody's glamorous and luxurious lobby was always a treat to gather in—before, after, or during the ducks. They settled in around the bar, each with a drink—except for Derrick, who got a Red Bull.

Cherry was a source of amusement for the ladies there—she'd clearly set her sights on Tony. She wore her special lucky lipstick that matched her hair, and her personality was especially sparkly.

"Cherry's really set her cap for Tony," Flo whispered to Evelyn.

"She drives me batty with all that. It's not like she's ever going to cheat on her Johnny," said Evelyn. "She just enjoys the thrill of the hunt. And why she puts up with all Johnny's nonsense is beyond me."

Tony seemed taken with Cherry, too. But then, Cherry—in full-throttle flirting mode—was well-nigh irresistible.

The lighthearted mood changed abruptly when the devil got into Rebecca Adrian again. Flo later wondered if Rebecca just didn't like seeing people have fun.

◇◇◇◇◇◇◇◇

"So tell me," asked Rebecca cajolingly to Cherry, who had finally removed her motorcycle helmet, since the threat of inclement weather had passed (although the threat of her falling out of her chair in front of the Peabody bar was rapidly becoming a distinct possibility), "are you ladies all for real? You give tours at Graceland? And you love each other like sisters and eat heaping piles of barbeque to maintain those skinny-minnie bodies? And you're all sweet as pie? It seems a little corny." Her swift smile minimized her cutting words. "Isn't there any dirt in there at all?"

Now Flo noticed that Tony kept some distance between himself and Rebecca. He asked the bartender for another drink. "That's it in a nutshell," said Flo in a rush. "Can I get you another drink, Rebecca?"

But Peggy Sue snickered. "We do love us our barbeque and we're all best friends. But sweet? I dunno about that."

Rebecca smiled encouragingly. "It would be a little weird if you were all like some sort of Stepford women."

"We've all had our little escapades, you know. Love affairs, scandals." Peggy Sue wiggled her eyebrows in an attempt to look devilish. It looked more as if she'd developed a debilitating tic.

Rebecca was disappointed. "Well, love affairs kind of go with the territory, don't they?"

"*And*," added Peggy Sue, holding her hand up to stop Rebecca. "One of us is an ex-con." Here she looked directly, but unsteadily, at Flo. A hiccupping giggle escaped her, which she soon swallowed when she heard the deafening silence from her friends and saw the satisfied smile on Rebecca's face.

"Ex-con?" asked Rebecca in a sweetly surprised voice. "I never would have guessed. What were you locked up for, Flo?" When she got no response, she said, "I see. Banding together with your vow of silence, right? That's okay. Peggy

Sue helped me supply the tad bit of seasoning I needed for my quirky Memphis barbeque story."

Flo's face splotched with red as she bent to get her pocketbook off the floor and wordlessly rushed from the hotel bar. Like four anxious ladies in waiting, the other Graces dashed after her. "Hey," called Tony, "do you need a ride home?"

Evelyn turned around. "I'm all right to drive, so I'll take everybody."

"Actually," said Cherry, "I'm going to walk home. It's only a few blocks to Harbortown. Thanks, though." She strapped on her helmet, figuring there was a high probability of a head-injuring stumble on her walk home.

Flo remembered Derrick fifteen minutes after returning home. And when she did remember, she gasped. In their hurry to escape the clutches of the wicked Rebecca Adrian, the Graces forgot they'd left Sara's nephew Derrick behind. He was visiting the men's room when they rushed out, a fact no one remembered as they scampered out through the glass doors of the Peabody, hollering at Flo to wait up. Flo cussed, picked up her cell phone (which had a very handsome Elvis skin covering it), and called Lulu. She decided she wouldn't bother calling Sara—that filly had a temper on her like you wouldn't believe. Lulu should best be able to break the news to Sara, anyway. Since she was Lulu's daughter-in-law and all.

When Lulu picked up the phone, Flo cut right to the chase. "I forgot him."

"Who?"

"Derrick. It was my fault entirely. Rebecca Adrian got me mad, and I stormed out and left Derrick behind with that woman. Want to string me up by my toenails?"

Lulu considered this proposal. "Maybe. What was he

still doing there? He promised me he'd just hang out for a few minutes with y'all and then he'd head over to Youth Group."

"Well, he didn't make it to church, Lulu, and I am so sorry. Want me to run by there and make him drive home? And I'll pinkie-swear not to take seventeen-year-olds again?"

Lulu softened at her anxious tone. "Don't worry about it. I can see how Miss Adrian could get anybody steamed. That girl likes looking for trouble, I'm sure of it. She'd better keep an eye on her back, though. Trouble has a way of catching up with you."

Sara Taylor was thinking about throwing some trouble in Rebecca Adrian's direction. Sara had a heckuva temper, which most people fortunately witnessed only short flashes of. Wisely, nobody made mention of the red hair and temper connection.

Sara stormed into the Peabody after getting Lulu's phone call. She realized after several minutes in the quiet lobby that Derrick and Rebecca Adrian weren't there. And, considering the bright lights of Beale Street just around the corner, Sara had a great idea where they might be. And it wasn't going to be at church.

Sara had just stridden around the barricades on Beale when she was nearly run down by her errant nephew. If she hadn't nearly been plowed over by him, she'd never have seen him at all—he was dressed in black as usual.

"Youth Group, huh?" Sara bellowed. "You *will* need to find God once I'm done with you." But a closer look at Derrick stopped her in her tracks. Instead of his usual sullenly sardonic face, he looked completely devastated. And . . . were those tears glinting in his eyes?

Sara threw an arm around him (difficult, since he was

taller than her) and redirected her fury toward Rebecca Adrian. "Where is that harpy? What did she do to you?"

"Nothing! Let's go, okay? I'm getting really tired."

Sara gave Derrick's arm a squeeze as they wordlessly walked to the parking deck and got into their separate cars. She couldn't imagine what could have caused such a transformation.

Back at the Peabody Hotel, Rebecca Adrian extinguished a cigarette against a "No Smoking" sign and picked up her cell phone. "Information? I need the number for Sebastian Taylor in Memphis, Tennessee."

Chapter

2

Seb Taylor was putting his feet up at home and still celebrating the fact that the restaurant had a back-door exit. He'd really needed to get home for that drink and cigarette this afternoon, and he wouldn't have stepped foot into that dining room again for all the money in the world.

What the *hell* was she doing in Memphis? Was it really a coincidence that she happened to be the Cooking Channel scout scoping out Aunt Pat's? *Of all the barbeque joints in all the towns in all the world, she walks into mine.*

The phone rang and Seb reached over to pick it up.

Derrick Knight's hurt turned into a pulsing fury, and his face returned to its regularly scheduled sullenness. Who did Rebecca Adrian think she was? He'd gone out with lots of girls—*girls*—not women a breath away from middle age. And they were *much* hotter than she'd ever been.

Just wait, he thought. Rebecca Adrian had better watch her back.

Sara tried tempering her fury at Rebecca Adrian. Whatever she'd done to Derrick (and he was not going to let on what that had been) was over. Sara at least needed to keep on good enough terms with her to get the art world contacts she needed and for Lulu to get a great review for the restaurant.

She'd waited a long time to show her art. And now she allowed herself to dream a little.

Graceland would kick her out. Kick her out and keep her out. Bar the big, beautiful doors. No more mirrored dining room. No more canary yellow TV room. No more jungle room.

And . . . she shivered. If Elvis knew, what would he think? Oh, she knew that he was dead and gone, of course. (Although she'd swear she'd seen him, in disguise and a bit older—and wearing that unfortunate white sequined jumpsuit. There *was* that funny business over his misspelled name on his gravestone.) What on earth would Elvis say?

Not to mention everybody else in the town. Or the far reaches of the entire United States of America, if Miss Rebecca Smarty-Pants had her way. Having the Graces know was one thing. They swore they'd keep it a secret. A secret until Peggy Sue got tipsy, then good luck with your secrets. You'd just pray to God your private life wasn't splashed across the front page of the Memphis paper.

But if Rebecca oh so jauntily put her ex-con background in her story to add a smidge of local color, the whole town of Memphis would know. Not to mention her no-good ex-husband who still looked for her in the wilds of Mississippi. Flo needed to convince Rebecca, and convince her good.

Southern Accents's transformation was astonishing, thought Susan Meredith, eyeing the large room through her round spectacles. She'd hastily removed the black-and-white photography exhibit. Now Sara's art covered the walls, pedestals, and shelves with a startling infusion of vibrant color.

Sara wasn't pacing, exactly, but jiggling a lot. She couldn't stand still; instead, she shifted from side to side, crossed and uncrossed her arms, and twisted her curly hair around a finger. And looked a little green around the gills.

"You should relax a little, Sara. Hers is not the be-all, end-all, final-authority opinion. Rebecca Adrian is *very* well connected with her ego. Other than that . . ." Susan shrugged her thin shoulders expressively.

Sara impatiently shook her head. "I think you're wrong, Susan. She told the Graces last night about all the people she knows in New York." She wove her fingers together, then pulled them apart. Sara had actually allowed herself some little daydreams involving hanging up her apron for good and spending all her days in the studio, squishing clay and slapping paint on canvases.

"Don't put all your eggs in Miss Adrian's basket, that's all. There are many avenues for developing a name for yourself and finding patrons for your art. None of them involve Rebecca Adrian."

Sara's rejoinder was cut short by the tinkling bell indicating Rebecca's arrival at Southern Accents. Unfortunately, from all appearances, Rebecca was in what could be described only as a peevish mood.

"Can we get a move on?" she asked, taking off her huge designer sunglasses. "I've got to get over to Aunt Pat's"—

she checked what looked to be a Rolex watch—"two minutes ago."

Hating that Rebecca Adrian succeeded in making her feel flustered, Sara wordlessly waved her hand to include the entire gallery. "Well," she started, "here it is."

Thankfully, Susan Meredith took over from there. "As you can see, Sara's art is a remarkable example of Southern folk art. She uses a whimsical approach to . . ."

But Rebecca cut her off with a dismissive slash of her hand. "Never mind all that. This wouldn't fly in a New York gallery. Never. It looks like someone tripping on acid made those teapots."

Sara prickled. "Some of us like coloring outside the lines, you know."

Rebecca squinted at the wall of paintings and made a move. "Plus the fact that the subject matter is completely parochial and clearly limited to local appeal."

Sara, God help her, did actually try to control herself. It was a powerful struggle between Good Sara and Bad Sara, and for a second or two, it looked as if Good Sara might win. She successfully slipped out the door of Southern Accents before she could say anything hateful to Rebecca Adrian.

But the devil got into Rebecca and wasn't going to have anything to do with Good Sara. Rebecca popped out the door behind Sara, followed quickly by Susan, and said, "What about this portrait here?" asked Rebecca, referring to a painting in the window of Big Ben. Sara was particularly proud of it, and Susan had begged her to show it for ages. "Did one of your daughters paint this one?" Rebecca snorted.

Sara wondered later if it was the snide reference or the way she implied that Coco or Ella Beth would produce poor artwork that made her blow her top. She never could decide. But whatever it was made her blow her top in a way she'd struggled to control for years. "At least I have somebody who gives a flip about me. Thanks for the pep talk. I'm just sorry I ever respected your opinion enough to go asking for it. People like you get off on putting everybody down to make yourself feel good. Have it your way. But when you're lying on your deathbed alone, look back and remember how you got there."

Susan's mouth flapped open and closed like a fish, which was such a departure for the always-composed Susan that it stopped Sara's tirade. Rebecca clearly wasn't waiting around to see if she was done yelling or not—her heels clicked as she stormed off down the sidewalk. People who had stopped to stare at the confrontation finally continued on their way.

Susan found her voice. "She doesn't know her Picasso from her Rembrandt, Sara. Rebecca Adrian wouldn't recognize great art if it bit her in the behind."

Somewhere under the cloud of misery, hurt, and anger, Sara appreciated Susan's attempt to make her feel better. She smiled reassuringly at Susan. But Susan was alarmed that the light had gone out of Sara's green eyes.

"She doesn't understand Southern folk art. Your work is beautiful," Susan added.

Sara looked around the gallery with an even more critical eye than usual. She saw her collection of oddly shaped ceramic livestock, the brightly colored canvases with misshapen figures in rural settings, the bloated, fantastically colored tea set. Where she once felt pride and hope, she now felt overwhelming fury and desperation. Damn Rebecca Adrian for taking her art away from her.

The day had been clearly destined for calamity in every way. Lulu reflected later that she should have picked up on the signs. There were certainly enough of them to indicate that the day would go to hell in a handbasket. But Lulu didn't put much stock in signs. So she didn't really pay attention when her car kicked the bucket on the way to the restaurant that morning.

She wasn't even on her usual route to Aunt Pat's, where friends and family would be sure to see her and would transport her the rest of the way. No, she was way off the beaten path.

"Shoot!" said Lulu as she steered to the side of the road.

"*Shoot!*" said Lulu when she realized she'd left her cell phone at home.

So there was Lulu Taylor, marooned motorist, walking down the road as her restaurant prepared for a possible Cooking Channel debut without her. Lulu had given up hope of ever making it to the restaurant when there was a honking behind her . . . the volume of which was so loud that she nearly fell into the street in surprise.

It was the red and green painted "Jesus Saves" bus from the Promised Land Church of Our Blessed Savior. "Hallelujah!" muttered Lulu.

The bus, which looked like it had escaped from *The Partridge Family* lot, pulled to the side of the road. "Lulu? You okay? What are you doing walking alone down the road?" It was Johnson Jones, his face puckered up with concern. Probably thought she'd gone ga-ga.

"Hi, J.J. My car broke down a little ways back. Is there any way you could give me a lift to Aunt Pat's or call Ben for me?"

"I can take you over there, Lulu. I've got to gas up the bus anyway. I'm taking the Promised Land's Sassy Seniors group over to Gatlinburg for a couple of nights."

"Well now, that *does* sound like a nice trip." Lulu beamed. Her day was back on track again. Or so she thought.

Everything was fine and dandy for a while after that. After the "Jesus Saves" bus dropped her right off near the barricaded entrance to Beale Street, she hurried to Aunt Pat's and discovered that the Graces had brought in bunches of red and white balloons and all wore "Aunt Pat's Is Where It's At" tee shirts in matching colors. Peggy Sue gestured to her shirt with a plump hand and said, "Not grammatical, I know. But our other tee shirt ideas were horrid. 'Aunt Pat's Won't Make You Fat,' 'Aunt Pat Was One Cool Cat' . . ."

Lulu hugged as many of the Graces as she could pull into her arms. "Y'all are the best. Thanks so much. It looks like we're having a party in here."

What everybody remembered afterward was what a gorgeous day it started out as. There was never a clearer sky of a brighter blue. The barbeque and sauce that day seemed blessed by the Lord Jesus himself. Even Ben, the most critical man you've ever come across, proclaimed it the best barbeque on the earth.

All the Aunt Pat's folks had an extra spring in their step. Lulu and Ben were sure the restaurant would be the blue-ribbon winner for Memphis barbeque. Big Ben, Morty, and Buddy had brought a couple of instruments and were giving an impromptu concert on the roomy front porch. The Graces were in rare form and cackling at everything anybody said. Ben was concocting the finest barbeque anywhere in the world. Lulu sailed around, chitchatting with everybody.

But when Sara slipped in the door, Lulu felt a smattering of drizzle on her parade. She looked completely wilted, like a flower blossom that some clod had crushed under the sole of her Manolos. Sara shook her head at Lulu's questioning look then hurried to the back office. Lulu's heart sank.

Now that her mind had opened to the possibility that

the day might *not* go according to script, Lulu noticed other problems. "Where did that Seb get to?" demanded Lulu, striding into the kitchen and putting her hands on her hips.

"Am I my brother's keeper?" asked Ben.

Lulu clucked. "He knew he was supposed to help us out today! He was going to win over Miss Adrian with his charm, and you were going to win her over with your sauce. Where could he have gotten to?"

Ben flipped over some ribs. "Have you noticed anything different about Seb, Mother? Since he returned from New York, I mean?"

Lulu watched as he halfheartedly swiped at some meat with the dry rub. "Ben," she said a little louder as she gently bumped him out of the way. "Move out of the way, baby—I'm stepping in for a few minutes. Whatever poor soul gets this meat . . . and I hope to high heaven it isn't Rebecca Adrian . . . isn't going to get the full flavor of the spices. We can't be afraid of the paprika, it *makes* the ribs." She gave her son a sharp, concerned look. "Why don't you take a break? Pull up a stool and relax and tell me what's on your mind. You know that always made you feel better when you were a little guy."

Ben pushed the stool over to the center bar and, chin propped in his hands, watched his mother scrub up, then expertly mix the brown sugar, dry mustard, garlic powder, salt, and paprika, and busily rub it onto the pork. She also managed to whip up a fresh pot of coffee for them. Ordinarily, he'd have been transported right back to his happy childhood while watching Lulu move around the kitchen. But today he had a problem weighing on his mind.

Lulu picked up the conversation again. "You were talking about Seb. I know what you were going to say, Ben. But I already had a word with Seb about it."

Ben looked relieved. "Well I am glad to hear that,

Mother. So he didn't mind talking about it? His problem, I mean. Is there something we can do to help him out?"

Lulu waved dismissively. "It's not all that much of a problem. I told him no more loud shirts with patterns on them. Especially the herringbone one. It makes Big Ben want to upchuck."

"For heaven's sake, Mother! I'm not talking about Seb's fashion sense."

Lulu knit her brows. "You mean his flirting with the Graces? I did tell him to cool it a little bit. But I think they kind of like it. At least, Cherry does. She fluttered those eyelashes a mile a minute. Although I saw Jeanne roll her eyes the other day—"

"Mother!" Ben broke off in exasperation. He gathered his thoughts and his patience together, and continued, "I mean, the way he's sniffling all the time."

Lulu looked perplexed.

"I just have to wonder, Mother, if maybe he didn't get caught up in some kind of trouble in New York. Like . . . drugs."

"Pah! Is this all because Seb won't go hunting with you?"

"No, it's because he's sniffing."

"Because of the pollen!"

"No, Mother, the pollen is long gone. It's May."

"I'm well aware of the month, Ben," said Lulu with dignity. "But there are plenty of other allergens out there: grass pollen, mold—"

"Sure, since Seb spends *so* much time in the great outdoors."

"Or he could even be allergic to B.B. and Elvis."

"The Labs? Come on, Mother. Seb grew up with dogs. I hardly think he's suddenly developed some major dog-fur allergy. I think maybe he's gone over to the dark side a little. Maybe he's more like Daddy than we thought."

Lulu sighed. "Daddy left when Seb was two. I hardly think he could have warped him that early in life."

Ben shook his head. "Daddy was a scoundrel, Mother. It's not like Seb would be the original black sheep of the family."

"Seb is *nothing* like your father. He's just . . . wayward." But she sounded uncertain.

"I'm just saying that maybe it was a genetic thing. You know—maybe it's not even his fault if he's going rotten."

"But you don't know for sure, Ben. Right? You don't know for sure that Seb is on drugs. He might be guilty of nothing more than gaudy dressing," said Lulu.

Ben just looked sad. "We've had a streak of scoundrels in the family, Mother."

Lulu said in a huffy voice, "I wouldn't go so far as to say that!"

"Think about it. Even your own daddy left."

"And Mama died of a broken heart. Thank the Lord for Aunt Pat, though. She didn't just step in; she loved me like her own. See, it all works out in the end. We just don't know what the plan is, that's all."

Ben said, "The point I was trying to make was about Seb. I'm wondering if he's one of those bad seeds. Like Daddy and Granddaddy. That's all I was trying to say."

"Let's talk about this later," said Lulu. "Or never. We've got some finger-licking barbeque to concoct!"

Word spread courtesy of the Graces that Rebecca Adrian was persona non grata as far as the Aunt Pat's people were concerned. Peggy Sue pulled the story out of Sara and felt it necessary to share the news with everyone, lest they be tempted to be pleasant to Rebecca Adrian. Nobody wanted to upset her enough for her to say ugly things about the barbeque to Cooking Channel, but nobody busted their buttons to rush to her side and visit for a spell.

Except for little Coco. Ordinarily, one of the patrons or staff would have rescued one of their own from the clutches of the wicked Rebecca Adrian. In this case, however, they felt like Cordelia Taylor could hold her own.

In fact, Coco was the ideal choice to provide entertainment while Rebecca's barbeque was prepared. For the first time since she'd arrived in Memphis, Rebecca Adrian finally seemed impressed with something.

"So," Rebecca asked Coco, "you started off with the Wee Miss pageant and won that title—"

"Still have the crown on top of my dresser. It's the tallest crown you've ever seen, Miss Adrian. It looks like I have the Emerald City on my head."

"And then you were in the Tiny Miss pageant and won that title—"

Coco shook her head and her blond curls danced. "No." She frowned. "I was first runner-up for the Tiny Miss. I was robbed, that's what everyone told me."

"Oh, brother," said her twin sister Ella Beth who'd come up to listen in for a minute. She quickly retreated to the kitchen to find Lulu.

Rebecca continued, "And then there was the Little Miss pageant. And that was last year?"

"It was. And I won that one, too."

"Aren't beauty pageants really expensive?" Rebecca was beginning to wonder if there were big bucks to be had with either barbeque restaurants or winning beauty pageants.

Coco shrugged. "Daddy says if it keeps me busy, it's okay by him. But he's not crazy about the dresses we have to buy. And Coach keeps telling me that Mama has *not* been as supportive as she could be. I could have used a real makeover this year because I'll be in the Miss pageant for the very first time." Coco glowered at Sara, who fortunately missed her look since she was trying to get orders from every person there and avoid Rebecca Adrian at all costs.

A few minutes later, the barbeque plate was ready. Lulu served it to Rebecca herself, and Ben came out of the kitchen to witness the event.

The plate fairly groaned with food. Ribs were piled up high, and the plate was loaded with red beans and rice, spicy corn bread muffins, and delicious coleslaw. Rebecca looked irritated. "You didn't have to bring so much, you know. There's no way I'm can eat all that."

Lulu looked surprised. "We didn't heap it like that just for you, honey. We fix all the plates like that."

The loud banter and chatting in the restaurant lowered to a hush as Rebecca Adrian took her first bite of ribs. She clearly played the moment up for all it was worth, conscious of the attention she was getting. Rebecca rolled the food around in her mouth for a moment.

"I believe she thinks she's at a wine tasting," murmured Ben to Lulu.

"As long as she doesn't spit it out," she answered.

"This," said Rebecca Adrian, pausing long enough to bring perspiration droplets to Ben's face, "is *excellent* barbeque. The pork is firm, but not dry. No charring on the bark. Smoky flavor from the dry rub, with accents of cumin, chili powder, and"—she rubbed her lips together—"paprika."

"What did she say?" bellowed Big Ben in his baritone voice.

"She said it was good," reported Buddy.

"We needed some expert from New York to toodle down here and tell us something we already knew?"

Once again, Morty neglected to summarily shush him, which was a far cry from his usual practice.

A miffed expression passed over Rebecca's face until she replaced it with her usual cool detachment. She was all business again and took out her black notebook to jot down a few notes.

"Glad you liked it," said Ben awkwardly. "What happens now?"

"Well, of course, there are other barbeque restaurants on our list," she said in a brisk tone. "But I've made my notes, and will report my thoughts and impressions to the producers." She gave a rather simpering smile. "They'll be in touch."

As Lulu asked her a little more about the process the network was using to determine the best barbeque, Flo finally caught up with Sara. It wasn't easy, since Sara was determined to flit in and out of the dining room with little contact with everyone—especially Rebecca Adrian.

Flo put a hesitant hand on Sara's arm. "I am so, so sorry about leaving Derrick last night. It's a good thing I never had any children of my own."

Sara couldn't be tart with Flo. "Forget it, Flo. I wasn't actually watching out for him myself. It's over and done with. Maybe it even taught him a lesson. After all, he should have walked out with you and been on his merry way to Youth Group. He's not a baby."

Flo swallowed. "Did anything happen to him?"

Sara sighed. "*Some*thing happened. But I'm not sure what it was. She's good at cutting people down a notch." She saw Coco talking animatedly with Rebecca. "I guess she's not doing any harm talking to Coco. Coco's completely undeflatable. Unlike me."

"Honey, when you walk through the door, it's like a breath of fresh air. You've always got this big, beaming smile on your face and have so much energy. Right now it's like that woman sucked the life out of you. Well, you have none of it, Sara. She just wants to bring everybody down. She probably doesn't even know anybody in New York. Braggart."

Sara made a face. "She sure wasn't impressed by Southern folk art. I guess she thinks we're all hillbillies, spending our days playing banjos at hootenannies."

"Or pulling beer out of our front-porch fridges," said Flo.

"Or that we have so many broken, beat-up cars that our yards look like used car lots."

"At least," said Flo, "you're not letting her get you down.

Peggy Sue gave me the lowdown on what happened. I really think that Miss Thing needs to learn a lesson."

"She's entitled to her opinion, Flo."

"But not entitled to present it in such an ugly way. Listen," said Flo, "the Graces are all planning on going by Susan's Southern Accents gallery tonight. She's going to have some wine and cheese, and we'll soak in your art and have ourselves a real party. We've all been dying to see it for ages—we couldn't be more thrilled." She gave Sara a hug.

A smile spread over Sara's freckled face. "Thanks, Flo." She squinted over toward the lunch counter where Rebecca Adrian held court with a crowd of admirers. "Uh-oh," Sara said. "Looks like more trouble. That's not Mildred Cameron's manuscript, is it?"

"Oh Lordy," breathed Flo. "I was sure her book was a figment of her imagination. She's been talking about that thing for forty years. I thought that manuscript was as fictional as the tooth fairy."

Sara winced. "It looks like she's offering it up for Rebecca's inspection."

Flo shook her permed head. "There's nothing about poor Mildred that can hold up to inspection, honey. She already has two strikes against her because she looks like the skinny, bug-eyed spinster on the old maid cards. Bless her heart."

Sara hurried toward the impending catastrophe, and Flo followed along beside her. "Maybe we can stop her."

"And just think," added Flo a little breathlessly, "it's a romance. Dear God."

It was too late. Mildred Cameron's honking voice squawked, "Miss Adrian, I've waited for years for someone to present my manuscript to a worthy New York publisher."

"Oh no," groaned Sara.

"And so," continued Mildred with rather touching dignity, "I present you with my life's work. My pièce de résistance." Her spindly arms, which clasped the bundle of raggedy papers to her flat bosom, abruptly proffered them to Rebecca Adrian.

"Looks like Abraham offerin' up Isaac for the sacrifice," whispered Flo.

"What the *hell*," said Rebecca, "is this?"

Mildred gaped at Rebecca in utter confusion. Had she not heard what she said? "My *manuscript*," she repeated loudly. You never could tell who was hard of hearing, thought Mildred. Maybe the lady had turned up her iPod too loud too many times.

Rebecca rolled her eyes and made a great show of reverently placing the papers on the lunch counter in front of her. She flipped to twenty pages in or so and read dramatically, "'She trembled like a trapped bird at his masterful touch. His sardonic eyes gleamed with his devilish intent. As he gripped her yielding softness—'"

Mildred Cameron gave a choked cry.

If it had been a slow-motion disaster, like in a movie, then maybe somebody could have stopped the super-sized iced tea as it catapulted toward Rebecca Adrian's fancy "casual" clothes.

But this wasn't the movies. And Mildred Cameron's drink was well on its way to being splashed all over Rebecca Adrian.

It was debated at some length afterward whether Mildred Cameron had intentionally covered Rebecca with the sweet tea. Some people thought Mildred had been aghast enough to do almost anything. But others thought that nobody on this earth would deliberately knock over a glass of Aunt Pat's iced tea. It was just that good.

Shoring up the evidence in favor of accidental drenching was Mildred's face right after the incident. It was a study in horror. Her eyes made perfect Os; her mouth was a replica of the agonized figure in Munch's *The Scream*.

But there was a flash of triumph in Mildred's eyes, too. Particularly at the choked-back laughter from everyone at the lunch counter.

Rebecca was livid. She surged up from her stool like a Fury, slammed both palms on the lunch counter, then whirled and bent into Mildred Cameron's face. It was about that time when all the snickering stopped. "In a couple of hours *I'll* be dry. But *you'll* still be untalented."

Even the whispers had stopped now, and a hostile silence enveloped Rebecca Adrian. Now she wasn't the only one who was livid. Lulu said with narrowed eyes and a lowered voice, "Don't you *ever* set foot in here again. I don't care if you like the damned barbeque or not."

Rebecca grabbed a full paper towel roll off a nearby table and sashayed across the crowded restaurant to the door. It was a slower than usual walk since her route was crowded with glowering patrons.

"Could this day possibly get any worse?" Lulu demanded of Ben. "We've got two dashed dreams, a devastated teenager, some royally ticked off Graces, and we will probably get completely overlooked for a plug on the Cooking Channel."

"Don't look now, Mother," drawled Ben, "but having Lurleen Ashton here won't exactly make things any better."

Lurleen was the co-owner of Hog Heaven, the leading competitor to Aunt Pat's. Her gung ho, cheerleading, way-too-sunny attitude made Lulu want to throw up.

She appeared to have a bunch of colorful flyers in her hands. "Miss Adrian?" she asked brightly, adroitly blocking Rebecca's attempted huffy escape. "Just making sure you're good and hungry. Because when you pop in down the street to Hog Heaven, you're going to have some of the best barbeque ribs you've ever put in your mouth. I was just wondering when you might be coming by today. You know, so I can lay out the red carpet and everything."

Lulu made a shooing motion at both of them. Lurleen smiled sweetly at her and followed Rebecca, who was only too delighted to push her way out the screen door.

Big Ben shivered, even though the weather outside had warmed up to nearly eighty degrees. "I got a funny feeling about what happened, Buddy. A goose walked over my grave."

Buddy said, "I know what you mean. That little thing is one wicked person. She's about as deep as a Dixie cup."

"I don't feel much like going home by myself. What're you doing this afternoon? Waving at cars?"

"No, I don't feel too much like waving. Seems a little jaunty, under the circumstances. No, I think I'll head home and watch the Weather Channel for a while."

"That so?" Big Ben brightened. "I do like the Weather Channel."

Buddy nodded sagely. "It's the most excitement you can find on television. Floods, tornadoes, droughts, snow . . . all on the same day in the same country. It's good stuff."

"Might be good enough to try out that fancy wine you've been holding on to?"

"The Domaine Vincent Dauvissat Chablis Les Preuses?"

"That very one."

"Watching the Weather Channel," said Buddy soberly, "is *not* a special occasion."

Big Ben's jowly face fell even further.

"I still have some of the sweet tea left over from the other day, though."

Big Ben pushed up from the table and hitched up his trousers. "Let's go!"

Tony the camera man walked out of the men's room and up to Ben. "Where's Rebecca?" Ben pointed to the door, and Tony said "What? She's gone?" He looked through the window in time to see the Cooking Channel van passing Beale Street.

He shrugged. "Might as well enjoy some lunch." He hopped up on a lunch stool.

"I'm so sorry, Tony," said Lulu. "I ran Rebecca off. I'd totally forgotten that she was your ride. This plate is on me." She rubbed her hand against the side of her face. "Can we give you a ride after lunch?"

Tony shook his head. "The Peabody is easy to walk to, Mrs. Taylor. I should get a little exercise, anyway. Not that your barbeque is fattening or anything," he added hastily.

"Well, it wasn't designed to be low fat."

Tony frowned. "We were supposed to be heading over to Hog Heaven later this evening. Did she say anything about where she might be going in the meantime?"

Coco chimed in. "She told me she was really tired and wanted to nap."

"Must need to sleep it off," muttered Flo.

Tony said thoughtfully, "She did tie one on last night. But I don't think I ever remember her napping in the middle of an assignment. Did, uh, anything else happen?"

Lulu sighed. "I hate to admit it, but she got under my skin, Tony. She flew off the handle at one of our customers when she accidentally spilled some tea on her. Well, I guess it was an accident, anyway. Rebecca was being so ugly to Mildred that maybe she thought a little spilled tea on Rebecca's designer clothes would be a good idea. I

fired off and told her she wasn't welcome to come back to
Aunt Pat's. She was cutting down people in my family and
some of my regulars. A Cooking Channel episode or even
a series is great for a while, but if you don't have your loyal
customers, you're going to go under. I lost my temper. I just
had this flash of a thought that came over me about how
Aunt Pat had always made the restaurant about friends and
family. She wouldn't have tolerated any meanness toward
her friends—and I couldn't, either. But I didn't handle it
as well as I should have." Lulu sighed. "Plus," she said in
a hushed voice that Tony had to lean over to hear, "she
was . . . *rude*."

Tony, who had heard Rebecca Adrian called a lot worse,
nodded his head. "She's definitely that. Don't worry about
it, Mrs. Taylor. You've actually had the guts to tell her off,
and she needed to hear it. Maybe she's gone off to sulk for
right now, but I bet she's going to respect you a heck of a
lot more for it later."

Tony continued, "The whole mindset is like that at the
Cooking Channel. You almost *expect* to run into people like
Rebecca there. I worked at Food Network for a while, and
it was a totally organized, nice place to work. The Cooking
Channel offered me more money, and I decided to jump
ship. Wish I'd never heard of them. They're just the ugly
underbelly of the cable world. Mean-spirited. Always looking for the gotcha angle. And lots of people like Rebecca
working for them—determined, ambitious, and sneaky."

He took a big sip from his iced tea. "Sometimes I gotta
wonder about her," said Tony. "Rebecca is tiny, you know.
So she wears these spiky heels and puts people down all the
time. Maybe she has one of those Napoleon complexes."

Lulu squinted thoughtfully. "She's trying to compensate
for being so little? It's got to be a tough business, right? I'd
think that she'd be at a disadvantage simply because she's
young and small."

Tony grinned as a waitress slid a plate piled high with ribs, slaw, spicy corn bread, and baked beans in front of him on the lunch counter. "As far as I'm concerned, Mrs. Taylor, Aunt Pat's *is* where it's at. I'll put in my two cents with the boss when we get back home. They know Rebecca goes off the deep end sometimes."

Tony looked around the restaurant at the dark-paneled walls jam-packed with pictures on every available inch, the red and white checked vinyl tablecloths, and the happily chatting patrons. "And if you don't mind, I'm not in any real rush to get Rebecca. Burning off some steam will do her good. I'll hang out here for a while with all of you. I guess we can still make it over to Hog Heaven tonight and deal with the crowds on Beale. I don't think they'll bar their doors if we're a little late." He smiled.

"Say," said Ben, as a dawning thought occurred to him, "do you ever do any hunting, Tony?"

Once it had been established that hunting wasn't a popular, or even legal, pastime in New York City (and that Tony—and really, for that matter, Ben himself—didn't really have the time to go driving off into the rural areas of Tennessee or Mississippi), they moved on to other topics. Then Ben had to get back to the pit to fix more barbeque, but Tony proved to be quite a popular draw for Lulu's patrons. Maybe, thought Lulu, the good folks at Aunt Pat's were trying to prove that they weren't ordinarily inhospitable. Except, of course, in the most extreme of circumstances.

By the time Tony had devoured his food, drained a beer, then eaten another order of ribs and had another beer, a blustery wind had struck up outside. Menacing dark clouds replaced puffy white ones and banded together to block out the sun. Everyone jumped at the crack, then boom of thunder soon followed by a deluge that blew up against the windows as the heavens split open.

Lulu looked thoughtfully out the window. "I'd say you might need a ride now, Tony."

"I'll second that."

"I'd drive you to the Peabody myself," said Lulu, "but I arrived at the restaurant today courtesy of the 'Jesus Saves' bus. So we'll both need rides."

Tony frowned as he looked at his watch. "She's really done a number this time. I've killed the whole afternoon here, and she hasn't even given me a call." He double-checked his cell phone to make sure he hadn't missed any messages and shook his head. Then he tried dialing her cell phone, but she didn't answer.

"I'm going to call the network," he said, "and see if they've heard anything from her. This is out of character even for Rebecca. When it comes to work, she's usually more on top of things."

Sara had come over and leaned on the back of her booth. "Do you think she went on ahead to Hog Heaven? She left at the same time as Lurleen Ashton."

Tony shook his head. "I don't see any reason why she'd do that. She knows I'd have to go back there later to do sound and light checks, and frame shots."

He dialed his producer at the Cooking Channel. "Have you guys talked to Rebecca this afternoon? She's gone AWOL . . . That's what I'm saying! . . . No, we're not done for the day, and I've been waiting for hours for us to go to the next location. We're supposed to be covering a different story in a couple days. . . . How am I going to manage that when we can't even wrap the barbeque piece?" He listened for a minute, nodding his dark head like his producer could see him. "Gotcha. Will do."

He snapped his cell phone closed. "Well, they tried to reach her this afternoon, and she didn't answer. If you don't mind," he added, "I'll take you up on the offer for that ride. They want me to round her up. We gotta get over to Hog

Heaven and make this a wrap today. If we get too far behind, then it's going to cost the network a bunch of extra money."

"Tony, would you mind if I go inside the Peabody with you? I'll make a really quick apology and won't hold you up a minute from going to Hog Heaven." At his puzzled look, Lulu added, "I'd feel better if I apologize. I don't usually act so ugly to my guests, even if they're rude."

Tony raised his eyebrows. "I promise you weren't out of line. Most people don't have the guts to tell her like it is. But sure, come on in if it'll make you feel better. You'll probably get the satisfaction of seeing your apologies put her in a worse mood."

"It's not that she didn't deserve it. She could have been tarred and feathered for all her foolishness, and it would have served her right. But I could have handled it differently."

Sara said, "I can give y'all a lift. But I must not be as emotionally mature as you, Lulu. They'll be making snowmen in Hades before that woman gets an apology from me."

Tony said, "I was telling Lulu that sometimes I think there's something wrong with Rebecca."

"I should say there is!" said Lulu indignantly. "Anybody who doesn't like the ducks at the Peabody doesn't have their elevator go to the top floor."

Tony's cell phone rang, and he wandered off a little ways to talk with his producer again.

"I just don't understand why she has to act so ugly to everybody," said Sara.

"Maybe the Cooking Channel wants to be something new and different to show how different they are from Food Network," said Lulu.

"I think they've already succeeded. They do this gonzo reality show where people send them tips about their friend or family member's awful cooking habits. Then they ring the poor devil's doorbell around suppertime and see what's cooking. Lots of pork and beans being put on America's dinner tables."

"But you're watching the show," said Lulu.

"Of course. It's completely hilarious. But now that I've seen in person how tacky Rebecca Adrian is, I'll never watch *The Foodmobile* again. I just wonder what screwed her up," said Sara.

Lulu clucked. "That's just your psychology minor talking again."

"Well, you've got to wonder why she's so mad at the world. Maybe she had to claw her way to where she is today. Or maybe she's around nasty people all the time, and it's rubbed off," said Sara. She pursed her lips in thought.

"I don't think it's anything all that complicated," said Lulu. "Maybe she's just constipated. Lots of people are, you know," she said defensively as Sara groaned. "That MaxLax stuff works pretty well. Maybe we need to go out to Costco and get her a pallet of it."

They looked out the window with some trepidation. Hail fell from of the sky. Cherry calmly tucked her bouffant hairdo up into her helmet. "Someday y'all will come round to my way of thinking," she said. "That there hail is going to bounce clean off my helmet. And my hair won't get a drop on it."

The same couldn't be said for Tony, Lulu, and Sara as they bolted for Sara's car in the parking deck. "Almost like divine retribution," muttered Lulu. But she couldn't decide who had triggered this vengeance. She hoped, since she was on her way to offer what she felt was a sincere, if abbreviated, apology, that it might be Rebecca Adrian who had caused the celestial distress.

Sure enough, the Cooking Channel van was in the Peabody's parking deck. Sara parked as close as she could to the entrance, and they hurried inside as the hail continued to fall and the thunder rumbled nearby. Tony's face flushed with irritation. "There's no excuse," he kept muttering. And, "Wait till the boss talks to her about this. She won't try something like this again."

It was past five o'clock so the lobby was empty of tourists. Sara twisted strands of red blond hair around her finger as they rode up the elevator. Tony glowered, and Lulu felt queasy. She was not a fan of scenes, and there had been far too many over the past twenty-four hours.

Tony led the way down the third-floor hallway and thumped on one of the doors. "Rebecca!" he bellowed. He waited and then thumped his fist on the door again. "Rebecca! I want to talk to you."

There was only silence from the room.

Tony tried the door, but of course, it was locked. He thumped loudly on her door again, and a couple of doors opened farther down the hall as people curiously peeped out.

"Are you sure this is the right room?" asked Lulu.

"Absolutely. My room is just next door."

Sara looked uncomfortable as other guests continued looking out their doors. "Can't we ask the hotel manager to let us in? Or security?"

"You don't think," asked Lulu as a thought popped into her head, "she killed herself, do you?"

"No way. She loves herself way too much. Besides, being banned from Aunt Pat's wouldn't have made her suicidal, you know."

"When you put it that way, it does sound a little silly."

"I'll run get the manager," said Tony. "He'll probably check on her since I'm her coworker and everything."

Ten minutes later Tony was back with the manager and one of the hotel's security men. The manager inserted a master key and cautiously opened the door a crack. "Miss Adrian?" He waited, listening hard but hearing no response. He pushed the door open farther. "Miss Adrian?"

He stepped into the room, then backed up a step. The security man pushed them back into the hall, but Lulu was able to see a sprawled figure on the floor of the room: Rebecca Adrian—quite obviously dead.

Chapter 4

"Do you think," asked Lulu in a hushed tone appropriate for being in the vicinity of a dead body, "this is a natural-causes kind of dead or a murdered-in-her-sleep kind of dead?"

"Well, it sure as heck didn't look natural to me," said Sara. Her freckles stood out like polka dots against her suddenly white face. "Upchuck everywhere, her body crumpled at a crazy angle."

Tony, whose olive complexion had turned as pale as it could get, wandered away to report to the Cooking Channel producers that Rebecca had actually had a fairly good excuse for being out of pocket for the afternoon.

The police and a forensic team, complete with cameras, hastily blocked off the third floor of the hotel. "I think," said Lulu, "that the police and those people walking around in space suits make it seem more likely that it was murder."

"Plus the fact, of course, that everyone hated her guts," said Sara.

"There is that," said Lulu, nodding.

A Detective Lyndon Bryce introduced himself to Lulu, Sara, and Tony as he rejoined them. He didn't look at all like what Lulu thought a detective should look like. Having her stereotypes disproved always made Lulu grouchy. He had a freshly scrubbed, youthful face with the slightest hint of blond stubble.

"If you don't mind," he said politely, "I'd like to get your statements from you real quick. Separately," he added. "Sometimes we remember things differently than other people, and it's better to hear the same story three different ways." He'd set up a space in one of the vacant hotel rooms with a sergeant taking notes.

Really, their stories weren't all that different. Best barbeque in Memphis. Food scout. Unlikable sort who made enemies fast. A few angry scenes. A sudden death. The police took notes, asked a few questions, and eventually let them go.

Tony was somber. "The network will notify her family. I feel bad about this."

"It wasn't your fault," said Sara.

"But I knew what she was like. Maybe I could have shut her up somehow—kept her from bugging everybody so much. I should've stuck a sign on her back, warning everyone to keep back."

Lulu said, "It wasn't your job to babysit her, Tony. Besides, some people can't be protected from themselves." She paused. "You're assuming she was murdered."

He shrugged. "What else is there to think? Why would Rebecca have a natural death? She wasn't old. Or sick. Just mean."

And dead, thought Lulu.

Lulu thrashed around in her bed that night. When she had finally fallen asleep, the docile, baaing sheep she'd counted had turned into fanged monsters that galloped through her dreams and gnashed at her heels. She looked at the clock. Five o'clock. Late enough to finally give up courting Morpheus and get out of bed. Her mind was a muddle of thoughts she wanted to process. And she had the oddest craving for some gingerbread.

The comforting familiarity of measuring and mixing relaxed Lulu. She made the coffee, strong and black, and read the paper while the gingerbread baked. It had finally cooled to the point of eating when there was a knock on her door. Lulu frowned. At six thirty? She gathered her pink robe around her neck and peeped out the curtain of the back door. Relieved, she saw Ben with what appeared to be a hairy rodent on a leash. Babette. Lulu opened the door.

"Hi, Mother. I was just taking Babette on a little potty stroll, and I saw your lights on. Is that," he inhaled deeply, "*gingerbread*?" The thought of eating gingerbread before dawn seemed to startle, then intrigue, Ben.

"Hot from the oven. I don't know why, but I had quite a hankering for it. Help yourself to a big slice."

So they sat at Lulu's kitchen table with plates heaped with gingerbread and a stick of real butter on the checkerboard tablecloth.

"I was working out in my head," said Lulu, "what happened yesterday. I'm sure the police will decide Rebecca was murdered. There's no way that child up and died on her own like that."

Ben nodded and stuck another forkful of gingerbread in his mouth. "I know. But that means . . ."

"Well, it means that somebody we know probably did her in. Because, who would follow somebody all the way from New York to commit murder? And that's what's really getting my goat. First of all, I hate it that somebody I know, love, and trust could be sneaky enough to commit murder. It's hard to stomach." She sighed deeply and tapped her fingers against her coffee cup.

"Rebecca was hateful enough to rile anybody up, Mother. The killer may not even have been acting in their right mind when they did it."

"Plus *we're* under suspicion until the police nab the culprit. We're all going to be looking sideways at each other. It's much worse than actually knowing who did it.

"She was probably poisoned," continued Lulu morosely. "All that being sick and the way her body was lying. And that can't be wonderful for the restaurant, either. Can't you see the headlines now? 'Poisoned! A Cooking Channel scout dropped dead today after eating barbeque ribs at Aunt Pat's.'"

Ben groaned. "And I'm the chef."

"But why should you be a suspect? You barely even met the woman. The only time you even spoke to her was right after the tasting."

"You're forgetting the fact that I might be upset that she turned my wife into a shadow of her former self. Oh, and she made my nephew, Mr. Tough Guy Derrick, cry like a little baby?"

"I mean she did nothing *directly* to you."

"Well, it can't be good that I cooked her food," said Ben. He put his elbows on the table and held his head. "Sara and Derrick are sure to be suspects, I guess."

"Considering it's public knowledge that Rebecca had a big scene with Sara and upset Derrick, I'm afraid so. Mildred, too."

Ben said, "Now hold on a minute, though. Mildred wasn't even around when Rebecca Adrian ate her ribs. She came up with that bundle of papers right before Rebecca got covered with iced tea and left."

"That's not what I'm remembering," said Lulu. "I think she was really enjoying that barbeque. She kept taking little forkfuls all along. Stuffing herself here and there. But it's still completely impossible. It's not like Mildred had poison stowed away in her pocketbook on the off chance that Rebecca was going to disgrace her in front of the entire restaurant." Lulu clucked impatiently.

They were quiet for a minute, concentrating on their gingerbread and their thoughts.

"Come to think of it," said Ben in the voice of a man about to make a phone call to the police, "Sara and Derrick weren't anywhere *near* Rebecca's food."

Lulu said, "Honey, you know I hate to contradict you on Sara. But that plate was getting loaded right back in the kitchen. And it was pretty obvious whose plate it was by the care we were taking to make it look just so. Sara hurried back and forth, and in and out through that kitchen a million times, picking up orders. And the restaurant was so crowded, I think anybody could have slipped something in her food while I was talking to her about the Cooking Channel. I guess it lets Derrick off, though. He was at school."

Ben cut off a big slab of butter and slathered it on a hunk of gingerbread. "I'm thinking Mildred, Sara, and Derrick couldn't have been the only three people with an ax to grind with Rebecca Adrian. I'm *hoping* that's the case, anyway."

Lulu dropped her voice like someone might be listening in under her kitchen table. "Flo had some kind of a run-in with her. She surely did. I don't know exactly what happened, but she said the whole reason she accidentally left Derrick at the Peabody to begin with was the fact that Rebecca had gotten her so steamed up."

"Well, *Flo* sure as heck wasn't lurking around in the kitchen."

"No, but she was right next to Rebecca the rest of the time after the initial tasting. And Rebecca kept right on eating, like I told you," said Lulu.

"I find it hard to believe, Mother, that Rebecca Adrian could hurt Flo's feelings. What did she do—insult Elvis's manhood or something?"

Lulu said, "Whatever it was, it was pretty serious. Serious enough for Flo to forget about Derrick. The only thing, though," said Lulu thoughtfully, "is that maybe she wasn't poisoned at the restaurant at all. Maybe it happened back at the Peabody."

There was a sudden explosion of yipping, and Lulu whipped her head around to see Babette skidding on the old linoleum as she raced off after whatever hallucination she was having. Ben jogged over and scooped Babette up, crooning soothingly to her.

Lulu studiously ignored the episode, which—if discussed at all—would end up with Ben saying that no one really *understood* Babette.

Ben struggled to remember the lost thread of their conversation as he absently put Babette's polka-dotted bow back on. "You said maybe Rebecca was poisoned *after* she left Aunt Pat's?"

"Why not? They have food and drinks at the Peabody, too. Somebody could have gone there and poisoned her food."

"Why would she be eating anything if she just polished off a huge plate of barbeque with all the fixings?"

"I thought you might want to join me in grasping at straws, Ben." Lulu looked crossly at her son. "Maybe someone spiked her drink there. We do use a lot of salt and paprika in the dry rub—she could have been thirsty and drank a bunch of Drano in her Coca-Cola or something. If you think about it, there are a ton of poisons within our easy reach every day. Cleaners, detergents, yard chemicals, insect killers . . ."

Ben pushed his plate away. "Okay, I'm done here. Thanks for the hopefully poison-free gingerbread."

Lulu wrinkled her nose. "What *is* that smell?" She twisted in her chair to look behind her. "Oh, for heaven's sake. Ben!"

Ben was already standing, hustling for the roll of paper towels and some cleaner. "Babette just gets a little excited sometimes, Mother. She can't help it."

"Excited about what? We're sitting here eating ginger-bread!" Lulu watched as the offensive spot on the linoleum was efficiently cleared away. "You know, Ben, seeing that poop has given me an idea."

"I may kick myself for asking, but what kind of an idea?"

"That poop was a sign from above. I'm meant to go clean up this poop we're facing. I need to shovel right through it until I find out who has put us in this predicament. The sooner we find out, the better."

"Mother, I thought you didn't put any stock in signs."

"That was before yesterday, Ben. Lord knows I should never have made it to the restaurant yesterday morning. I should have pulled those covers right back over my head, rolled over, and gone back to sleep."

After reviewing the possibilities, Lulu decided that the first order of business was to talk to Mildred. First of all, she wanted to make sure that she felt comfortable coming back to the restaurant. It was never good for business to lose one of your regulars, no matter the reason. Lulu also wanted to pick her brain a little about Rebecca's murder.

But first she had to get there. Ben had had her car towed to a garage yesterday morning, but the repair wasn't done yet. Lulu winced at the thought, because the length of time a mechanic had her car usually corresponded to the size of the bill she was due to receive.

Fortunately, Lulu caught a ride with Sara to Mildred's

house. "Want to come in and visit with me?" Lulu asked her.

Sara made a face. "No thanks. It'll be too much like a Rebecca Adrian rejection support group. When you're finished visiting, call me on my cell phone, and I'll swing back around and take you to Aunt Pat's. I have a couple of errands to run anyway."

And so Lulu found herself alone on Mildred's front porch. She rang the doorbell. "Ding dong! Ding dong! Hello! Hello!" sang an oddly high-pitched voice from inside the house. It was kind of early, but Mildred's paperback exchange bookstore opened early, too, and it certainly sounded like someone was awake. Did Mildred have her mother squirreled away in her house? Lulu thought her mom had died ages ago.

The lacy curtains in the front window pulled aside, and Mildred's homely face with its thick spectacles peered out. Lulu waved cheerily like she didn't have a care in the world and had nothing better to do than visit with Mildred on the day following a prominent customer's murder.

Mildred smiled tentatively at Lulu and slid back the series of chains, sliding locks, and deadbolts that secured her humble castle. Lulu gave her a little hug when she finally came out. "Sweetie, I'm so, so sorry about yesterday! I couldn't sleep a wink last night for thinking about it. Could I come in for a few minutes and ease my conscience?"

Mildred, ordinarily not the most demonstrative person, couldn't refuse Lulu's charm and hugged her back, spindly arms awkwardly cinching Lulu's waist. As she ushered Lulu into her dimly lit living room, Lulu felt like she'd stepped back in time to the Victorian era. Everything had a little frill attached to it—the lampshades, the curlicued frames around prints of *The Lady of Shallot* and maidens delicately sniffing roses in English gardens. Gilded bird cages contained various talking birds, which explained the high-pitched talking Lulu heard. Lacy tablecloths covered end tables, and the windows were all encased with lace. Old, chipped crystal bowls held faded bits of potpourri. As usual, Lulu felt a pang that this woman who thought the world of romance had not found any of it herself.

Mildred's hand fluttered to her head as if to keep her thoughts from flying away. "Lulu, I don't want to be a bad hostess, but could you follow me into the kitchen for a minute or two? I was putting together some food for supper tonight before I leave for the bookstore."

Lulu said hastily, "Of course! Here, let's go in and maybe I can even lend you a hand."

The kitchen itself wasn't all that modern, either. There was no microwave to be seen, and the appliances looked like they might have been labeled "harvest gold" and "avocado green" at their 1975 debut. An ancient toaster oven on the counter looked prepared to burst into flames at any moment. The only thing that lent a hint of modernity to the room was the slow cooker Mildred hovered over. Although, thought Lulu, come to think of it, this particular slow cooker might be a 1970s incarnation itself.

Mildred said apologetically, "It'll just be a minute." Lulu watched as she put some half-defrosted chicken in the bottom of the slow cooker, dumped a bag of frozen broccoli on the top, and sloshed a can of cream of chicken soup over the two other ingredients. Mildred turned it on low. "There," she said. She looked uncertainly at the appliance. "That should become supper by the end of the day."

Would it? wondered Lulu. She doubted it would be a *good* supper. She trailed Mildred back to the living room— which looked more like an old-fashioned parlor. Lulu perched stiffly on a damask sofa and smiled as Mildred settled her gangly length into a toile armchair and smiled tentatively at Lulu.

"It's all right, Lulu; don't worry about what happened

yesterday. It wasn't your fault, after all. I should have known," she said, giving a dismissive sniff, "that Rebecca Adrian wouldn't understand romance. She's clearly not a reader."

Lulu was relieved to see that Mildred had come to terms with the incident. She must be better adjusted than Lulu had thought. "Exactly. She was heartless, so how would she have known about matters of the heart?"

Lulu felt a stab of pity for Mildred. She'd been heading for that fall for a long time. She was relieved it wasn't as damaging as she'd thought.

"Anyway, I'm thinking about giving myself a little change of pace. I thought," Mildred said eagerly, "that I'd write a murder mystery. Maybe one set in Victorian times."

Lulu said, "That sounds like a wonderful idea. Have you been thinking about this for a while?" Lulu found it hard to imagine that Mildred had been thinking about anything other than her constantly revised romance novel.

Mildred looked deflated again. "Not really. But when Miss Adrian was being so nasty about the romance, I mulled over some of the other things I could work on. After all, owning a bookstore means that I've read a whole lot of different books. It's not the end of the world."

Lulu said, "Now with mysteries, does that mean that you need to do some research?"

Mildred perked up. "That's what I'm saying, Lulu. I've got so many mysteries in my bookstore that it'll be a cinch. But I did think"—Mildred drew herself up importantly—"that maybe I could look into some true crime cases here in Memphis. Even if I'm writing something from Victorian times, I could find out how detectives do their jobs and how suspects act. Maybe I'll even spend some time riding around with the police."

Lulu gave a snorting laugh. "Sounds like you'll have

plenty of research that you can do right around the restaurant." Lulu clucked. "I mean, it's not the biggest shocker in the world that nasty woman is dead, considering how ugly she was to everybody, but . . ." Lulu saw the color drain from Mildred's face. "Oh! You didn't know."

Mildred shook her head. She reached into her dress pocket and took out a frilly handkerchief and blew her nose with a honking sound. "When? Yesterday?"

"She died sometime after I booted her out of the restaurant. It . . . wasn't a natural death. I think she must have been poisoned," said Lulu.

Mildred looked a bit like she'd eaten some poison herself. Pure nausea crossed her face. She closed her eyes for a few seconds, leaning back into the armchair.

Lulu frowned at Mildred's reaction. She certainly didn't *like* Rebecca Adrian. Maybe it was the sudden violence of the death that made it difficult for Mildred to take in. But if she was this sensitive, then how would she handle writing death scenes for mysteries?

"I guess the police will want to talk to me," she said in a quiet voice that was very unlike her usual adenoidal tones.

Lulu considered this. "I suppose they will. Considering the events of the day and all. But I can't imagine you have anything to worry about, honey. We were all right there watching you when you talked to Miss Adrian." Mildred winced at the public nature of her humiliation. Lulu hurried on. "You didn't put anything in her food. And your drink pitched all over her, after all. She left immediately after that."

Lulu's words didn't seem to comfort Mildred. "She did leave right after that," said Mildred. She spoke in such a low voice that Lulu had to lean in to hear her. "But I left right after that, too. Do they know when she took the poison?"

"I'm not sure. I'm not even sure it *was* poison. I'm making wild, unsubstantiated guesses. Don't listen to this old lady, honey. I didn't come over here to rile you up, after all—I wanted to apologize for the whole mess and ask you to please visit us as soon as you're ready. I'll guarantee you a plate on the house." Lulu knew that would bring her in. Award-winning barbeque would win out, hands down, over that vile concoction in the slow cooker.

Mildred was insistent. "Can you find out what the police think? What happened to her and whether they think I have anything to do with it?"

A tall order, thought Lulu. Besides, the police were most likely going to come calling on her anyway, just to check in. "I'll see what I can find out, honey. Pink, the policeman, comes to the restaurant almost every day, so I'll see if I can't squeeze some information out of him." She looked at her watch. "Let me call Sara real quick and ask her to swing by and get me."

Mildred wasn't even listening to her. She looked like a broken twig in that big armchair. Lulu quickly called Sara, then patted Mildred on the knee. "You don't have a thing to worry about. I'd never have mentioned it to you if I'd known you were going to be so upset. Do you have an alibi for yesterday afternoon?"

She looked at Lulu with blank eyes.

"You know—did anybody see you out yesterday afternoon? Did you go back to the bookstore?"

"Dora looked after the store for me all day yesterday," she said quietly. "I took the day off to work on my writing and to talk to Miss Adrian."

"Are you sure nobody saw you out anywhere yesterday afternoon? Did you run by the drugstore or over to the grocery store?"

Mildred didn't even respond. She looked like she was deep in thought.

"Honey? I was wondering if anybody *saw* you yesterday afternoon?"

Mildred looked up at Lulu with clear blue eyes. "Yes. Yes, I saw quite a few people."

"Well, that's a relief, isn't it?" said Lulu quickly. "You make sure to let that Detective Bryce know all about it, and you'll be in good shape."

Lulu hesitated, then added, "Maybe you should take a day off today. Just put your feet up? You look like you've had such a shock."

Lulu's phone trilled. Sara letting her know she was outside.

"Honey, I've got to run. Sara's taking me to Aunt Pat's today."

Mildred stood so quickly that she nearly knocked Lulu over. "Can you call me?" she asked with a piercing intensity. "Can you let me know what Pink says?"

It wasn't really a question at all. Lulu said, "Of course I will. I'm not sure he's going to be at the restaurant today, though."

Mildred slumped.

"How about if I give him a buzz, even if he doesn't come in," said Lulu, walking toward the door. "I'm sure he can fill me in with some basic information." Mildred wasn't really listening again, so Lulu slipped out the door. She turned to wave before she shut the door behind her, but Mildred had already left the room.

"Bye-bye! Bye-bye!" whistled a parrot. It was an oddly mournful sound.

"Sounds like she's behaving even odder than usual," said Sara to Lulu. "Why do you think the news hit her so hard?"

Lulu shook her head. "I guess she thought she'd be the major suspect. She had that big scene with Rebecca in front of everybody. And then she waffled back and forth about whether she had an alibi or not for yesterday afternoon."

"Well, if we go by the big-scene standard, I should be suspect number one. I had a huge falling out with her. And I definitely had time to put something in her food. I was in and out of the kitchen, and passed right by her plate about fifteen times. Add that to the fact that I hated her guts, and I've got motive and opportunity."

"You didn't do it, did you?"

For a second, Lulu thought she caught a fleeting shadow cross Sara's face. Then Sara said stoutly, "No indeed. I'd have strung her up by her skinny neck. Poisoning was too good for her."

Lulu gave the smile that Sara was looking for, but inside Lulu was worried. Was Sara hiding something, too? Sara had a very hot temper. And Lulu didn't think for a minute that Sara was sorry that Rebecca had puked all over her designer duds, no matter what Sara said about poisoning being too good for her.

"But," Sara continued, "I really doubt Mildred murdered Rebecca. Somehow I just don't see her going to Rebecca's hotel room and forcing arsenic down her throat. Did she threaten her with her overwhelming strength?" Sara snorted. "The only thing I hate is that the paper this morning even mentioned Aunt Pat's in the same article with a suspicious death."

Lulu nodded sadly. "Well, I don't think we'll lose any regulars over it. We've been around so long that I think folks know we don't serve poisoned barbeque most days. And anybody who knew Rebecca Adrian couldn't be too surprised by her sudden death. That was one mean woman."

Chapter

5

"You'd think," said Lulu to Seb, "that people would be a little more concerned about eating here. Aren't they worried they could end up with food poisoning or something?"

There was a damper on the usual lighthearted chatter at the restaurant that afternoon but lots more unfamiliar faces. Lulu figured that some people were curious about the newspaper article that morning. It hadn't said anything too atrocious, but it definitely mentioned the connection between the dead television scout and Aunt Pat's.

Seb gave his cigarette-induced gravelly laugh. "When I looked over the paper this morning, there wasn't any kind of mention of salmonella, Mom. People want some dirt, that's all. They're not worried about their personal health."

The mention of personal health reminded Lulu of Ben's suspicions about Seb. She wracked her brain to remember what you were supposed to watch out for with drug use. It had been a while since she'd had teenagers. She peered closely at him. Wasn't she supposed to look for sweatiness and dilated pupils?

"Something wrong, Mom?" drawled Seb. "Should I wipe my nose or something?"

He certainly sounded surly. Wasn't irritability supposed to be an early sign of drug use? Could he have killed Rebecca Adrian in a drug-fueled rage? "Why weren't you here yesterday afternoon for the barbeque tasting, Seb?" He rolled his eyes at Lulu. "No, I mean it. You're part of the family . . . although sometimes you try not to be. You couldn't have spared a few minutes to watch the tasting?"

"Mom, if I'd been here, I'd be a suspect now just like all of you, wouldn't I? Besides, I did come in yesterday— but not during the tasting. I worked in the office yesterday morning."

Lulu frowned. "What time was that? I don't remember you being here yesterday morning."

"Before the big 'Jesus Saves' bus brought you in. I just had some paperwork to take care of. Nobody was here."

"You were *up* before anyone got to Aunt Pat's?"

"You don't have to act so shocked, Mom." Seb sounded affronted.

"Well, I believe you're the same baby I birthed, and I never do remember you being an early bird. You even slept through your first feeding of the day."

"Things do change as we get older," said Seb.

"Hmm." Maybe Seb *was* on drugs. Lulu wondered if insomnia was a symptom of drug use. "And what were you doing yesterday afternoon?"

"Taking a nap. I was sleepy after getting up so early to come in. I'd done my paperwork after all, right? What's wrong, Mom? You don't think I had anything to do with that food scout's death, do you? Why would I have killed the woman? Remember—I *like* women." He grinned. "I'm not running around poisoning them to death."

"So you *slept* all yesterday afternoon?" Lulu guessed that explanation would have to do, but she wasn't happy about it.

Lulu surely couldn't think of any reason at all why Seb would kill someone he hadn't even met. But she was convinced he was hiding something. In fact, she was starting to wonder if everybody she knew was hiding something. First Mildred, then Sara, now Seb. The whole idea gave her a sickening feeling down in the pit of her stomach. The sooner she figured out who killed Rebecca Adrian, the better for all of them.

Lulu was never more delighted to see Pink Rogers in her life. She patted herself on the back for her inspired idea some years ago to offer half-priced food to police officers and firefighters. Despite the large amount of barbeque Pink consumed, he stayed fit and trim. And he always had a warm smile and kind word for everyone at the restaurant. Lulu loved having a guardian angel in the guise of a Memphis police officer. When he was off duty, Pink favored wearing pastel button-downs, although a more masculine man you'd never meet. Of course, being six feet seven and two hundred and fifty pounds meant you could afford to be secure in your masculinity.

Pink headed over to his usual seat on the barstool, where the lunchtime patrons sat shoulder to shoulder, but Lulu quickly herded him to a booth to sit with her. She wanted a little bit more privacy than the barstools afforded. "Oh no, come sit over here with me. I want to talk to you, and I can't hitch myself up on those stools anymore. My hitcher is broken."

Pink raised his eyebrows but followed Lulu to a booth. One of the waitresses came over quickly, and Lulu said, "Pick whatever you want, honey. It's on the house today."

Now Pink looked suspicious. His usual fifty percent off wasn't a bad deal at all, but free food was unheard of. He placed his order, then said, "Spill it Lulu. This must have something to do with the shenanigans over here yesterday. The scout?"

Lulu had the grace to blush. "It was a *trying* day, let's say. But, yes," she said in a lower voice, "I wanted to press you for some information. Nothing that you'd get in trouble for giving me," she hurried on. "But it's not like I'm going to go to the paper or anything. I'm just trying to figure out which way is up."

Pink nodded and took a long gulp of his sweet tea. "Fair enough. What's on your mind?"

Lulu said, "First of all, is it murder? I mean, it didn't look natural to me, but I'm not someone who'd know."

"It was murder." This was said in the discouraging tone of one who does not want a whole lot of questions asked.

"Right," said Lulu. "So, I'll move on to the next question. Was it poison?"

"It was poison." Same tone but same friendly face.

"Not like an accidental poisoning?"

Now Pink grinned. "Explain to me how you accidentally poison someone? Your red beans and rice doesn't have mushrooms you found in the woods somewhere, does it?" He appeared unconcerned by the possibility. "I wish I knew how you make those. I'd be making it to go with my dinner every night. When I'm retired, I want to come work for you, Lulu. You can show me all your kitchen tricks, and I can be Ben's sous chef."

Lulu beamed at him, then said, "Honey, you're welcome to work at Aunt Pat's when you're done crime fighting." She frowned, trying to collect her thoughts again. "Oh. Okay, scratch that accidental-poisoning idea. Let's see. Was it something . . . she ate?" Lulu's lined face looked anxiously at Pink.

He wanted to relieve her mind but couldn't. He said gently, "It was something she ate or drank. The forensic team is working on it. And to answer your next question, it wasn't some sort of slow-acting poison that's been eating at her since she left the Big Apple. She was either poisoned here or soon after she arrived at the Peabody."

Lulu leaned forward. "And so the suspects for this murder are . . ." She trailed off, hoping Pink would just fill in the blank. When he didn't, she said, "Mildred Cameron wanted me to ask you if she was a suspect."

Pink said, "Now, Lulu, you know I can't go into details about the case. I'm not even assigned to this one, anyway."

"I guess there's no mad stalker who followed her down from New York City? No rabid ex who decided to do away with her while she was in Memphis? No serial killer around here who has this MO?" asked Lulu.

The plates of ribs, red beans and rice, and spicy corn muffins arrived at the table. Pink thanked the waitress and waited a minute until she'd left. "No, there's nobody like that around, Lulu. I'm sorry. The most likely suspects are going to be people she interacted with or had any type of conflict with over the last couple of days. We'll retrace her steps, question different people, and check out her cell phone for incoming and outgoing calls." He took a big bite from his ribs. "You didn't, of course, hear any of this from me. We've been chatting about our mutual love of blues music, right?"

Lulu mustered a smile. "That's right." The smile faltered. "Restaurants don't like being linked to poisonings."

Pink didn't immediately answer since he had a huge mouthful of coleslaw. He swallowed it up and then gave Lulu a reassuring smile. "I'm obviously not too worried about the food here. I think you'll find that most other people won't be, either."

◇◇◇◇◇◇◇◇◇◇

The lunchtime rush ended and Lulu moved out to the screen porch, sat in one of the big wooden rocking chairs, and petted B.B., who smiled his happy Labrador smile. The roomy porch was one of Lulu's favorite parts of the restaurant. It held several picnic tables and three rocking chairs with high backs and checkered cushions. Sometimes, when the weather wasn't hot and the band wasn't too big, they'd stack up the tables in the corner, and the band would play right there on the porch. The music would mingle with the barbeque's smoky scent, pulling people right off the street. Lulu watched people walking up and down Beale Street until the afternoon heat made her doze off in her chair.

The screen door slamming abruptly startled her awake. In came Cherry, helmet still in place from her motorcycle ride, spitting mad.

"That cow, Lurleen! You won't believe what Hog Heaven has done this time!"

Lulu struggled to transition into consciousness. "Lurleen? Why? What happened?"

"They have a fuchsia pig dancing on Beale Street, outside Hog Heaven. It's carrying a sign that says 'Eat Hog Heaven's delectable, *safe* BBQ! God Bless America.'"

"Well, for heaven's sake. Although I can't say I'm surprised. That Lurleen is never up to any good. I don't think people will really think our barbeque is bad, though. Or that we're somehow un-American here." Lulu didn't sound completely convinced.

"I was thinking," said Cherry, "that Lurleen wasn't up to any good yesterday. After all, she was here when Miss Adrian got poisoned." Lulu made a face, and Cherry said quickly, "Sorry, Lulu. I mean, right before Miss Adrian got sick."

"So were a lot of people, Cherry. The dining room was jam-packed."

Cherry shook her helmeted head impatiently. "But she might really have done something to it. She was right here, after all."

"Well." Lulu considered this. "It doesn't make any sense, Cherry. We can't accuse Lurleen Ashton of murder just because we don't like her advertising techniques. I just don't see it happening. She wasn't anywhere near Rebecca's food. And what good would a dead television scout be to her? She planned for Hog Heaven to be Rebecca Adrian's very next stop. Miss Adrian was supposed to be blown away by their food and crown Hog Heaven the king of Memphis barbeque. Why kill her before she even got there?"

"I don't know, Lulu. But I'm sure in my heart of hearts that Lurleen had something to do with it all." Cherry looked huffy. "Weren't you upset about her and Seb being an item when he moved back down here? Maybe she had a jealous fit."

"Cherry, that was like a two-day fling before Seb came to his senses. After I gave him a little talking to, he realized the error of his ways in courting Lurleen Ashton. I really doubt Lurleen would still be jealous when their relationship ended months ago."

"Still, though. I had to go over there for my cousin's birthday dinner last month, and when I asked for a water, they brought me *bottled*, not tap! Who do they think they are? Stuffy snobs. Like I wanted to pay three dollars and fifty cents for something I can get from the spigot. She's greedy."

To Lulu's relief, Cherry eventually wandered inside to order some ribs. Lulu didn't think she could follow Cherry's twisted logic for another minute. Besides, it was Lulu's favorite time of the day—three o'clock, when the school bus dropped Coco and Ella Beth off right at the barricaded entrance to Beale.

As usual, she had sweet tea and some spicy corn bread out on the table for their after-school snack. Ella Beth tore through the door, ponytail bobbing. The screen door closed with a bang behind her. She gave Lulu a big hug, then buried her face in B.B.'s neck as he yelped his welcome. Cordelia ran to the screen door, then, aware that she had an image to uphold, slowed down to enter the porch at a much more sedate pace. She also hugged Lulu, careful not to mess up her elaborate hairdo.

"How were your days, girls?" asked Lulu.

"Fine," answered Coco absently. "Is Miss Adrian here?"

Lulu's heart skipped. She'd forgotten in all the hubbub yesterday that they hadn't even thought to update Coco and Ella Beth. And apparently Sara had put them straight to bed without discussing the day with them.

Lulu must have looked poleaxed. Ella Beth noticed Lulu fumbling for words. "Is something wrong, Granny Lulu? Did something happen?"

Coco raised her eyebrows at Lulu's uncharacteristic lack of words.

"Well, I'm sorry to have to tell you this, children. But there was . . . an accident. I'm afraid Miss Adrian has passed away."

Coco tilted her head to one side like an inquisitive bird. Ella Beth, always one to call a spade a spade, said, "She's dead? What kind of an accident? She was in a car wreck?"

Lulu shook her head, frustrated with her clumsiness around the children. "No, sweetie. She got really sick yesterday afternoon and then died very unexpectedly. It wasn't anything contagious," she assured them. "Let's try and find your mom, Coco. Maybe she can discuss it with you a little." Lulu's indignant conscience fussed at her for unloading the problem on Sara. But she felt better about doing so when Coco melted into her mother's arms.

The news of Rebecca Adrian's demise didn't seem to

upset Ella Beth in the slightest. After all, she'd mentioned she didn't like the woman. Besides, Ella Beth had a much more pragmatic approach to life than most nine-year-olds. Or ninety-nine-year-olds. Lulu settled down in the rocker next to Ella Beth, and they rocked in companionable silence on the porch. Beale Street surprisingly was still quiet. But it wouldn't be long before the evening crowds poured in, the music cranked up, the graceful back-flipping boy street performers started, and the neon lights turned on. Ella Beth pulled off a piece of corn bread and buttered it.

Ella Beth finally said, "Miss Adrian wasn't very old."

"No sweetie, she sure wasn't."

"And she didn't seem at all sick yesterday. She felt good enough to be mean as a snake. I didn't hear a single cough out of her."

"Well, that's true. I guess it goes to show you never can tell," said Lulu. She would be much more comfortable if this conversation took a philosophical or even a theological turn. "Sometimes, it's just your *time*, sweetie. Life and death. . . . these are things we don't completely understand in this life. Maybe, one day, in another sphere, we'll know some of the deeper mysteries of our existence."

Ella Beth looked at her grandmother sternly. "Did somebody do her in?"

So much for the philosophical shift. "Mercy, Ella Beth! Whatever gave you an idea like that?"

"Nobody liked her. Except Coco, but she's dotty."

Lulu hesitated but then realized that not being fully upfront would probably result in a more prolonged interrogation. She sighed. "We don't exactly know what happened, Ella Beth. But it certainly looks like somebody poisoned her. I guess she must have messed with the wrong person. Not that there's anything for *us* to be worried about," she added hastily.

"Of course not. We don't go around insulting people and acting all la-di-dah. No one wants to do *us* in."

"Yes, well, that doesn't mean she deserved what happened to her," said Lulu. She noticed an aha look on Ella Beth's pixie face. "What is it?"

"Nothing," said Ella Beth quickly. "I was just thinking about Miss Adrian and all. I'd better catch up with Coco and start on my homework."

Catch up with Coco? Homework? Now Lulu wondered if even little Ella Beth was hiding something from her. No, she fussed at herself, you've gotten completely paranoid. Snap out of it!

Coco glared across the office at Ella Beth. "Stop looking at me!"

"I'm really just thinking and looking into space. Your face just happened to be occupying the space where I was staring," said Ella Beth.

"Well, stop it! What are you doing?"

"Coco, can you keep a secret?"

Although the lunch traffic had been steady, the dinner crowd was thinner than usual. When Susan Meredith shut down Southern Accents for the day and went to Aunt Pat's, she didn't see the steady stream of people coming in and out that she usually did. After eating supper, she settled in a rocker next to Lulu's.

"It looks quieter than usual," she said to Lulu.

Lulu nodded. "Lunch was busy, but that might have been people who were looking to get some gossip about Miss Adrian's death." She rocked for a minute in reflective silence. "How were things at the gallery today?"

"One of the reasons I came in was to talk to Sara this morning. Southern Accents was really buzzing. I've never seen people so excited by an exhibit. They went on and on about the vibrancy of the show. Word of mouth yesterday afternoon and today brought in a lot more people than I usually get during the week." Lulu raised her eyebrows. "That's what I was telling her," said Susan. "Rebecca Adrian didn't know two cents about art. Too bad Rebecca couldn't have been murdered *before* she filled Sara's mind with all that negative energy."

"You assumed it was murder?"

"Lord knows I felt like murdering her myself yesterday. But," she added, stabbing her finger in the air, "I *didn't*. And there are plenty of patrons who can attest to the fact that I was knee-deep in tourists all afternoon."

"Oh, honey, I didn't mean that you did her in," protested Lulu. "I was commenting on the fact that you thought it was murder."

"Well, if I felt like stringing Rebecca Adrian up by her neck, then everybody else probably felt the same way. *Sure* she was murdered. Why else would a healthy, twenty-something, hateful creature end up dead at the Peabody? If I'd been Sara, I'd have had murder on the brain for sure. Right after I left Southern Accents for the day, I went straight home to meditate and do some yoga. I can't tell you how stressed out I was. And Sara must have been even more stressed out than me."

"But Sara didn't kill her, of course."

"Of course," said Susan. "Because she wasn't even at the Peabody. She was . . ." Susan waited for Lulu to fill in the blank on Sara's alibi.

Lulu rocked violently in her rocking chair for a minute. "Well, she was working at the restaurant, naturally. She wasn't anywhere near the Peabody until we all discovered Miss Adrian's body together."

"And the poisoning happened at the Peabody?" asked Susan.

Lulu said, "Honey, we just don't know. It could've hap-

pened to her barbeque ribs here and not kicked in until she
got back to her room." She spoke in a quiet voice in case
any of the few customers in the dining room should happen
out on the porch.

"I don't see how that could have been possible. The dining room was full of people. Somebody would have noticed someone putting poison in her food."

"You know how packed the restaurant is at a regular
lunchtime. It was even busier yesterday for everyone to see
the scout's reaction to the food. Her plate was constructed
in phases and kept warm. Someone could have sneaked
into the kitchen and messed with it. Ben was slaving in the
pit. Waitresses were rushing in and out picking up orders."
Lulu shrugged.

Susan reached over and squeezed Lulu's thin arm.
"Don't you worry about a thing, Lulu. No one in their right
mind is going to boycott Aunt Pat's because of this. Oh,
maybe they'll take a break for a few days, but then they'll
be hankering for the best barbeque in Memphis." Susan
glanced up and quickly put a hand to her hair, smoothing
down some errant blond flyaways.

Lulu followed her gaze and wasn't surprised to see Seb
coming over. It was obvious that Susan had a crush on him.
Her whole demeanor changed when Seb was around. When
Seb first came back to Memphis, Lulu crossed her fingers
and toes that he would renounce his alley cat ways, settle
down, maybe even bring Susan officially into the family.
But now Ben had Lulu worrying over Seb's sniffling and
whether he might be a druggie. Lulu was now wondering
whether her son was good enough for Susan.

"Hi, Seb," Susan said, smiling brightly. "How's everything going?"

As usual when speaking to someone of the female per-
suasion, Seb automatically hugged Susan closely before

sliding smoothly into the booth next to Lulu. "Well, hi there, darlin'!" he said to Susan. "Haven't seen you here lately. Where've you been hiding yourself?"

Idiot! thought Lulu unkindly. Susan had been at the restaurant daily in the last week. If *he'd* spent more time at work, maybe he'd have run into her. Lulu hosted most uncharitable thoughts about her second-born.

Susan didn't share Lulu's opinion. Her eyes twinkled at Seb through her John Lennon glasses. "Oh, I've been around. Although lately it's been really hard to pull away from Southern Accents. Your sister-in-law is a smash hit."

Seb frowned. Lulu could tell he didn't have a clue in the world why Sara and Susan's gallery would be mentioned in the same sentence. As irritated as she was with her son, she hated seeing him look so oblivious.

"You *know*, Seb. Sara's art." Lulu pressed hard on Seb's toes under the table with her foot. "Susan finally talked her into showing it at Southern Accents yesterday. You'll have to run by and see it," she added in a more threatening than encouraging tone.

Seb grunted from the pressure on his foot, then said, "Yes, ma'am, I'll have to do that." Then he flashed his slow smile, and Lulu saw Susan melt right then and there. Lulu gritted her teeth.

Susan gulped and tried to pull it together. "Your mother and I were talking about business at the restaurant."

Seb raised a dark eyebrow. "Business is great. I worked on the numbers today. They look fantastic."

Susan blushed. "Well, yes. I mean, I'm *sure* it has been great." She looked to Lulu for a lifeline.

"Sales look great for *before* the murder, Seb." Lulu was knocking on the wooden table. "We seem to have gotten ourselves mixed up in a poisoning, so we can't be feeling cocky about our numbers."

Seb shrugged. "People want barbeque, Mother. I doubt they're really going to think about it. The lunch crowd was good."

"Because people are curious, Seb. There are television cameras out there and reporters. They just want to see what's going on. But what'll happen after that?"

Seb lost interest in the conversation. "I'm sure there'll still be plenty of guests tonight and tomorrow, too. We've got a great band lineup. They'll be here when the music starts playing."

"No, they won't, because there won't *be* a blues band. They cancelled tonight's appearance, and the one for tomorrow night cancelled, too. I guess they're afraid they might be murdered while they're playing." Lulu finally noticed that Seb had his laptop bag with him. "Where are you going, by the way?"

"It's quitting time," drawled Seb calmly.

"Is it? Well, I guess I'll have to take my watch by Bing's Clock Shop, because by my watch, Aunt Pat's is open another four hours."

Now Seb frowned in irritation. "I'll check back in later, Mom." He quickly exited the screen porch, letting the door slam behind him. Lulu clucked. That was the last she'd see of Seb for the rest of the day, she knew it.

Susan stared at the spot where he'd last stood. "I'd better go, too, Lulu. Call me later when you get the chance?"

Lulu rocked violently in her chair. Everything about this day had gone wrong from the start. *Before* the start. She couldn't wait for the moment when she pulled those cotton checked sheets up to her chin, laid her head on her feather pillow, and put today to bed for good.

Then she saw three familiar figures coming into the porch. Big Ben, Morty, and Buddy. She couldn't do anything else but smile at the sight of her friends. They hugged her, then peeked into the dining room.

Buddy shook his head. "Can't believe how empty that room is. I never thought I'd see the day."

"More food for us!" grinned Morty, rubbing his good-sized belly.

Lulu turned serious. "It's been a rough day for us. Once the curiosity seekers left, we didn't get our regulars back. The live blues acts cancelled their gigs 'out of respect for the recent events.' The tourists have been walking right on by when there's nobody lined up to get in. I guess they figure the more-popular-looking places look like better bets."

Big Ben gave a harrumphing cough. Apparently the cough was a signal to the others to tell Lulu something. "Do you think," asked Buddy, "tomorrow evening would be a good night for a blues concert on your porch? We thought we'd revive the Back Porch Blues Band. Gratis, of course. Nothing too big or fancy," he hurried on, "but a size such as three blues musicians in their eighties could comfortably handle."

Lulu felt tears welling in her eyes. She nodded.

"We didn't want to take up too much of your space, honey," said Morty. "This joint is going to be hopping with paying customers as soon as we start to play and they start smelling that barbeque cooking. I'm going to get my boys to bring in some bongo drums, and we'll have a guitar, a bass, a trumpet, and a harmonica. There'll be some heavenly music pouring out on the street."

Lulu hid a smile, knowing Morty's boys were at least sixty-five years old. "They'll be battering down that screen door to get in."

"We figured you could use some help with your advertising right now. Since you don't have any dancing fuchsia pigs to draw in customers," said Buddy. "Although why that woman thinks anyone wants to dwell on pigs before eating pork is anyone's guess."

Lulu hugged them all again.

"This reminds me of that time, back in the day, when we put on a concert in the park. We were the headliners, man, and people poured into the park by the hundreds," said Morty in a dreamlike tone.

"Funny," drawled Big Ben, "how I never manage to remember any of these events."

"Well, I hate to say it, Big Ben, but I think your memory has slipped some as you've gotten older. Or maybe you're just blocking out the gigs altogether. You know, since all the pretty ladies were coming up to me." He winked at Lulu. "I was always the debonair one, you know."

Lulu hid a smile. If any one of the three qualified as debonair, it was Buddy. If he'd wanted to turn on his charm, the ladies would have come in droves. But no one had managed to turn his head since his wife of fifty years had died several years ago.

Buddy cut Big Ben off before he could stutter out an indignant retort. "We're going to grab us some food before the hordes come. And they will come, I know it. Especially after a special concert by the kings of blues."

Chapter

6

"Ben, are you listening to me?" asked Sara. Since this was the second time she'd asked that particular question, exasperation fairly dripped from her words.

Ben, whose mind only seconds ago had been happily engaged in a daydream involving an eight-point whitetail buck, an excellent vantage point, and a trusty rifle, startled guiltily. "Yes," he said.

"Yes *what*?"

Ben crinkled his brow. "Yes, ma'am?"

Sara ran her fingers through her curly red hair until it poofed out around her head like a fiery halo. "No, Ben. I mean, what are you *yes*ing? Didn't you listen to what I said?"

Ben was suddenly intensely interested in Aunt Pat's food inventory list.

Sara frowned at him with great irritation. "I was just saying that your mother has moped around for a couple of days now. Now she's determined to find out what really happened and clear the names of the innocent," said Sara.

"That could be a good thing," suggested Ben. "After all, you're one of the primary suspects. Considering the brouhaha in Susan's gallery and everything."

"Well, that's certainly true. It's not something your mother needs to be worrying herself over, though. The police will figure it out and probably in no time flat. I hate seeing Lulu so sad. I think that a diversion for the day is in order."

"What kind of a diversion?" asked Ben nervously. He hoped this wasn't the sort of diversion that entailed him driving his mother to the mall and giving feedback as she tried on a variety of floral-print cotton frocks. Her dresses all looked the same to him. "I need to be cooking on the pit today, honey. We have a huge takeout order to put together." Please, God, he thought. It's amazing how quickly you can fall from a happy hunting daydream into a suburban-mall nightmare.

"The Graces," said Sara complacently. "They'll make the perfect diversion for your mama. I don't know what they'll find to do, but I'm sure it'll be entertaining."

Peggy Sue was Sara's go-to Grace. "Sara, honey, we'd be *delighted* to take Lulu out and show her a good time. She needs to get away from the restaurant for a little while. It's not healthy to mope around and ruminate on bad stuff."

"I think she's trying to solve the case," said Sara. "You know how she's always looking out for 'her children.' I think she wants to figure out who did it, get them tossed in the clink, and get on with life as usual."

"Sounds like a pretty good plan, actually," said Peggy Sue in a considering voice. "But if she's getting too wrapped up in it all, she should take a step back. We were going to go out anyway today for a happy little outing. Because you know," she spoke in a hushed voice as if somebody was listening in on the conversation, "Flo is not doing well."

"Flo isn't?"

"Oh, honey, not at *all*. We don't know what's wrong with her. We know it has to do with Miss Adrian's murder, of course, but we don't know if she feels guilty about it because she had a run-in with her before Miss Adrian ended up deader than a doornail, or if she knows something, or if she *did* something . . ." Peggy Sue broke off. She sounded a little guilty now herself. "Not that we think that Flo could hurt the very nastiest of *flies*, mind you, but . . ."

"I know what you mean, Peggy Sue. And I'm starting to think that Lulu's right. The sooner this case is wrapped up, the better."

The plan, in theory, was a sound one. It involved Peggy Sue picking up the still car-less Lulu and the other Graces, and heading on a fun-filled trip to the mall with food, shopping, and makeovers.

But implementing this plan was harder than Peggy Sue expected. By the time she'd finally rounded everybody up, her face glowed with perspiration, and she had to perform major reconstruction on her heavy makeup.

Cherry hadn't picked up on her house phone or cell phone. Peggy Sue had hopped in her VW bug and drove over to check in on the out-of-pocket Grace. It turned out that she was tackling her yard work early in the day before it got too muggy. Peggy Sue was greeted by the sight of Cherry, helmet firmly on her head, bouncing around on her riding lawnmower at a tearing speed and seeming to be thoroughly enjoying herself.

Peggy Sue pulled into the driveway and managed to flag her down after several attempts. Apparently Cherry's peripheral vision was somewhat compromised by her Elvis helmet. It was clear, though, that she was the safest lawn-mowing homeowner in Memphis. "What're we doing?" she asked. She looked at her Elvis watch. "It's only nine fifteen."

"I think," said Peggy Sue, "that the best course of action would be a trip to the mall. Serious measures have to be taken because we have two people to cheer up. Lulu is so fit that she won't have a problem walking all over the mall. And Flo . . ." She shook her head. "Flo needs a makeover."

"Has it gotten *that* bad?" asked Cherry in a hushed voice. "I just don't see her as needing a makeover intervention. Flo is always really put together."

"Well, honey, it looks like something done took her apart. She needs some reconstructive makeup of the emergency variety," said Peggy Sue. "And fast."

Cherry took off her helmet and patted her hair. Her bouffant do was a don't. "I need thirty minutes, Peggy Sue. I can't leave my front yard half mowed, and I can't go to the mall looking like something the cat drug in."

"I'll sit in my car and call the other Graces." A guilty flush spread over Peggy's Sue's neck and generously exposed chest. "I feel like this is partly my fault. I never should've said what I did that night at the Peabody. You know," she muttered, "about Flo's background."

Cherry looked around swiftly as if the squirrels and chipmunks might be taping their conversation. "The less said about that, the better. Besides, Flo forgave you for it. She knows it was the margaritas talking and not you."

"Just the same, I do feel awful about it. The next day I was actually sick with an upset stomach, headache, and all," said Peggy Sue. "I don't think my tummy will settle down until the police put somebody away for that murder."

Cherry thought it might have been more like a swift-acting, frightening hangover that attacked her, but she had more sense than to say that to Peggy Sue. She didn't need a mad Peggy Sue on her back—that was for *sure*.

"True. Although I think that if anybody needed killing, it was that Rebecca Adrian. She got what was coming to her."

"You don't think . . ." Peggy Sue hesitated. "Never mind. Flo's got a heart of gold. She'd never hurt anybody. I don't care what happened in her past."

Jeanne and Evelyn quickly signed on for a trip to the mall. They'd been there yesterday, but who cared? It was always fun to have a girls' day out.

Then Peggy Sue called Lulu. Sara had asked her to make it look like it was the Graces' idea to go shopping and not hers. Peggy Sue had totally agreed with that line of thought. After all, it wasn't a stretch. At some point, the Graces and a shopping expedition were bound to happen. Lulu's battle with the blues would not have gone unnoticed by their sharp eyes, and a trip to the mall was their favorite remedy.

Lulu was, fortunately, easily convinced. "Sweetie, that sounds like fun. I'd love to escape for a while. My car is still at the shop, though."

"That's no problem at all, Lulu. There'll be six of us going, so we'll either take Cherry's old minivan or else we'll do two cars. See you in about thirty minutes."

As soon as Cherry was clean, garbed in jangly bracelets and tight but cute clothing, and had her helmet in place since she was driving a car, Peggy Sue and Cherry drove around Memphis, collecting Lulu and various Graces, all eager for a day at the mall.

Flo, however, was not easily reached. First they tried her house phone. Then they left imploring, loud messages on her answering machine. Her cell phone must have been either turned off or out of batteries.

But the Graces were not easily dissuaded. They'd come too far with their plans to have them dashed by a fallen Grace. Jeanne snapped her fingers. "I got it!" she said. "I've got Flo's house key still. I had to keep her cat for her a few months ago when she went on that church retreat. I never did give the key back to her."

Jeanne, always the cleanest-living Grace and the one who adhered closest to Christian values, carefully avoided mentioning the cat's name.

Evelyn, however, had no such compunction. She hooted. "I just *die* whenever that cat is mentioned. Who else but Flo would name a cat Dammit?"

Lulu said, "I think the cat named itself. Considering that's the only thing it would *sometimes* answer to."

Evelyn was still giggling in the third row of the minivan as the car headed back to Jeanne's house. "Here kitty, kitty, kitty! Heeeeeeerre kitty, kitty kitty. Heeeeeeeerrrreeeeee kitty, kitty, kitty. Come here, Dammit!"

Jeanne gave her a subduing look as she hopped out of the minivan and ran inside to dig out Flo's house key from the depths of her junk drawer.

It was a good thing the Graces broke into Flo's house, thought Lulu. Because Flo definitely needed resuscitation. "Dear Jesus," hissed Evelyn. "She looks like holy hell." In a loud voice, Evelyn said, "Flo, sweetie! How stunning you look in that muumuu. I've never seen you in that chartreuse color before. It suits you, it really does."

Flo's eyes bored holes into Evelyn, which she carefully ignored.

Cherry picked up where Evelyn left off. "I do believe that's the most perfect thing I've ever seen—for sitting around the house. Oh, and look at this . . ." Cherry turned her back to Flo and held up a blanket-type thing for the viewing pleasure of the wide-eyed Graces. "A Snuggie. Look, everyone: Flo has a Snuggie."

Flo remained stoically silent.

Jeanne coughed. "I have a Snuggie, too. A sage green one. Although your royal blue one is very pretty."

"And they are," said Peggy Sue, "*wonderful* for watching soap operas in your den. But we're going to go to the mall. Flo," she spoke loudly as if Flo had acquired deafness along with her crippling deficiency of good fashion judgment, "we're all going to the mall for the day."

Flo looked one step away from catatonic.

Dammit, the cat, abruptly materialized in Flo's rather chaotic den. It glowered at them with raging hostility before bounding into the dimness of Flo's bedroom.

"Could y'all give me a few minutes with Flo? Alone?" asked Cherry.

Peggy Sue whispered to Cherry, "I could stay and talk to her with you."

Cherry shook her helmeted head. "That's okay. Just go on out with the other girls back to the car." Flo didn't seem to harbor any hard feelings against Peggy Sue for her drunken expose the other night, but at a time when Cherry needed to persuade her to do something, she didn't want to take the chance.

"Honey," Cherry said after the girls had retreated outside, "I know you don't feel like going anywhere or doing anything. I can *tell* that you're hurting." And how, thought Cherry, wincing again at Flo's appearance. "But I need you to rally yourself for a little while. The Graces have been assigned a mission," said Cherry with all the patriotic pride of a World War II munitions-factory worker.

There was a flicker of life in Flo's eyes.

"Lulu," said Cherry with great dignity and seriousness, "is in trouble. She's all depressed, and you know how older ladies don't like to take happy pills. It's our duty to revive her. We're going to take her for a day at the mall. We'll do makeovers and eat and have a grand time. What do you think?" she asked imploringly. "Can the Graces count on you? For Lulu?"

Cherry's call to action seemed to jumpstart Flo. At least temporarily, and enough to stand up. Flo reached for the Snuggie.

"Uh-uh. Let's put something a little bit peppier on. It'll cheer Lulu up." Cherry directed Flo to the bedroom and sighed with relief as she encountered no resistance.

"She's *driving*?" squeaked Jeanne in alarm. "Why on earth is she driving? The minivan seats seven."

Cherry shrugged. "She said she might want to leave before we do. She'll meet us at the food court."

"Is she okay to drive?" asked Peggy Sue. Her husband was a policeman, and she thought about that type of stuff a lot. Actually, he was an office-park security guard, but same thing.

"Well, sure she's okay to drive."

"I mean, she's so *disheveled*."

"She's disheveled, Peggy Sue, not tipsy."

"Shouldn't we wait and follow her?" asked Evelyn. "Make sure she's okay?"

Cherry drove off down the street. "I don't think we'd better. She's just real sensitive right now. If we act like she's not in her right mind, that could be a deal breaker. We'll meet her at the food court. Maybe we can hit a few shops before we meet her. It might take a few minutes to pull herself together."

It actually took a lot of few minutes for Flo to pull herself together. The Graces and Lulu yo-yoed back and forth between different stores and the food court. No Flo. Jeanne called Flo's cell phone, but it was still either off, dead, or she was studiously ignoring it.

"This," said Peggy Sue, heaving a tremendous sigh that threatened to rend her too-tight top, "is incredibly discouraging. Here we are, trying to have a happy day to distract Flo, and Flo goes MIA. Should we organize a search party?"

"She's not all *that* late," said Jeanne.

"No? When in the past would Flo MacDonald be late for a day at the mall? Can you imagine our Flo dawdling on her way to a makeover or to eat some greasy fast food? No, something must be wrong." And Peggy Sue kept tapping her cute designer shoes impatiently on the mall floor.

Finally, Flo found them in a store not far from the food court. Well, what passed as Flo, anyway— really a shadow of her usually sleek, chic, funny self.

Jeanne was all for pretending that no delay had happened, but there was no way Peggy Sue was going to allow that. "Where the *hell* were you? We've gone in and out of five stores for the past hour, trying to hover near the food court. They probably think we're running some kind of shady shoplifting scam."

Flo looked unnerved. "It was that stupid chicken truck."

"'Scuse me?"

"A chicken truck that was driving ahead of me. Full of chickens. I didn't see it and clipped my bumper on it. Had to stop, had a report drawn up, blah, blah, blah . . ."

Peggy Sue was incredulous. "You couldn't see a chicken truck ahead of you? With white feathers floating out of it? On an eighteen-wheeler truck bed?"

Flo preferred not to acknowledge this question. She walked ahead of them a little ways, wandering toward the food court.

"Okay," said Peggy Sue in a low voice to the others, "I don't know where she's been, but she looks like the cat dragged her in after spending the night carousing. Can we do the makeover first?"

Evelyn groaned. "I'm starving *now*! But I'll agree this qualifies as an emergency." Flo turned around to look balefully behind her to make sure the women were still trailing behind her. "Look—Flo doesn't even have her eyelashes on!"

The Graces gasped. Flo's signature look involved the daily use of fake eyelashes. Lulu thought Flo might have chosen sight over fashion for once. It couldn't be easy to view the world through that synthetic thicket. Although hitting the back end of a chicken truck didn't inspire confidence in her overall visual abilities.

Jeanne wrung her hands. "Oh dear. We can't take her to lunch looking like that! Even the food court people would be gaping at us."

Since the Graces appeared to be too deep in shock to do anything but stand agog, Lulu caught up with Flo. "Honey?" she asked.

Flo looked at Lulu with bleary eyes that didn't look like they'd seen sleep for a while.

"We thought we'd do makeovers now—won't that be fun? The girls thought my look could use a little updating. Maybe you can sit at another stool and get yours done at the same time. I know we rushed you out the door before you had a chance to apply makeup today."

Evelyn thought this was laying it on a little thick. After all, Flo in her right mind would know that the Graces would *never* presume to tell Lulu she needed her look updated. That would just be plain *rude*. Lulu was an older lady, at least ten years older than most of them, and older ladies were always welcome to look however they damn well pleased—that was one of the few perks of being old.

Lulu could wear all the floral print dresses and clunky shoes she wanted to.

But Flo appeared to be too far gone to even register this complete falsehood. She nodded listlessly and allowed herself to be led to the makeup counters at Belk's.

Evelyn tried to make conversation. "Y'all, we are going to have the best time! I have a friend who works over at the Lila Fleur counter and she's a genius when it comes to makeovers. Your face becomes a *palette* for Natalie . . . it's very exciting!"

"Is that so?" asked Lulu. "Wonder what she'll think to do with me?" But even Lulu felt a little excited. With marble floors, beautiful bright lighting, and heavily made-up women bandying about overpriced products, you couldn't help but feel glamorous.

Flo was helped onto one of the tall stools at the Lila Fleur counter, and Lulu climbed on the other one. Lulu felt like she was playing along with the makeover to be a good sport, but then she saw that a lit-up magnifying mirror was right in front of her. She was horrified by what she saw in the mirror. "Natalie," she asked urgently, "what can you do for me?"

An hour later, Flo and Lulu both had enough layers of makeup on to completely hide any possible flaw, real or imagined. They carried bags full of makeup and "free gifts" they'd gotten for spending gobs of money at the makeup counter . . . courtesy of Evelyn who'd insisted it would be her special delight to treat them for the day.

Flo definitely looked better on the outside. This was due in part to the fact that Peggy Sue had brought a huge hair brush with her and brushed and combed and teased Flo's hair until it was whipped into shape. Then Peggy Sue aimed enough Aqua Net at Flo's head to effectively destroy several ozone layers. That was due to the fact that Flo kept running her hand nervously through her hair.

Yes, they'd done everything possible to take care of Flo's outward appearance, but her insides were obviously still a disaster area.

"Can we get something to eat?" Flo asked.

Cherry looked relieved that Flo was actually talking. She whooped. "Finally! I'm so hungry I'm about to start gnawing on my arm. Let's see—in the food court we have that Chinese food place, the burger place, the chicken place, the pizza place . . ."

Flo gestured to a restaurant that bordered the side of the food court. "How about that place?"

"The one with the wooden door?" Cherry squinted over at it. The restaurant's entryway was an intricately carved wooden door with an Old English–looking sign on the top. "It looks kinda fancy. Who has restaurants with doors inside a mall? Maybe it's expensive. It *looks* expensive." She stared suspiciously at the door.

Flo was already tugging at the handle.

Much later, when Lulu and the Graces analyzed where the outing had gone so horribly wrong, they pinpointed that very moment. If *only* they'd noticed that the restaurant had the word "tavern" in its name. If *only* they'd been quick thinking enough to claim boredom with the mall and drag Flo off to a wholesome afternoon of mourning Elvis at Graceland. Unfortunately, they instead sealed their fate by crossing the threshold of Ye Olde English Tavern. They sat in a large round booth and proceeded to watch Flo drink her lunch.

When Flo left the table for one of many trips to the restroom, Lulu said, "Okay, you girls have got to level with me. I thought I might be the reason for this emergency shopping trip, but it looks like Flo is the one who's in dire need of some help.

"Don't be shocked," added Lulu when the Graces exchanged guilty looks. "I just had a wild guess that my friends were trying to make me feel better. Morty, Big Ben, and Buddy are doing the same kind of thing; they're having a shindig tonight, free, to draw in some customers. I love y'all for being so sweet."

Lulu hugged as many of the Graces as she could reach.

"But now I need the lowdown," Lulu said seriously. "What's put Flo in this state? Why'd she have that run-in with Miss Adrian the night before she was murdered?" She saw the Graces' eyes open wider. "Yes. I've talked to the police, and I understand that it *was* murder."

Peggy Sue's blue eyes welled with tears. "It's all my fault," she wailed. She dissolved into sobbing while Jeanne patted her soothingly on the back. Cherry put her Elvis helmet on. Maybe she was afraid the lusty crying would bring down the roof.

Jeanne said, "I *knew* we should never have been at a bar that night. It goes to show that nothing good ever comes of drinking. I am hereby renouncing my life of casual drinking."

Evelyn rolled her eyes, and no one else reacted at all to Jeanne's declaration. Jeanne gave up drinking every couple of weeks. The woman barely drank a thimbleful to begin with.

"It wasn't a bar, Jeanne. It was the Peabody! We only had a couple of drinks," protested Cherry.

"*You and I* had a couple of drinks, maybe. Peggy Sue had quite a few drinks."

Peggy Sue howled louder, mascara rivers streaming down her rouged cheeks.

Lulu frowned sternly. "Now cut it out, Peggy Sue. Get control of yourself. Flo is coming back from that bathroom at any moment, and you do not need to be a puddle. Tell me what happened, somebody, please."

Cherry and Jeanne filled her in on Flo's blowup with Rebecca. Peggy Sue tried keeping a stiff upper lip but gave loud, sporadic hiccups. She wiped her eyes a few times and blew her nose on her napkin when they got to the part where Peggy Sue told Rebecca about Flo being an ex-con.

"We should have told you before," said Cherry. "When Flo said to keep it a secret, she didn't really mean from friends like you. She was afraid that if more people knew about it, word would spread, and then *everybody* would know about it."

Lulu took a sip of her water. "I'm surprised that Flo cares that it's kept such a secret," she said. "I've never known her to really care a whit what people think of her. She's a very brave woman."

The Graces looked at each other as if trying to decide if they should leave it at that or reveal another secret about their friend. Peggy Sue shook her head. She wouldn't be the one to spill the beans this time.

Cherry looked behind her to make sure that Flo wasn't making her tipsy way back to the booth. "It's not only because of her reputation. I mean, she cares more than you'd think about people's opinion of her. She doesn't want to lose her gig as docent at Graceland." Cherry, Jeanne, Evelyn, and Peggy Sue all looked horrified as they considered the possibility of being ejected as docents.

"Flo is trying to escape from her past," said Evelyn. "She has an ex-husband who she tried to bump off. And now he'd give anything to return the favor. Except that *he* wouldn't fail. Flo would be deader than a doornail if Virgil knew where she was. And Rebecca, that harpy, was going to use Flo for a little local color on the Cooking Channel show."

"But then she was murdered before she produced the show." Lulu stopped short of saying what was on everyone's mind—what if Flo had killed Rebecca to shut her up? "But how would Virgil know where Flo is since Rebecca didn't air it?"

"That Cooking Channel story was quirky enough to make national headlines. Remember all those cameramen that camped out for a while outside the Peabody and Aunt Pat's? Flo even saw herself on CNN. So she stopped being worried about all of Memphis finding out about her secret and started worrying more about the piece she saw on CNN. And worrying that Virgil now knew where to find her."

Lulu rubbed her eyes. "Well, thanks for leveling with me. I won't say anything to anybody, although I do think y'all should have a little chat with the Memphis police." The Graces' voices clamored in protest and Lulu said, "No, I mean it. You won't even have to call the station. They'll end up coming to you. Flo had an argument in the Peabody Hotel with Rebecca Adrian the night before she died an unusual death. The police will want to talk to Flo and will want to talk to y'all, too. I'd tell the police myself, but I wasn't privy to the knowledge, firsthand."

Evelyn looked at Lulu with surprise. "Privy to it? Aren't you little Miss Law Enforcement?"

Lulu colored. "Oh, you know. I'm just trying to look out for my children . . . and my friends."

Cherry's forehead furrowed underneath the helmet. "But won't that mean more trouble for Flo? They'll know she had a record. I mean—Flo changed her name as soon as she left prison to start fresh and escape from Virgil. But she'll have to level with the police. And when they find out that she's an ex-con, they're going to make her suspect number one. Who knows; maybe her ex-husband will end up finding out about it and track her down."

Lulu shook her head until the carefully wound white hair was in danger of falling down. "She can't hide information from the police. The way she's acting right now is clearly guilty or worried. And if she tries to hide her true identity from them, they're going to find out. And then they really *will* be suspicious."

At this point, Flo weaved to the vinyl booth and carefully navigated the curved seat. She looked solemnly at them, then put her head down on the table.

"Check please!" said Lulu to their passing waitress.

"Clearly," said Lulu to the Graces, "we need to commandeer Flo's car and get her back home to bed."

Cherry looked horrified. "She'll miss Graceland today!"

Flo groaned.

"Some things can't be helped," said Lulu briskly. "Now, Flo, where is your car?"

Flo groaned again.

"Your car, Flo. Do you remember where you parked it?"

Flo lifted her head from the table and studied the ceiling as if it would provide her with inspiration. "My car."

Evelyn knit her brows. "Your sedan, honey. The one you hit the chicken truck with a little while ago."

Flo groaned a third time and put her head back down on the table. Her muffled voice said, "I don't remember where I parked."

This stopped the Graces and Lulu cold. It was a huge parking lot.

Lulu said, "Do you remember if you parked on the Sears side or the J.C. Penney side?"

"No."

"Well, surely you remember if you walked a long way to get to the food court or not. Maybe you parked right outside the food court?"

"Don't remember."

Lulu and the Graces looked at each other. "All right," said Lulu. "Let's peek right outside the food court entrance, and maybe we can see it." Flo sprawled across the table. "Maybe one of us should stay here with Flo and the rest of us can look."

Jeanne shifted uneasily in her seat. "Our waitress is giving us the evil eye and talking to her manager. She keeps pointing at Flo. I'm thinking we need to keep moving . . . Flo, too. Oh, somebody grab her cosmetics bags!"

The five Graces and Lulu took Flo on a forced march to the food court entrance. Flo started wailing. "I'm sorry! I don't know where that car is."

Lulu had endured entirely too many waterworks episodes for one day at the mall. "Buck up, Flo. We'll find your car and get you home, and you can take a nice nap. There's nothing to be upset about; I lose my car all the time. I always have to hit that button on my key ring and look for the headlights to blink at me."

"Hey," said Cherry in a hopeful voice, "Flo, do you have an alarm on your car like that?"

Flo looked balefully at Cherry and then unexpectedly upchucked in a convenient trashcan by the entrance. An ignominious end to what was intended to be an uplifting day with friends, thought Lulu.

Cherry flagged down the mall security car as it made its rounds around the parking lot. Lulu and Cherry rode through the various parking decks until they finally located Flo's car (with a dinged front bumper). Finding the car took a while, and Flo was napping on the curb, propped against Jeanne, when they returned to the food court entrance.

Jeanne drove home with Flo in Flo's car, so she could keep an eye on her for the afternoon. Peggy Sue drove everyone else to their respective houses and then took Lulu back to the restaurant. Lulu had never been more relieved to see it.

Peggy Sue said sadly, "Well, here we are. I'm sorry, Lulu. I thought we'd have fun today. I never would have brought you out if I'd known that Flo was going to flake out like that. Now you probably feel worse than ever."

"It's just very out of character for Flo," said Lulu. "I don't think of her as a heavy drinker."

"She *isn't*. That's why a few glasses of wine knocked her on her butt. That night we were out with Miss Adrian, she hardly even touched her drink." Peggy Sue blushed. She was probably wishing she'd been the same way. But she wasn't going to be like Jeanne and swear off drinking. Summertime wasn't summertime for Peggy Sue without a pretty pastel frozen beverage with a miniature umbrella sitting in it. And, in Memphis, they were barreling toward summer.

"Don't worry about it, Peggy Sue. And don't beat yourself up about what you said that night. Sometimes things are meant to happen. We just might not know the reason right away."

Peggy Sue hugged her. "You are so right, Lulu. I'm going to have to get over it. I've bawled me a river over it." She looked at the restaurant. "Hey, it looks like the guys are already setting up for their gig. Be ready for crowds."

Lulu squinted at Aunt Pat's and saw a new notice on their sidewalk sign about the blues trio playing that night. She hoped Ben had already fired up the pit. Lulu had a feeling Aunt Pat's was going to be packed.

Chapter 7

There was nothing like the blues to cheer a body up, thought Lulu. Morty's voice was deeply resonant and full of regret, Buddy and Big Ben played strong and true, the bass throbbed, and the beat was contagious. When Morty played a harmonica solo, it brought down the house with applause.

Best of all, the restaurant was chock-full of people. Lulu breathed a sigh of relief to see everybody back in the dining room, listening to music and stuffing themselves with ribs, spicy corn bread, and red beans and rice. Morty winked saucily at her, and Lulu smiled back at him. Yes, sir, life was good. She sat down on the screen porch in one of the rockers and listened to the music. Both Labradors, B.B. and Elvis, came over and rested their heads against her for a rubbing. After the day she'd had, she'd happily plant her rear end in that rocker until the cows came home. Beale Street was crowded, with people jamming the street outside. They carried huge cups of beer with them as they slowly walked up and down the street, taking in all the

neon lights, the music, and the scent of fine Southern cooking that wafted out the doors.

Unfortunately for Lulu, resting and enjoying beautiful
music wasn't in the cards. Right when she thought all the
oddities of the day were fading like a bad dream, Derrick
bolted from the restaurant and plowed through the screen
porch door, letting it slam behind him with a bang. Morty
briefly stumbled through his lyrics before picking back up
where he left off (although there was a short interlude of
him humming).

Sara tore out after Derrick, red curls bouncing on her
back. The screen door slammed again, and the Labs hid
their heads under a table. The dogs' law of physics was "If
I can't see you, you can't see me!"

The trio kept playing, although Buddy's eyebrows shot
all the way up his black face. Lulu shook her head at him.
Funny how you could communicate without words after so
many years. No, there'd be no need for Lulu to run after
Sara. Lulu was sure that Sara would be back any minute,
because Derrick wasn't going to be caught by Sara.

Sara, red in the face and with glittering eyes, opened the
porch door. She cocked her head to the back of the restaurant in a gesture Lulu interpreted to mean that she wanted
to speak with her in private. "Let's go to the kitchen," said
Lulu. "The girls are hanging out in the office."

Lulu did stick her head in the office for a second to see
if Seb was there. Which he wasn't. Lulu said, "Before we
talk about what happened with you and Derrick, have you
seen Seb at all today?"

Sara, already seething, said, "No, and I could kill him. I
know I shouldn't say that, considering, but I'm that furious.
But first let me tell you about Derrick." She leaned back
against the big counter.

"Okay. Let me hear it." Lulu winced in anticipation.

Sara softened a little when she saw Lulu's reaction. She

remembered that she had only just that morning told Ben that Lulu needed to escape from her worries about the murder, and here she was loading her down with all her anxiety and frustration. She rubbed her freckled face with the palms of her hands. "I know he's my nephew and I shouldn't say anything. But when he comes in with all that black on, it's like he's sucked all the sunshine out of the room," complained Sara.

"It's just a phase," said Lulu soothingly. "He had a huge adjustment from Chicago to Memphis. Think about how different the kids must be up there."

Sara stared gloomily out the kitchen window. "Are they? It seems like teenagers are difficult anywhere at any time. I wish he'd at least *try* to be a little more cheerful. And that goatee is so scruffy it looks like a five o'clock shadow. Today was a real disaster. Ella Beth was walking down the street today and saw Derrick going into the tattoo parlor."

"Oh no," sighed Lulu. "Well, do you need me to talk to him? I can give him the lowdown on how skin sags in one's later years. That eagle tattoo might end up looking like a chickadee."

"Well, luckily, Ella Beth told Coco, and Coco ran all the way here to let me know. Coco has a thing about tattoos, you know. I caught up with him and pulled him out of there." Sara rolled her eyes. "Look, Lulu, I don't want to unload on you. It's nothing—typical teenage rebellion stuff, I'm sure. Why don't you tell me about your day?"

Lulu paused. That was one thing she really *couldn't* do. She'd sworn herself to secrecy. Any tales Lulu told involving Flo and a drunken ramble about the mall would be quickly analyzed for content. *Why* was Flo drinking? *Why* did Rebecca Adrian's death affect her so badly? And Lulu had promised not to say anything. "Actually, the Graces took me shopping today. Sort of a surprise treat. It was . . .

very nice." Lulu was so preoccupied with lying that she didn't notice Sara had turned bright red.

"Well, that's wonderful! I'm glad you had a nice day out. Listen, don't worry about the thing with Derrick. I shouldn't have dragged you off the porch about it. I just get really mad, sometimes, you know? I'm trying to do the right thing by him for my sister's sake, and sometimes I feel like he's throwing it all back in my face." That wasn't the extent of the problems she was having with Derrick, thought Sara guiltily.

Ben was pulling ribs out of the brick wall pit and putting them back in as fast as he could. Considering how many years he'd been cooking, though, his multitasking abilities were very good. "You know what that boy needs?" he asked.

"I'm almost scared to ask," said Lulu.

"He needs to hunt some turkeys," said Ben, thumping his spatula against a baking sheet.

Sara's brow furrowed. "Wearing *what*, Ben? He's only got the black shirts and baggy black pants."

"I've got plenty of extra camo! He could borrow some of mine."

Lulu tactfully decided not to bring up the fact that Derrick was thin as a rail. And that Ben . . . wasn't.

"And really," added Sara, "I'm not sure it's a great idea to arm Derrick, Ben. Especially considering that scene he and I had."

Sara quickly changed the subject. "Hey, how is Flo doing?" Lulu shifted uncomfortably. "The last time I saw her, she was really apologetic about forgetting Derrick at the Peabody. It sounded like she'd really had a run-in with Rebecca. Which," she added wryly, "wasn't hard to do."

"Oh, I think she's fine," said Lulu, crossing her fingers behind her back. "You know—the whole thing is wearing on all of us."

"I'll say," said Sara. "My initial reaction to hearing Rebecca Adrian was dead was a 'ding-dong, the witch is dead,' type thing. And now I feel really guilty about it all."

Lulu looked at her searchingly. How guilty was guilty? Guilty because she'd harbored ill feelings about someone and they ended up dying? Or guilty because she had something to do with it? Lulu said, "Well, you have nothing to worry about. You were driving me over there so I could apologize to the woman, so you were playing an important role in reconciliation, after all. And don't worry about Derrick. He's having a rough time adjusting to a new place, that's all. And seventeen is a difficult age. Things will turn around, you'll see."

Sara grinned. "Now you forget all about my ramblings, Lulu. Please go back out on the porch and enjoy the blues. You deserve a break. I think I might, too. I'm going to go ahead and take the girls home and try to make up with Derrick."

Ben scooped some ribs and baked beans into a takeout container and handed it to Sara. "Here, bring some food home to him. That's definitely the way to a boy's heart."

Lulu happily retreated to the porch with a bowl full of sliced peaches sprinkled with some brown sugar and pecans. The sweetness of the treat and Morty's soft voice soothed her. She rocked and let the crooning blues music wrap around her like a blanket until the restaurant closed down for the evening.

Lulu had high hopes that a day ending peacefully would somehow carry over into the following morning. But dashed hopes were all that were in store for her at Aunt Pat's.

"All right! Where's my brother?" demanded Ben. He looked ferociously mad, which did not jive with his Captain Kangarooish appearance. "He wasn't here yesterday, and now he's not here again this morning. I've got to get some food ordered, or we're going to have to shut down from lack of supplies."

Lulu knit her brows. "It couldn't be all that bad, Ben."

"But it is. Otherwise, our customers are going to be placing orders, and the waitresses will be saying, 'Oh sorry—we're out of ribs. And coleslaw. And corn bread. But we do have some great sweet tea and baked beans.'" Ben's face displayed a rainbow of colors, none of which indicated a clean bill of coronary health. No wonder Sara said yesterday that she could kill Seb. Considering Ben's rage, Seb better watch his back or else he might be kicking the bucket himself.

Lulu was already calling Seb's cell phone. It went immediately to voice mail. "Seb? It's Mother. I need you to get yourself to work right away. We need inventory from our vendors, and it's too expensive to have it overnighted. Call me."

Ben was in orbit. "And now we can't even get in touch with him!"

"All right, all right. Let me look at the computer and see if I can place the orders. It can't be all that hard. I know we have some software to help us out," said Lulu.

"I'd have done the ordering myself, but I assumed that Seb was taking care of it. Since it's his *job* and everything," said Ben with more than a touch of bitterness in his voice. "And now it's time for me to fire up the pit and get some ribs smoked. I don't have time to worry with the inventory."

"Just hustle back into the kitchen, Ben," said Lulu, propelling him out of the office. "I'll see what I can do with the business end of things."

The business end of things quickly made Lulu extremely vexed. She'd found the inventory list (which indicated some shocking shortfalls) and pulled up the software that helped them place their orders from the vendors. The only problem was that the computer was offline. She couldn't seem to connect to the Internet. Indeed, the entire machine seemed to have been possessed by the devil. An exorcism was clearly needed.

With great reluctance, Lulu picked up the phone and dialed their Internet provider, World Net. She crossed her fingers that her call would stay somewhere in America. Whenever she was diverted to India, there was a tremendous language barrier—mostly with the technical help not understanding a word she said.

First, of course, she had to make it past the automated customer service representative. "Please tell me why you called today. You can say things like: about my bill or can't connect to the Internet."

Lulu hesitated. These programs could never seem to interpret her accent. "Can't connect to the Internet," she said carefully.

"I'm sorry. I didn't understand that. Please tell me why you called today."

"Internet!" said Lulu.

"I'm sorry. I didn't understand that," repeated the robotic voice on the other end of the line. "Could you please repeat why you called today?"

"Human!" It was time to cut to the chase.

"Hold on one moment, and I'll connect you." The machine sounded miffed, if that were even possible. Although, thought Lulu, some automated machines sounded more human than some of the people she'd gotten on the line.

Fortunately for Lulu, the call center apparently had a location somewhere in the South. Now the problem wasn't that they didn't understand *her*. It was more that *she* couldn't understand *them*.

"Okay, ma'am. I'm sorry to hear about your problem today. First of all, let's go to the start menu and click on 'run.' Then we're going to type a command in."

For a while, Lulu was able to follow, albeit slowly. Unfortunately, this changed not long after that. "Okay, we're going to see if we can ping the external address interface."

"Pardon?" asked Lulu.

"Well, it could be your modem or NIC card. Or maybe it's the signal on our end, although we haven't had any reports of outages in your area."

Lulu grunted.

"Or maybe you have a virus," said tech support.

Lulu was indignant. "I certainly do *not*! I feel absolutely fine. It's not my fault the computer is acting this way."

There was a pause on the other end. "I meant that maybe your computer has a virus—a Trojan or malware. Hey, let me ask you—is there anybody there who maybe is a little more familiar with computers than you are?" The tech support man sounded anxious.

"Ben can't come because he's working the pit."

"Umm-hmm."

"And Seb . . . well, this whole problem is Seb's fault. And we don't know where he is at all. I'm about to file a missing person's report on him," said Lulu.

"Okaaay." There was another long pause. "Can you look and see if anybody else is there who can help us out?" This time there was a pleading note to the representative's voice.

"Hold on just a minute," said Lulu. She got up from the desk and peered out the office door. She was surprised to see Derrick in the empty dining room, sitting with his head resting in his hands. Wasn't there school? Ella Beth and Coco were at school, she knew. With no time to really focus on truancy right now, Lulu called urgently to Derrick. There was no response. She called his name again. No response.

Lulu quickly remembered that when Derrick didn't answer her, it wasn't a cut and dried case of disrespect. No, it usually meant that he was plugged in.

Lulu strode right up to him and put her fingers to his ear. Sure enough, there was some sort of headphones plugged in there. She unplugged Derrick, and he lifted his head in surprise.

"Derrick? We have a computer emergency on our hands!"

Derrick had a confident air as soon as he sat down in front of the computer. Lulu smiled at his relaxed, self-assured manner. Lulu was sure the tech-support person on the other end of the phone line was relieved to have him there, too. Satisfied that her problem was in expert hands, Lulu focused on getting the dining room ready for the lunchtime crowd. Until, that is, the Memphis police came in. And they didn't seem to be there for the half-price plates that law enforcement got.

Lulu laid her dishrag back in her wash bucket at the sight of Detective Lyndon Bryce's freshly scrubbed face. "Mrs. Taylor? Hope you're doing well this morning. I just wanted to check in with you about your son."

Lulu's brow wrinkled. "About Ben? He's cooking ribs in the kitchen right now. You're welcome to talk to him while he works." Her mind spun. What the heck could the police want with Ben? Everything was falling apart around her ears.

Detective Bryce shook his head. "No, ma'am. We're actually interested in speaking with your other son. Sebastian Taylor."

Lulu put her hands on her hips. "Well, if you find out

where he is, you let me know. I'm interested in speaking
with him, too! He's vexed the life out of me today."

"He's not here?" asked Bryce.

"Afraid not. He was *supposed* to be here yesterday afternoon and this morning. But he's off gallivanting somewhere, I'm sure. And now we've got computer issues out
the wazoo!"

Detective Bryce appeared to not want to delve too far
into the computer problems plaguing Aunt Pat's. He handed
her his card. "If he does come in today, could you please
call me and let me know? Or have him call me directly."
He registered Lulu's anxious expression and added gently,
"It's strictly procedural, I promise."

Lulu puffed out a sigh of relief. "Well, I am glad to hear
that. He's mischievous, mind you, but I don't think he runs
around killing people he hasn't even met. I'll be sure to
give you a call if I see or hear from him."

A waitress hurried by, carrying a big tray loaded with
ribs with all the fixings. The sergeant's stomach rumbled.

"Sweetie, do you need a meal? Here . . . Pam, can you
grab a to-go plate for the sergeant here?"

The sergeant, with a swift, sideways glance at Detective
Bryce, shook his head. "Um, no, ma'am, I shouldn't . . ."

Lulu patted his arm, "Now, hon, it's not poisoned or
anything! You don't have to worry your head about that.
We cook with love here." After a beat of hesitation, Lulu
said, "And a plate for Detective Bryce. Because his stomach is next in line to grumble, I'm guessing. Nobody can
resist the sweet and spicy smells from Aunt Pat's kitchen."

A few minutes after Detective Bryce and his
sergeant had made their departure Derrick poked his head
out of the back office. Lulu blinked with surprise at his
pleased smile.

"It's up and running," said Derrick.

Lulu whooped and gave him a hug that made him gasp. Ben stuck his head out the kitchen door. "What was that noise? Did a wild animal get in here?"

"Just me," said Lulu, "getting excited over the fact that Derrick is a computer genius. He's got the computer back online."

Derrick looked hesitantly at Ben.

But Ben whooped, too, and gave him several hearty thumps on the back. "Excellent job, Derrick! Excellent job! Once I finish getting this takeout order done, I'll run in there and do some ordering. We're going to be in big trouble if we don't bring in some more stock."

Derrick said slowly, "Uncle Ben, if you like, I could give it a try. I saw the sheet listing the inventory you wanted to order. And the software doesn't look too hard to figure out."

Ben's face had a relieved expression on it. "That would be fantastic, Derrick. I'm . . . uh . . . not sure why you're not in school, but you've saved Aunt Pat's today. Another twenty-four hours of this and we'd have had to tell everybody we were out of half the menu before they placed their order." He looked at the wall clock. "I'd better get back into the kitchen."

Lulu said, "And I'm going to treat Derrick to some milk and cookies before he gets started ordering from vendors. I think he needs a little break." Ben nodded absently and pushed through the kitchen's swinging door.

If anybody needed some grandmotherly TLC, it was Derrick. She wasn't sure what the status on his actual grandmothers was, but she was always happy to step into a role that she really enjoyed. In a few minutes time, she'd settled Derrick in a rocking chair on the screen porch with a plate of chocolate chip cookies, a tall glass of milk, and two very interested Labradors.

After rocking quietly for a few minutes (the better to munch cookies), Lulu said, "I really appreciate your helping us out this morning, Derrick. I don't know what we'd have done if you hadn't stepped in. The tech-support people would be ready to shoot me by now."

"No problem. I like computers. And I was glad to help you out." He scratched B.B. behind his ears. "I'm sorry I've given you a lot of trouble," he added in a muffled voice.

"Trouble?" scoffed Lulu. "You've been no trouble at all."

Derrick looked sideways at Lulu. "Well, you know. The police fine for that vandalism."

Lulu arched her brows. "That desire to express yourself artistically? With highway overpasses as your palette?"

"And then I stole those garden gnomes from that lady down the street."

"A wayward beautification effort," said Lulu.

"And all the speeding tickets, of course," added Derrick.

"You have an admirable bent toward punctuality," Lulu helpfully interpreted.

"And now I've cut school the last few days," finished Derrick.

"Maybe because the shock of the murder has left you feeling sick and upset?" This analysis was apparently more on target, since Derrick nodded in agreement with it.

They rocked quietly again, Lulu waiting on him to speak first. "Aunt Sara is worried about me," he said slowly. "She knows something else that I did, but she didn't want you to worry. I'd rather if you knew about it, though. The day Rebecca was killed"—his face flushed angrily as he said her name—"I didn't go to school that day, either."

"No?" prompted Lulu as he paused.

"No. I lurked around the restaurant for a while, watching from a distance. I don't know why I was doing that. At first I told myself I only wanted to know how the barbeque tasting went."

Lulu nodded. "Maybe we should have taken you out of school early that day anyway. To let you be part of it. Ella Beth and Coco, too."

Derrick's eyes shifted away. "That was only part of it, though. The other part was that I wanted to get back at Rebecca." He reddened again.

Lulu stopped rocking. Would this turn into a full-fledged confession? Had this troubled boy done something to haunt him the rest of his life? "What *did* happen that night?" she asked. "The night before Rebecca Adrian was killed."

He hunched his shoulders forward in his familiar slump at the memory. "It's like she set me up to humiliate me. The Graces had left the Peabody and Tony wandered off, I guess to his room. Rebecca flirted with me and said she'd like to go out on Beale Street and see what it was like at night. So we walked to a blues club. People were dancing near the band, and I asked her if she wanted to dance. Then she started ripping into me. She had this weird look in her eye—like she loved every second of me being embarrassed."

Lulu nodded. "That's *exactly* how she was, Derrick. She also humiliated your Aunt Sara, Flo, and Miss Cameron, the writer and bookseller. That was her hobby—putting down other people to make herself feel good."

Derrick considered this while he gulped down another cookie. Lulu bided her time, knowing he'd talk again when he was ready. Lulu was thrilled that Derrick was finally opening up to her. Ever since he'd arrived, he'd looked like the most miserable teenager that ever lived. But anyone abandoned by their own mother would have to feel that way. It made Lulu feel weepy just thinking about it.

She was fighting tears, thinking Derrick would not appreciate her pity, when she heard an ominous snarl. The .

Labradors edged back from them, and Lulu looked down
to see tiny Babette growling at her with teeth bared. Lulu
growled back, and Babette exploded in yipping, running
behind Derrick's legs. He scooped her up and held her,
crooning until she calmed down.

"Well, I'll be," said Lulu. "Who'd have thought it?"

He shrugged it off. "Babette and I are buddies."

"I wish I knew your secret. I keep having nightmares
that Babette's going to murder me in my sleep."

"Yeah. It'd be a lot better if everybody liked me this
much. That's why Rebecca got under my skin so bad. I'd
had enough of it. I get bullied at school since I'm new and
don't fit in. I'm not even sure how I fit in with Aunt Sara
and Uncle Ben. They had me dumped on them and already
have two kids of their own. Then, when Rebecca made fun
of me . . ." He worked to get control of himself. "I'd had
enough. I decided to get back at her. I followed her Cooking Channel truck to the Peabody. When she went inside, I
slashed her tires." He gave a huge sigh as if a large weight
had been taken off of him.

"How did Sara find out about it, Derrick? Did you tell
her about it?"

"No. Well—but she called right afterward, checking to
see where I was. So I came out with it."

Lulu gave him another cookie. It was amazing how fast
they disappeared. And that Derrick stayed beanpole thin.
"I think," said Lulu slowly, "this is a good place to turn
things around for you. We *want* you here, Derrick, and are
happy to have you as part of the family. You don't know
what a huge help you were today."

She took a deep breath, "But to move ahead, we'll put
the past behind us. Do the police know you slashed Miss
Adrian's tires?"

He shook his head.

"I'm guessing Sara is completely overwhelmed and

doesn't know what to do. We should let the police know," said Lulu firmly, "as soon as possible. They're bound to find out anyway, and it'll be much worse if they have to come to you first about it. Is there anything else you need to let the police know?"

Derrick shook his head, and his long bangs flopped into his eyes, covering them. Lulu watched him wearily. The secrets everyone kept exhausted her. "Just you running around with a killer on the loose gives me the chills." Lulu was being literal—she rubbed her hands against her arms to warm herself up. "Now listen, because I want you to be sure—how about the murder scene? Is there *anything* you saw at the hotel? Anything that the police need to know to help them solve this case?"

Derrick hesitated. Lulu waited.

"Not really. I mean . . . I saw one of the Graces at the Peabody."

"Did you?"

"Yeah. The one who acts crazy sometimes."

Cherry, thought Lulu. "Okay, honey. Thanks for letting me know. I'll try to get to the bottom of it. This is probably something completely innocent, but I'll find out, just to make sure. Nothing else?" The head shake again. "Okay, if you're sure about that, then let's go ahead and get this cleared up. Detective Bryce left me his card today with his phone number. We'll give him a statement. Then we'll start turning things around for you. Like . . . school tomorrow, for a start." Derrick frowned and Lulu hurried on. "I know it's rough over there for you. Sara and Ben should have a little talk with the principal to let him know what you're going through. They'll get it stopped, don't you worry. Or else Sara and Ben can try enrolling you in another school. We'll work it out. And, by the way . . ." added Lulu.

Derrick raised his eyebrows questioningly.

"That spray painting you did on the overpass was very

good. Since you're interested in art, why don't I ask Sara if you could spend a little time in her studio?"

Derrick grinned and gave her an awkward hug before hurrying away, Babette still in his arms. Lulu smiled. Maybe things weren't so bad after all.

Chapter

Shoot! Lulu's mouth dropped when she saw Tony being seated in the dining room. Where were her manners? With all the hubbub, she'd completely forgotten about Tony's existence. And he was a stranger in town! What must he be thinking about them all?

Tony raised his eyebrows in surprise as Lulu rushed over to his booth and sat down opposite him. "I am so *sorry*." She clucked. "I should have followed up with you and seen how you were doing. What did the police say? What did Cooking Channel say?"

Tony laughed. "Don't worry about it. I didn't expect you to check on me, you know. It's been okay. The worst part was talking to Rebecca's parents on the phone. The network broke the news to them, but then I didn't feel right not calling them to give them some more information." He shrugged uncomfortably.

Lulu winced. She could only imagine how awful it would be to get such bad news about your child.

"Her dad was pretty broken up over it all." Tony frowned

at the memory. "But Mrs. Adrian sounded cold as ice. She might have been upset, who knows? Sometimes people react different when they're grieving. But she reminded me of Rebecca."

"What're they planning on doing? I know they've got a funeral to plan."

"I think they're waiting for the autopsy and that type of thing. The body . . . Rebecca . . . needs to be released. Then their funeral home in New York can make some arrangements. That's what Mrs. Adrian said, anyway," said Tony.

"How about *you*? Do you have to stay here in Memphis, or can you go back up to New York?"

Tony said, "The police said I could go home and back to work. They could tell there was nothing going on between me and Rebecca . . . no romance, no professional jealousy. There was nothing except normal aggravation from dealing with her in close quarters every day. I didn't have any gripes with her; I simply didn't like her."

"Where are you going from here?" asked Lulu.

"I've got to get back up to New York and talk to my producer up there. Kind of a debriefing. Then I'm going to go back out with another scout on another assignment. Different town," added Tony. "Sorry. They're going to take a break from the Memphis production for a little while. Until everything calms down, you know. Then they'll send me back here with another scout to taste the barbeque and do some filming."

"What have you been doing since . . . ?" asked Lulu.

"Well, first thing I had to do was to go get some new tires for the truck. Damned thing. Some kid or someone must have slashed the tires. It's absolutely unbelievable."

Lulu flushed. "I might know a little bit about that, Tony. Actually, I found out a little tidbit about it this morning."

Tony studied her face thoughtfully. "Was it Derrick?" he asked in a low voice so no one could overhear them.

Lulu sighed. "How'd you guess?"

"Rebecca was in a hell of a mood that night at the Peabody. She was bent on putting everybody down around her. I wondered if Derrick was heading for a fall. She was leading him on: putting her hand on his arm. Smiling and winking at him. That was her thing, you know—sort of like a cat playing with a hurt mouse. I left that night right after the Graces did because I was sick of dealing with Rebecca for the day." He rubbed his eyes. "I shouldn't have left him alone with her. He's only a kid."

"It's not your fault, Tony. Dealing with rejection is one of those life lessons we all have to learn sooner or later. And Derrick has already had enough rejection from his mother to last a lifetime. Maybe things will look up for him from here on out."

Tony's order came to the table. He took a big bite of corn bread and chewed it while he thought. He washed it down with some sweet tea. "So the poor kid was trying to get back at her, right? That's what I'd have done when I was his age and hanging out in the city."

Lulu nodded. "He shouldn't have done it. But that's all he did." Lulu hoped her voice sounded more positive than she felt.

Tony took a swig of his sweet tea. "You know the cops think the person who slashed the tires might be a murder suspect, don't you? I'm only asking because the last time I talked to them, they didn't seem like they knew who did it."

"I was just telling Derrick that we were going to have to call the police this afternoon . . . soon as the lunchtime crowd thins out a little." Lulu stood and gave Tony a quick hug. "I'm sorry your trip to Memphis was so eventful—for all the wrong reasons!"

"None of it was your fault. I got such a warm welcome from everybody here. It made me feel great. Usually Rebecca gets all the attention because she's the scout and everyone wants to butter her up. But you guys were nice just because you're nice people. I'll enjoy seeing you again when I come back with the new crew."

"Lulu, was Tony here?" asked Cherry. Lulu noticed Cherry had her very cutest bright-colored coordinating short set on, extra jangly bangles, and no helmet. This was a sure sign that the mating season was underway.

"Honey, I'm sorry, but he left a few minutes ago. He's wrapping up his time in Memphis."

Cherry groaned. "I missed him *again*! *Un*believable. Well, I guess it just wasn't meant to be."

"You've been trying to catch up with Tony?" Lulu looked confused.

"Lulu, you've been single for so long I guess your love radar broke. Tony is the best-looking single guy to strut into Aunt Pat's for years. I even went back to the Peabody to find him. But he wasn't in." Cherry made a face.

Lulu felt a wave of relief wash over her. *That's* why Cherry was at the Peabody . . . trying to make moves on Tony. She'd have to let Derrick know. "You're right, Cherry. Besides, you wouldn't have liked a long-distance relationship."

"*Relationship?*" Cherry grinned wickedly. "Who said anything about a relationship?"

Lulu sat ramrod straight and right next to Derrick in the restaurant's office as the police talked to him. They had their old friend and regular customer, Jed Sharpe, there to serve in the lawyer capacity. He was delighted to be paid for his services in free ribs with all the fixings. And that was a great deal for Lulu, because he was one of the finest lawyers in town.

"So what we're saying," reiterated Jed to Detective Bryce, "is that Derrick here made an obvious mistake—one that he's very repentant for." Derrick certainly did look sorry, thought Lulu. Or sick maybe. His face was completely white and perspiration dotted his forehead. He obviously realized this was much worse than his other scrapes with the law. This time, there was a dead body involved.

"But," continued Jed, "he was not responsible in any way for Miss Adrian's death. It's unfortunate that his childish act of revenge coincided with the day of her murder. But he had nothing to do with it."

"After all, Detective," said Lulu, "I don't mean to be disrespectful, but don't you think if one of the Taylors wanted to kill somebody, we'd take one of our knives to them? We have one of the finest knife collections in town, you know. Why'd we go to the trouble of looking up poisons if we have the perfect weapon at the ready?"

Jed hushed her, but Lulu was rewarded by the trace of a smile on Detective Bryce's lips.

The detective asked a few more questions. They mostly centered on where Derrick had been and what he had been doing the afternoon that Rebecca was killed. Unfortunately, Derrick's actions that afternoon were comprised of slashing tires and skulking around the Peabody and the barbeque restaurant. Lulu grimaced. They had been so wrapped up with their own dramas that afternoon that no one had given a thought to Derrick's whereabouts, even after school hours. If only they'd thought to call his cell phone and ask him to come back to Aunt Pat's.

Since the police had no direct evidence that Derrick was involved in Rebecca's murder, he was free to go. But Detective Bryce cautioned him sternly before letting them go.

"Young man, we're keeping an eye on you. You're free to go, but you need to keep yourself out of trouble. We're not done with you."

Derrick nodded. He relaxed as the police left the restaurant. Lulu put an arm around him and said, "Jed, you saved the day. I can't tell you how much we appreciate your help. You come in as often as you like, and we'll heap a plate with the best barbeque ribs in town."

Jed grinned. "That's a great trade for only a few minutes of my time." He patted Derrick on the shoulder. "I think they're done with you, son. The police don't have anything to link you to that murder. And you had nothing to do with it." He looked piercingly at Derrick.

Derrick looked away from Jed. "No. I had nothing to do with it."

Lulu just hoped Derrick was telling the truth.

The day plummeted downhill when Lurleen Ashton popped her head in through the office door not long after the police left. She gave what she fondly considered a sweet smile, but what was closer to a simper. "I wanted to stop by and make sure y'all were okay, Lulu. I saw the police cars outside and that unmarked cop car, too. I sure hope there wasn't more trouble here. Mercy! Between food poisonings and being suspected of murder, you've had a nutty week at Aunt Pat's, haven't you?" She shook her head until the black strands brushed against her shoulders in mock concern.

Lulu gritted her teeth. She just couldn't stand this woman. Every bit of her, from her dyed-black hair to her over-the-top implants to her knock-off designer shoes, was fake, fake, fake. And everything that came out of her mouth was fake, too. She lied through her teeth every chance she got. And Lulu hated most of all that fuchsia pig that danced outside Lurleen's barbeque restaurant.

Lulu collected herself with some difficulty. She answered sweetly, "I appreciate your concern, Lurleen. You're right; the police were back over here. But you know how we give our public servants a big discount on our barbeque."

Lurleen raised her super-plucked eyebrows. "They were here for a bite to eat? I thought I saw that detective who's investigating the murder here. As I was coming in," she explained hastily.

Lulu had to wonder how much time Lurleen spent observing the comings and goings at the restaurant. How could she possibly have seen who was leaving unless she'd been hanging out near the front of Aunt Pat's? The Memphis police had left a good fifteen minutes before she came in. She looked into Lurleen's all-too-innocent green eyes and summoned up her Christian principles to give the other woman the benefit of the doubt. Maybe she was making cell phone calls and was wrapping up her phone conversations before coming inside.

"I guess detectives have to eat, too," said Lulu noncommittally.

Lurleen said, "He must have taken it to-go, then. Or else, he's chucking down his food a little too fast!" She giggled and then added, "I'm surprised the detective wasn't worried about eating here. After all, he's investigating a murder, and clearly the victim was poisoned here. It's awfully brave of him. No offense."

"None taken." Lulu felt her blood pressure shoot up. "You know, the police haven't actually determined where she was poisoned. It could have been after she left the restaurant. This was just one of the places she ate that day. In fact," Lulu noted sweetly, "I remember that Rebecca left with you that afternoon. Did she follow you back to Hog Heaven?"

Lurleen flushed. She waved a hand with fake-tipped fingernails dismissively. "Oh, that. You know, I was here to narrow down when she was doing her tasting at Hog Heaven that afternoon. I wanted to roll out the red carpet for her, that's all. She didn't go back with me. In fact, she took off down the street. I guess to the parking deck."

Lulu knit her brows. "Didn't they have a scheduled time to come by Hog Heaven? They did for coming here."

Lurleen pinched her red lips shut. Then she said, "Well, I'm sure I don't know, Lulu. Maybe she wasn't sure how long the tasting was going to take here. Maybe she wanted to leave enough time to go back to the Peabody and brush her teeth before going to Hog Heaven," she added cattily. "You know—cleanse her palate."

Lulu had heard just about enough nonsense for one day. And she was very much afraid that her prized self-control was about to come to a catastrophic end right here in the Aunt Pat's office. "I do appreciate you coming by, Lurleen. Do you really have to go?"

Lurleen gave a tight smile. "Yes, I guess I must. By the way, have you seen Seb?"

Oh, please, thought Lulu, don't let Seb be messed up with this vixen. That's all they needed. "Actually, no. I haven't seen him lately, Lurleen. Why are you looking for him?"

"Oh, I only wanted to talk to him about something. Business related, you know."

Lulu watched her go. Was everyone looking for Seb? She'd had enough of calling his cell phone and not getting an answer. It was time to have a little face-to-face talk with her younger son.

Seb wasn't delighted to see his mom's face when he peeked through the peephole in his front door. "No one's home!" he said advisedly.

"That's interesting," said Lulu. "Because I have a paycheck in my hand for the last week. If no one is here to claim it, I'm going to put it back in the Aunt Pat's kitty. It'll prove handy when we hire our new office manager."

The door opened and Seb, or an unreasonable facsimile of him, leaned on the doorjamb. "Dear Lord. What on earth happened to *you*?" gasped Lulu in horror. "Did you have a life-threatening encounter with the murderer?"

Seb's hair stood on end like he had just risen for the day. The hair covering his face was decidedly more than the stubble of a day-old beard. It appeared that he'd slept in his clothes and hadn't even picked very nice clothes to sleep in. And, Lulu wrinkled her nose, he seemed in need of a good scrubbing.

Seb looked at his mother with bleary eyes. "Nothing, Mom. Nothing happened to me. Can't a man relax at home without his mama coming to drag his butt out of bed? Jeez."

Lulu pushed past him into the house. "Not when it's the middle of the afternoon. What's going *on*, Seb? Have you got the swine flu or something? And could you please explain why the police are looking for you?"

Seb raised an eyebrow. "The police are looking for me? They must not be looking very hard because I've been right here all along."

"Right here, but not answering your phone? Or your door? Because they've been trying to contact you."

Seb didn't answer, just rubbed his eyes.

"And I've been looking for you, too. You'll notice that your paycheck is a little bit smaller than usual. I've subtracted out the hours you didn't work. I'm going to divert that money to Derrick, your substitute."

Seb snorted. "I doubt Derrick has the ability to do much filling in."

"Actually, he's done remarkably well in your absence." Lulu sniffed. "The computer has never run better. And he's placing orders to vendors for us. Now the restaurant won't go under while you're having your lost weekend."

Seb spun on his heel and tromped into the kitchen. Lulu followed him like a worried mother hen. She was sorry she'd followed when she took a gander at the kitchen. It looked like the home of someone who should be confessing his slovenly habits on Oprah. There was dried up food on plates, dried liquids in glasses, and not a surface to be seen that wasn't stacked high with tilting piles of dirty dishes and silverware. Lulu put her hands on her hips.

"And what's the meaning of this? I didn't raise you to live in squalor." Lulu took off her rings and put them in her pocketbook.

"What are you doing?" asked Seb suspiciously.

"What are *we* doing, you mean? We are going to clean up this foolishness. That's what *we're* going to do. Then you're going to have a shower while I dig up some edible food in this kitchen."

Seb opened his mouth to protest, but when he saw Lulu's face, he had second thoughts. He obediently rolled his sleeves and filled the sink with hot water.

Two hours later, the kitchen sparkled and Seb, while in no way sparkly, was at least clean and shaven. He wolfed down a plate of scrambled eggs and a couple of pieces of toast while Lulu unloaded and reloaded the dishwasher.

Lulu was ready to continue her interrogation. She peeked into the den to see if it was clean enough to sit in. After looking, she decided to stick with the kitchen. She sat down at the small kitchen table and smoothed out her floral skirt. Seb smiled at her.

Lulu smiled back and said, "So did you murder Rebecca Adrian?"

Some bit of egg or toast made its way down Seb's windpipe, and he commenced a coughing fit. Lulu waited patiently for the coughing to end.

Since Seb didn't seem in any hurry to answer her question, Lulu pressed on. "Did you? Because I simply can't think why the police would be interested in talking to you since you'd never even met Miss Adrian. At least, not as far as I'm aware."

"I cannot believe," said Seb with an affronted tone, "that a mother would accuse her loving son of committing such a heinous crime."

"I haven't accused you at all, Seb. I'm just asking. What is the police's business with you? And, on a similar note, what's happened to make your house resemble a place pigs would be proud to call home?"

Seb looked very tired. Which was odd, considering he'd recently awakened and it was five o'clock in the evening. "I'm guessing the police want to talk to me because my phone number is on Rebecca Adrian's cell phone."

"Excuse me?"

"Because Rebecca called me, Mother. Yes, she called me."

Lulu blinked at him. "Why on earth would she have called you? Did you slip her your phone number on her barbeque plate? What have I told you about fraternizing with our guests? First the Graces, then people well on their way to getting murdered . . ."

"For God's sake. I didn't try to pick her up, Mom. I was trying to avoid that snake at all costs."

Lulu was completely agog. "How do you know she's a snake? Was a snake?"

"Because, Mother, she was my girlfriend in New York."

Lulu clutched at her throat. "No!"

"Yes. And she knew that I'd had to serve time in the city on a drug-dealing charge." At his mother's look of horror, he added, "You thought I was in Munich for a special finance training seminar."

"No!"

"Yes. And she called me the night before she died, and I met her at the Peabody."

"*No!*"

"And while I was in her room with her, she tried to blackmail me about my drug-dealing past."

"*N—*"

"Mother, *stop*! Enough with the *no*s. Yes, all those things happened. But do you know what?"

"No." Seb glared at Lulu and she said, "I mean, what?"

"I laughed in her face. I really did. Because if there's one thing I've discovered about coming home, it's acceptance. Here in Memphis, I'm just Seb. I'm not somebody with a complicated past or somebody who served time. I'm just one of the Taylors. Being a Taylor and growing up at Aunt Pat's means that everybody automatically knows all about me and how I was raised. Lord, that sounds like something from *The Waltons* or something." He shrugged. "I told her where she could go and what she could do with her blackmailing. I left the Peabody. And I didn't go back."

"Well, honey, that sounds so sweet with the family stuff and your finding your identity. But—you need to level with me. Because if you really didn't care what Miss Adrian said and if she really didn't have any power over you, why haven't you been to work? Why were you filthy and unshaven? Why should your kitchen have been condemned by the board of health?"

Seb rubbed his nose in intense irritation. Lulu wasn't sure if he was irritated with Rebecca or with Lulu or with himself. "Because she *does* have power over me. Not because of the blackmail, but because I still have . . . had . . . feelings for her."

Now Lulu looked more stunned than she had during

the entire rest of the conversation. "*Feelings?* For Rebecca Adrian? Like, *loving* feelings?" Lulu could certainly understand hateful feelings and hurt feelings where Rebecca came into play. Loving feelings she couldn't begin to grasp. It was like trying to understand quantum physics.

"Yes, Mom. Loving feelings. Or, at least, very complicated feelings. Complex feelings that I've been trying hard to work out over the past few days: her sudden appearance back on the scene, the fact she was betraying me, and then the fact that she was murdered." He gulped. "It's been a lot to absorb."

Lulu was still having a hard time absorbing Seb's attraction to Rebecca Adrian. But she wanted to feel sympathetic. Clearly, he'd had a rough few days. She gave him a hug, and he hugged her back, hard. While his ear was very close to her lips, she said softly, "You know what you need? What would help pull you out of your slump? Going out with Susan Meredith."

Seb groaned and pushed away from his mother.

"I mean it, Seb! I really do. If you actually knew what a nice girl was like, you'd never waste your time on someone who was going to end up murdered. And at the Peabody, too! Why someone would get themselves murdered in such a classy place is beyond me."

"Mom!" He buried his face in his hands and shook it from side to side. "This is all a nightmare. This can't be happening."

"Susan's gallery is very sweet. And she's been really kind to Sara, showing her art and all. She's a nice girl," said Lulu.

"She's a yoga-practicing, meditating, organic-food-growing hippie. And don't you think 'girl' is a bit of an exaggeration? She must be forty-two if she's a day."

"Well, you're no spring chicken at thirty-eight, Seb. You know what—never mind. I don't want to see Susan get hurt. When you grow up a little bit and are ready for a real relationship, cross your fingers that she's still going to be around. Because she might be married to Trevor Baldwin by then."

"Trevor? For Lord's sake, Mom. Why would somebody smart and pretty go out with that mealy mouthed guy? He doesn't have a lick of sense."

"Because he's a decent man. He works very hard, saves his money, and has a nice mama and daddy."

Seb rolled his eyes. "Well, if that's the kind of person she's looking for, tell her to go for it. He sounds right up her alley."

This only served to irritate Lulu more. She decided to move on to her next line of attack, which covered something sudden, unwelcome, and appalling. "While we're on the subject of women, why is Lurleen Ashton looking for you? I certainly hope you know better than to get involved with that vixen again," said Lulu sternly.

Seb made a sound that was halfway between a sob and a laugh. "Good God, Mother."

"It's not me being nosy—she *asked* about you. At Aunt Pat's." Lulu made Lurleen's inquiry sound like something dirty.

"Mother, she's on the committee that's organizing our high school reunion. Remember how she was in high school? She was a cheerleader, homecoming queen, and student body VP—exactly the kind of person who organizes reunions. Not that I have any intention of attending the damned thing. And I have no desire to see her because we had a really nasty and abrupt end to a one- or two-day relationship. So I'm *avoiding* her. I hope you didn't tell her where she could find me. When we went out, I was in an apartment at the time."

"No, I certainly didn't. For one thing, I didn't know

where I could find you myself. It seemed like everybody in Memphis was looking for you. Besides, the less I see of Lurleen Ashton, the better." Lulu drew herself up and abruptly changed the subject. "You, on the other hand, will call up the Memphis police department and explain your connection with Miss Adrian and your presence at the crime scene."

"Well, it wasn't a crime scene then, Mother. It was just a hotel room."

"And they're going to look at your past and judge you against it. I *knew* you never should have left Memphis. Here you're around people who love you, but as soon as you left, all the vultures of the world swooped down on you out of the heavens." This flight of her fancy intrigued Lulu, and she mulled over her own imagery.

Seb gave a pained sigh. "Is this interrogation over? Because I think I'm ready to take some Advil and crawl back in bed."

"Which you can absolutely do—the first part, anyway. Take some headache medicine, and then we're calling the police. They need to hear this right from the horse's mouth."

Where Detective Bryce had been willing to see a troubled youth in Derrick, he wasn't nearly as understanding with middle-aged Seb. In fact, he positively glowered at him the whole time. Lulu thought a glower looked really funny coming out of Bryce's sunny, boyish face.

Lulu had been all about calling Jed back and having him come to be Seb's mouthpiece, but Seb would have nothing to do with it. "Mom, think about it—I didn't have a motive anymore. When I told her to go ahead and tell everyone about the drug stuff, I really didn't care. Why would I have killed her?" Lulu agreed that she couldn't think of a reason, but she hoped that Detective Bryce wouldn't have more imagination than she did.

"But you did have a motive, didn't you?" Bryce finally asked.

Seb frowned questioningly at him.

"Your motive was to keep her quiet. To keep her from saying anything about your past your family."

"But," said Seb, "I just finished telling you that I didn't care whether she said anything or not. I told her to feel free to spill the beans."

"And I'm supposed to believe that?" asked Detective Bryce.

"Why not? It's the truth," snapped Seb. Lulu hoped he wasn't about to blow his top. She wondered if that's what Bryce wanted to see happen. It could be a ploy to get more information out of him.

"Why didn't you go right to your mother and fess up? It seems to me that you'd have immediately told your family about your prison time in New York. After all, you wanted to make sure they heard it from you first. Instead, the woman who is threatening to blackmail you is murdered, you disappear, and no one finds out a thing about your background until your mother pulls it out of you."

Seb only glared at him.

"He didn't disappear, though, Detective Bryce," said Lulu. "He was right here all along, filthying up his house. Peek in his den if you don't believe me." Seb rolled his eyes at her.

Lulu continued, "If he'd killed Miss Adrian, wouldn't he have run off and tried to build a new life somewhere else? Why would he be hanging out in Memphis? And he didn't *have* to tell me today about her attempt to blackmail him and his prison time. I wasn't going to find it out now that she's dead. He could have just told me that Miss

Adrian got his phone number because she thought he was cute." Both Bryce and Seb looked at her blankly. "Well, she could have thought that! He's not a bad-looking boy, just a little rundown."

Seb broke in before the conversation turned into a litany on what he should do to spruce himself up. "Look, have you got any evidence against me? Because really, that's what this all boils down to. And I don't think you have it."

Apparently, Detective Bryce didn't think he did, either. His blue eyes looked tired for a second, before he briskly stood and moved toward Seb's door. "If you think of anything to add to your statement, call me." His tone suggested he was far from finished with Seb.

Lulu looked at her watch. "Heavens, I've got to get back to the restaurant for the dinner rush!" She clucked. "Tonight's band should be arriving any minute, too." Thank goodness her car was in working order again. Right now, she loved Seb just as much as always, but she sure didn't like him very much.

"Hey, Mom, do you want me to come in to work? Get some things done in the office?" asked Seb hesitantly. He didn't seem to *want* to go in but more like he thought he *should* go in.

Lulu looked at him severely over the glasses she wore to drive with. "Not a bit. I don't think you're customer-ready right now. You're not even back door ready. You look like you've been run over by a Mack truck, frankly. Your original plan was a better one—go to bed. Go directly to bed. Do not pass Go. Do not collect two hundred dollars."

Seb gave a faint smile. "I used to love it when we played Monopoly."

"That's probably because you usually won. Even when you were a little guy," said Lulu.

"Well, I was always good at figures," said Seb with an attempt at a modest tone.

"You were always good at robbing the bank." Lulu sniffed. She held her head high as she walked out the door—but turned to wink at Seb.

Lulu softened a little. "You can come in tomorrow, though. I'm sure there're some things we can find for you to do."

Chapter

9

Lulu was so absorbed by meeting and greeting all her guests in the crowded dining room that she didn't even notice she was being shadowed.

In fact, it took close to an hour before she finally glimpsed a small brunette head dodging back behind the back of a recently vacated booth. Lulu figured she'd made a colossal mistake by not staying more on top of Derrick, and she was determined to communicate more with Ella Beth and Coco. She plopped down in the booth opposite the scrunched-down Ella Beth. "Is there something you needed to talk to me about, sweetie?" asked Lulu.

Ella Beth shook her head. She clutched a bug viewer magnifying glass. "No, Granny Lulu. I'm looking for clues, that's all. And keeping under cover. You really shouldn't be drawing attention to me, you know."

Lulu knit her brows. "Clues to what, honey?"

Ella Beth looked at her with some incredulity. "To the mystery, of course. The mystery of Miss Adrian's death. I'm going to crack the case and find out who done it. This

magnifying glass helps me look for clues to the killer.
Dusty footprints, a torn piece of clothing, or smudged fingerprints. You know."

Lulu didn't want to break it to her that there were so
many footprints, fingerprints, and DNA traces scattered
around the dining room that she never would be able to dis-
tinguish what should be there and what shouldn't be there.
She leaned over the table and squeezed Ella Beth's hand.
"You did a great job for your last case."

"The case of the disappearing cell phone? Yes, and that
was a tough one. Daddy should never have put it on vi-
brate. When he called it to see where it was, it didn't ring.
It took me forever to find it for him. And don't forget my
private-investigation talent for keeping undercover. I was
the brains behind the bust of Derrick at the tattoo parlor."

Lulu said, "You surely were. So are you a solo detective,
then? Where's Coco? I haven't seen her around tonight."

Ella Beth shrugged. "She's watching some TV show in
the office."

Clearly, Coco had no interest at all in playing along
with her sister's detective work. How could twins be so
different?

"Have you made any discoveries with your case,
sweetie?"

Ella Beth brightened. "Could we be a crime-fighting
duo? Most detectives have sidekicks."

"Well, sure. I'd be proud to call you my sidekick."

There was a long pause. "No, Granny Lulu. I was thinking that *you* could be *my* sidekick. Since I'm the one with
the detective kit and all."

"Of course, of course. What was I thinking?" Lulu
shook her head woefully at this evidence of her mental
shortcomings.

"Since you're here, this will be a good time for a secret

meeting. Let's share our findings on the case of the mean TV scout. Do you have an update to share, Granny Lulu?"

"My update?"

"What you've discovered so far," said Ella Beth. "Because I know you've been working on it."

Lulu looked startled. She needed everyone to think she was a garrulous, gossipy old lady. Or, perhaps, that she was on a mission to clear the good name of Aunt Pat's barbeque. If everybody in Memphis knew she was trying to solve the case, she'd be running into one brick wall after another. They'd all be protecting their secrets. What if the killer tried to bump Lulu off because she knew something he didn't want her to know? She shivered.

"Don't worry," said Ella Beth breezily. "Nobody else knows. Except Daddy, maybe. I'm just especially observant. After all, I'm a detective, so I notice things."

"Well, now, that *is* a relief. Because, if I'm a private eye, I'd like to be a *private* eye," said Lulu. "But, no, I really haven't discovered anything, honey." After all, she certainly wasn't going to tell her nine-year-old granddaughter about Flo having been in prison. Or, for that matter, her uncle Seb having been there. Or her cousin Derrick's proclivity for slashing car tires. She'd just keep those little tidbits of information to herself.

Ella Beth looked rather disgusted. "Nothing? You haven't found *any*thing out?"

"Afraid not, sweetie. I'm a real crime-fighting dunce."

"Well *I've* found out something. But you can't tell anybody. Because we're in the investigating stage and don't need to scare off any suspects."

Suspects like your mom? wondered Lulu.

"I found out," breathed Ella Beth, after looking around her in all directions, "that not everybody was where they said they were the day Miss Adrian was murdered."

Oh, so she did know about Derrick playing hooky. Lulu guessed that was to be expected. After all, they were living like siblings now.

"Good work!" said Lulu. "Do you think it'll give us a clue to the murder?"

"No," said Ella Beth. "But it might mean somebody needs to make sure Derrick's grades aren't dropping like crazy."

Lulu wondered if Ella Beth might be bitter over the fact that she was at school while Derrick was skipping for days in a row. Although it didn't seem like she was when she said, "By the way, Derrick has been really cool lately. He even helped me with my homework yesterday."

Lulu raised her eyebrows. "Since when do you need help with your homework?"

Ella Beth shrugged. "I didn't actually need any help. But it meant Derrick and I got to spend some time together, and he was totally pumped that he could help me out."

"That's really sweet of him."

Ella Beth nodded. "And then he even drove Coco to her dance practice when Mama and Daddy were too busy. Good thing he did—Coco was fit to be tied that no one could take her. She needed to practice her routine for the next pageant." She added thoughtfully, "One day, Coco will be a beauty queen, and I'll be the most in-demand investigator in Memphis."

Lulu gave Ella Beth a quick hug. "By the way," she said, "I have something else I'd like you to investigate for me."

"What's that, Granny Lulu?"

"Your math book. I seem to remember your mama saying she needed you to work on homework. But all I've noticed is you with a magnifying glass."

Ella Beth looked miffed. "All right. I guess I can take a break for long enough to do some math. But if I get a fresh lead, then I'm outta there."

"Deal," said Lulu.

"And, Granny Lulu? Did you happen to make any cookies today?"

"Sweetie, you know I wouldn't forget about you! I made your favorite chocolate chunk cookies. And this time I didn't even eat a one. Although they were right tempting there on the cooling rack."

A huge grin spread over Ella Beth's freckled face as she hurried off for the kitchen.

"Remember to share some with Coco!" called Lulu. But Ella Beth was already conveniently out of earshot.

Lulu headed back into the dining room after her tête-à-tête with Ella Beth. The supper crowd was dying down, but the night crowd was coming in—drawn by blues and barbeque. This crowd was more likely to have a side order or a dessert and a drink while listening to the band. Lulu saw Mildred Cameron entering the restaurant.

Despite Mildred's eccentricity, Lulu really liked her. After all, she was *nice*. And nice went a long way with Lulu. Mildred looked around her tentatively, making sure no one appeared to be talking about her or laughing at her or recalling her last fateful appearance there.

But no one did. Actually, *studiously* no one did. In the South, if someone is going to talk about you, they'll do it only in the most loving of ways and certainly not where you can see them doing it. In fact, there was a chorus of hellos when she walked farther into the dining room. Lulu's was one of them.

Lulu slid into the booth opposite Mildred, and Mildred looked relieved for the company. Lulu was happy to see that it was Normal Mildred and not Zombie Mildred that had come to the restaurant. Lulu had really been worried about her at the tail end of their visit the other day.

"We really missed seeing you here, sweetie. The Graces were all asking me when you were coming by, and Big Ben asked if I'd talked to you. It hasn't been the same here without you, honey!"

Mildred blushed but looked pleased. "I missed everybody, too. And I found out I can't write as well when I'm all holed up at home." She shyly took out a notebook. "I think I put little bits of all of y'all in my stories."

A waitress hovered nearby, and Lulu said, "A pulled pork sandwich with red beans and rice, coleslaw, and a couple of spicy corn muffins. That *is* what you want, right? And an iced tea?"

Mildred nodded shyly, and Lulu said softly to the waitress, "On the house, please, Maggie."

Lulu leaned toward Mildred and said in a low voice, "I know you were worried about the police visiting you. Did you get my message about Pink?" Mildred nodded. "He just couldn't give me much information . . . you know, he's not supposed to. And he's not on that case, anyway."

Mildred said, "It went okay. I was terrified at the beginning, but that Detective Bryce is really a nice man. And it ended up being good research for my mystery."

Lulu reflected that Detective Bryce's innocent-looking, freshly scrubbed appearance might work to his advantage in some circumstances—like putting shy, old maid booksellers at ease. Lulu reached over and gave Mildred's hand a quick squeeze. "Good for you!"

"I've made up my mind that nothing she could say is going to make me feel bad about my manuscript or myself. Miss Adrian was . . . mean."

"Or something," agreed Lulu sympathetically. "She seemed to have a lot of different issues. Tony was telling the Graces, Seb, and me that Rebecca was so secretive she couldn't even take a cell phone call without getting up and walking away. She sprang up right in the middle of a conversation we were all having. So she didn't even have basic *manners*."

"Detective Bryce asked me what I'd thought of her. He really was interested in my opinion about Miss Adrian." She added, almost to herself, "I wanted to kill her."

"You didn't tell the police that, right?" asked Lulu. Surely Mildred had said something like, "I was furious" or "I was so mad."

"Well, of course I told Detective Bryce that," she said, looking puzzled at Lulu. "He *asked* me. The police *asked* me."

Lulu sighed. Mildred's honesty might end up getting her in trouble.

Mildred looked around her, patting her slightly greasy locks. "I was wondering—is Seb here? I was hoping to talk to him for a few minutes."

You and everybody else in Memphis, thought Lulu. "No, honey, I'm afraid he wasn't . . . uh . . . feeling well today. I told him to stay at home instead of contaminating the populace here at Aunt Pat's. But I think he'll probably be here bright and early tomorrow morning." At least he'd better be. Otherwise he was going to be her dearly departed younger son.

Mildred drooped with disappointment. "Oh. Well, I guess I could come back and talk to him tomorrow morning before going to the bookstore."

"Is there something you want me to ask him for you?" asked Lulu. Surely Mildred wasn't setting her cap for Seb. If pretty Susan Meredith wasn't turning Seb's head, then poor Mildred didn't have a chance in hell.

"No, that's okay, Lulu. I'll try to catch up with him later." She looked like she was worried about something and opened her mouth for a second before snapping it shut again. More secrecy.

Then Mildred leaned forward in a secretive way. "But

the new book? The mystery? It's coming along really well.
I'm already a couple of pages into it! I think mystery might
be the way to go for me. And I'm really going to research
this one and make it really accurate—what it's like to be
a suspect, and how a murderer thinks. That kind of thing."

Lulu could only imagine how long it was going to take
to complete a whole new manuscript, especially if there
was research involved. Mildred's last project had taken de-
cades to complete. "I'm so happy for you, Mildred! See,
you've figured out a way to make some pink lemonade out
of those sour lemons you were dealt."

Lulu felt world-weary about this case. She
couldn't even imagine how Detective Bryce could investigate crime for a living. And he still looked boyish! He must
have a painting in his attic that was turning monstrous, like
Dorian Gray.

Lulu wondered if maybe she should take a little break.
The secrets everybody toted around were really wearing
her down. When the phone rang with Evelyn on the line,
Lulu decided that the two of them must have some kind of
cosmic connection.

"I just had the best idea!" bubbled Evelyn. "We'll do a
girls' day out tomorrow. My house on the lake. We'll have
brunch, go out on the boat, have some drinks and some
food, and *relax*. What do you think?" Evelyn demanded
Lulu's opinion in a tone that indicated she'd allow no
argument.

Lulu was a little bit leery of this idea. The last planned
girls' outing had ended with Flo throwing up in a trashcan,
and Lulu and Cherry driving around with security looking
for her car.

Evelyn added, as though reading Lulu's mind again,

"And this time we'll have *fun*. We need," Evelyn pronounced, "to escape from Memphis."

Evelyn had quite an impressive house right on Pickwick Lake, as did many of Memphis's well-to-do residents. But the thing about Pickwick was that it wasn't exactly local. No, it would take them close to three hours to get there. She opened her mouth to offer a quick excuse.

"Now wait, Lulu. I'm sensing a *no* coming. This won't be a day trip, and you won't have to drive. We're going to have an overnight excursion. A house party."

Lulu hesitated. "Aren't some of us under suspicion of murder? Shouldn't we stay in Memphis?"

"It's not Bora Bora, honey! And, we're not *all* under suspicion. Besides, no one told us to stay here in town, did they?"

Not as far as Lulu knew. She wasn't sure what Flo had been told. Lulu was tempted to say no, but realized it might be the best opportunity to ask some questions. The Graces always knew the inside track on everything and everybody. Besides, Evelyn was rolling in money, and her lake house was a sight to behold.

As though anticipating more doubts, Evelyn said in a wheedling tone, "Tommie's gonna cook the brunch." Tommie was Evelyn's long-time housekeeper and girl Friday.

Lulu's tummy rumbled on cue. "You've got yourself a deal, Evelyn. I'd never pass up a meal from Tommie."

"Great! It's a plan, then. The weather looks like it's going to be perfect. I'll call the ladies. Make sure you pack a bathing suit and a towel."

The day started out just as Evelyn said it would. The sun shone as if nighttime would never come. The car ride over seemed quick with such lively companions. Evelyn was the perfect hostess. They sat out on her huge screen porch with ceiling fans blowing. This, actually, was not Lulu's strict definition of a screen porch. Such a definition would include a description of the area that was attached to the front of Aunt Pat's. This place was more of an outdoor living room with comfortable brand-new sofas that aspired to be shabby chic.

Evelyn's housekeeper, Tommie, strode out with a tray of Bloody Marys. She wore a buttoned-down pink blouse, a floral skirt that stretched over her stomach, and large white tennis shoes. And a somewhat put-upon expression.

"Y'all know my executive assistant, Tommie, don't you?" drawled Evelyn.

Tommie beamed at the chorus of hi's, then mock-scowled at Evelyn. "Executive assistant? I'll execute *you*! I saw that pile of clean laundry wrinkling up there in the dryer. I'm darned if I'll pull that heavy iron out. How long has that stuff been in there? Since the last time we were at Pickwick?"

"Probably. Well, throw a wet washcloth in there and run it a few minutes. The wrinkles will fall out," said Evelyn carelessly.

While the ladies were visiting on the porch, Lulu couldn't resist checking out Evelyn's kitchen. Sure enough, the kitchen was drool worthy. It was massive, with tons of granite-covered counter space and enough cabinets to store any kind of kitchen gadget that you wanted to. Lulu couldn't resist opening a cabinet door. Sure enough, there were slicers and processors and blenders that seemed to mean business. There were vegetable steamers and egg slicers and fondue pots . . .

"It does beat all, doesn't it?" Lulu jumped guiltily and turned around to see Tommie standing behind her, laughing. "I didn't mean to scare you, Lulu."

"Do you really know how to use all these gadgets, Tommie?"

"Mercy, no! But Miss Evelyn likes to have them around, anyway. For when *she* cooks." Tommie smirked. "Elbow grease works just fine for me with the dicing and slicing. And not much cleanup, either. Some of her cooking toys are the devil to clean, let me tell you."

She motioned to Lulu to follow her. "Take a look at this. You'll appreciate this part of the kitchen." She opened an oak door and made a sweeping gesture to Lulu at the huge pantry inside. Half of one wall was devoted to spices and oils of every kind and description. There were exotic looking pastas and rice and jarred fruits and vegetables. Lulu was overwhelmed. "This looks bigger than our storeroom at the restaurant!" She shook her head. "I'm going to have to get out of here before my face freezes this way."

"What way?"

"Green! With envy."

Tommie laughed. "Well, how about if you come around and see what I'm cooking up for y'all for lunch."

"I thought you'd never ask! What's that lovely aroma I've been smelling?"

"That is my very own Vidalia onion pie," said Tommie with a great deal of personal satisfaction.

Lulu gave a big smile. "I haven't had onion pie for ages, Tommie. Aunt Pat used to make a heavenly sweet onion pie, but I never watched her make it. What's in yours?"

"Oh, I like to put in some cheese . . ."

"Cheddar?"

"Oh, honey, Miss Evelyn got over the cheddar. Now we're into the goat cheese. But cheddar would work just fine. Then we got the heavy cream . . ."

Lulu gave a happy sigh.

"Or, if you're watching your figure, the half-and-half.

We've got ourselves a few eggs, some nutmeg, some butter to cook up our onions in . . ." She tapped her foot while she tried to summon the other ingredients.

"Bacon?" asked Lulu hopefully. "I've been having the biggest hankering for bacon lately."

"Bacon!" said Tommie, thumping the granite counter. "That's exactly right."

"That sounds like the *perfect* lunch."

"That's not the lunch, sweetie, that's just a side item. No, we got the famous Tommie fried chicken as the main course. Y'all are having a special, pampering girls' day. So get ready for some pampering from the kitchen."

Evelyn hurried in. "'Scuse me, y'all. I've got some cutting up to do."

Tommie put her hands on her hips. "Something I can do for you, Miss Evelyn? Because I'd rather not have you messing around my kitchen."

"No, just cutting up some limes and lemons, that's all."

Lulu winced at the glass cutting board that Evelyn whipped out from the cupboard. "Ooh, honey, don't cut on that."

Tommie heaved an exasperated sigh. "You're gonna destroy those knives. Use the wooden board for cutting."

Evelyn was already done and hurrying out of the kitchen with a bowl of cut-up limes and lemons. Tommie said, looking after her, "She means well."

"Those knives don't deserve the treatment they just got." Lulu clucked.

"Don't you worry," Tommie said, "I guard my kitchen from Miss Evelyn's clutches. She's got nothing to do with the brunch y'all are about to enjoy."

Tommie's food was manna from heaven. There was a breakfast casserole of eggs, bacon, cheese, and hash browns. The buttered grits on the side were the perfect texture—not too soupy, not too dry. There was a big bowl of peeled, sugared peaches, topped with blueberries. And she'd made the world's lightest biscuits, which had come straight from the oven.

Lulu felt a nap coming on. "Now this," said Cherry as she crawled into a convenient hammock there on the porch, "is living."

Nice to see how the other half lived, thought Lulu. Not many people would opt to have a saltwater pool (complete with underwater barstools and table) right on the lake. Evelyn—or maybe, Tommie—had hung hummingbird feeders right outside the porch.

Cherry gave a contented, "Ahh."

"Oh, no-no-no! Out of the hammock—it's time for some fun!"

Cherry groaned. "But an after-brunch nap *is* fun, Evelyn. What planet do you live on?"

"Don't be grouchy, Cherry."

"Then let me take a nap! I'll be a kinder, gentler version of myself."

Tommie started collecting the empty dishes.

"Tommie, tell Cherry to agree with me."

Tommie snorted. "Sugar, do yourself a favor and give in. Miss Evelyn *always* gets her way."

Evelyn pleaded with Cherry, "Tell you what—you can have a nice little naptime right *after* your waterskiing adventure."

Cherry sat up in the hammock. "We're going to ski? Okay, I'm in." She reached out to pluck her helmet from a nearby chair.

Peggy Sue patted her perfectly coiffed curls apologetically. A couple of hours on a boat and you'd never be able to tell she'd spent an hour at the salon yesterday.

◇◇◇◇◇◇◇◇

The boat was a roomy model that zipped through the water. Evelyn took off a flowing caftan to reveal a widely patterned zebra-inspired suit. She sported large sunglasses and dripped with diamonds. Most of the other Graces had swimsuits with sequins, underwires that did astounding things with their anatomy, and wild colors. Except, that is, for Jeanne. She wore a one-piece that was even more of a granny suit than Lulu's.

Lulu decided her water-skiing days were over but received full entertainment value for her day by watching the others ski. Evelyn piloted the boat and didn't ski, but she dangled an arm over the side to feel the spray.

The escape from Memphis had worked a remarkable change in Flo. She was much more like her old self, although a little quieter than usual. Lulu was relieved to see she hadn't gone wild with the Bloody Marys that morning.

"Both Cherry and Evelyn," said Flo in a lazy voice, "are completely crazy. Look at them—jewelried to the hilt. And waterskiing and hanging their arms overboard."

"And Evelyn is even crazier than Cherry," said Lulu matter of factly.

"How do you figure that?"

"Because Evelyn's jewelry is *real*."

Cherry finished skiing, and Evelyn helped pull her back onto the boat. Cherry gave a big whoop. "Now *that*," she said, "was some real exercise. And a heckuva lot more fun than the treadmill." She wrapped a huge Elvis towel around her wet swimsuit.

"Time for our picnic!" declared Evelyn.

"*More* food?" asked Lulu, wishing she'd brought a Tums with her.

"Why not? We deserve it! Tommie packed us a bunch of really different things so you can either eat light . . . or pig out like I'm going to do!"

Evelyn took the boat to a shady cove and threw down the anchor. She opened the huge cooler. "See? It's like a treasure chest." Sure enough, there were bottles of wine, a corkscrew, Lucite wineglasses, deviled eggs, pasta salad, fried chicken, potato salad, Tommie's delectable-looking onion pie, and both pimento cheese and vegetable tea sandwiches.

Everyone helped themselves from the cooler, and Evelyn poured them all glasses of wine before finally lounging back and proposing a toast. "To Memphis! And Elvis!"

They all took good-sized gulps from their glasses, even pious Jeanne, who felt it would be somewhat mean-spirited not to drink to Elvis.

"This potato salad," said Flo, "is the best stuff I've ever put in my mouth. Tommie is going to have to share her secret with me."

"I'm first in line to hear that secret," said Evelyn. "That's Tommie's insurance that I won't ever get rid of her. If I couldn't have that potato salad for lunch every day, I'd turn into a shadow of myself." She tilted her face toward the sun. "Ahh," she said, chestnut hair gleaming in the sun. "Now this is perfect—wine and gossip."

"Gossip?" frowned Jeanne. "But we're not gossiping. Our mouths are full of food."

"But," said Evelyn wickedly, "we're about to *start* gossiping. It's a girls' day out, after all. And gossiping can be fun."

Lulu thought gossiping would be okay, only if it stayed in the territory of the murder. She really didn't have any interest at all in hearing the dirty laundry of other Graceland aficionados being aired. She hurriedly interjected, "Well, I don't know if it qualifies as gossip or not, but I can't seem to stop talking about Rebecca Adrian's murder, y'all. It was just too close for comfort. And the police don't seem to really have any leads to find out what happened."

Lulu quickly found out that her chosen subject of gossip was not appreciated. Flo resumed her haunted look, Jeanne seemed stricken, Peggy Sue looked guilty, Cherry choked on her sandwich, and Evelyn looked gravely disappointed.

"I'm sure that murder is *not* a good picnic topic, Lulu," said Evelyn. But she relented at Lulu's hangdog expression and sighed. "Okay. I'll admit it is the most interesting subject du jour. And . . . I did have something to tell you, although I was going to pick a better, less-public time." She hesitated.

"Well don't stop there!" said Lulu. "For heaven's sake, spill the beans."

"I was at the Peabody myself that afternoon," said Evelyn, pausing for dramatic effect. She got it, too.

"*What?*" chorused everyone.

"This is the gossipy part of my story," Evelyn explained. "Yes, I was at the Peabody, having an assignation with a gentleman I've been seeing for a little while." They all gaped at her. "Not in a *room*. In the lobby, for heaven's sake. We were having afternoon drinks. And you know how vast that lobby is, filled with sofas and arm chairs and tables and people. And ducks. The woman was there, but she clearly either didn't see me, didn't recognize me, or didn't care."

"Rebecca, you mean?" asked Lulu in a hushed voice that somehow seemed more appropriate when speaking of the dead while on a springtime picnic.

"Yes. I didn't know she was there until she came right up close to me, talking on her phone. She was wandering off and talking on the phone, just like she did at Aunt Pat's that day. Except I guess she didn't see me there with my back to her because she walked right toward me. And she was fussing at some loan creditor. Really letting them have it for harassment." Evelyn gave an emphatic bob of her head. "And we thought she was rolling in money with her Chanel sunglasses and designer clothes."

This news, however interesting it might be, wasn't a major surprise to Lulu. Rebecca Adrian had tried to blackmail Seb, after all. And she had a feeling about the very next thing Evelyn was going to say. Sure enough: "So then she wrapped up her rant and went back to her table, when what should happen but yet another phone call for Miss Thing. She wanders over near me again, and you'll never guess who she's talking to this time." Evelyn peered at Lulu anxiously.

"Seb?" she said quietly.

Evelyn leaned back. "How'd you guess, Lulu? I thought Seb and she had never even met each other. I know he's a smooth operator, but—"

"Actually, it's a smaller world than we all thought it was. Apparently Seb and Miss Thing dated each other for a while in New York. Crazy, isn't it?" Lulu said.

This time it was Lulu that everyone gaped at. "Really? He went out with that woman?" asked Cherry. "I thought Seb had more sense."

"Well, maybe he does, but not when it comes to women."

Evelyn broke back into the conversation to take the spotlight again. "Well, I've been meaning to tell you about this, Lulu, like I mentioned. But it sounds like you already knew. I guess the police know, too?" When Lulu nodded, Evelyn said, "Just as well. We know he didn't have anything to do with her death, but the police would want to know they were old flames."

Cherry said, "Actually, I might have some information, too. I didn't know I did, though. I heard Seb on his phone the morning of the tasting. I'd gone to the gas station to fill up my bike. Seb was there, but I saw he was on his phone, so I didn't try to say hi. Then I was really glad I didn't say hi when I realized he was having a blazing argument with somebody on his phone. It sounded like women troubles, which didn't really surprise me at all, knowing Seb. All I could gather on my end was that he'd been accused of cheating on somebody."

Lulu tried to digest this tidbit. "So you're thinking he had an argument with Rebecca Adrian? That maybe she was ragging him for cheating on her in New York a while ago?"

Cherry said, "Well, that could have been true. But the explanation that I like so much better is that maybe Seb and *Lurleen* were arguing the morning Rebecca died. Since we know that Seb and Lurleen were an item, maybe Lurleen got real jealous of Rebecca—maybe she thought they were trying to reignite an old flame. She could have gone all *Fatal Attraction* on him and killed her competition!"

Lulu said slowly, "As appealing a solution as that would be, I just don't see it. That seems like an awfully severe reaction to the possibility of some cheating."

"Maybe it's something to tell the police, though. The next time we have to talk to them," said Cherry. There was no reasoning with her when she was being insistent. That was her theory, and she was going to stick with it, no matter what. "And you know what? That woman needs a makeover. Is she *trying* to look like Wonder Woman? She's got those clunky gold bracelets on and keeps wearing Fourth of July colors for that dumb Hog Heaven Loves America theme of hers. I keep thinking she's got an invisible jet parked out back somewhere."

"She's a brazen hussy," said Jeanne with some degree of venom.

Evelyn heaved a dramatic sigh. "Well, if you're going to be a hussy, Jeanne, it's best not to be a meek one. My sympathy lies with Seb, though. Like him, I used to be unwise with my relationships. But then I realized that I needed to really think about who I went out with. Not treat it like a fling, but like the beginning of something that could last a lifetime." She flung back her head and let the wind blow her hair back around her shoulders. "Love is too important to treat cheaply."

Suddenly, their quiet picnic was interrupted by the roar of a Jet Ski and an enthusiastic, "Hoo-boy!" Lulu blinked as Evelyn did an abrupt about-face and started waving to the sunglassed younger man on the Jet Ski. "Hey there! I'm thinking about buying one of those things. Mind if I go for a test ride with you?"

"Sure, sweetheart! Hop on!" he shouted as he pulled up to the boat.

"Evelyn," said Lulu, "uh . . . what about us going back to the house?"

"Y'all will be *fine*! Enjoy your picnic, and I'm sure motorcyclin' Cherry can maneuver that boat home when you're done." Her last words were nearly swallowed whole by the ruckus the Jet Ski made as the young man soared away on the top of the water.

"Well, my *God*," said Peggy Sue. "And off she goes with a handsome stranger on a Jet Ski. So this is how the other half lives."

"Sounds like an invitation to fornication to me," said Jeanne. She pressed her lips together tightly. Then she said, "I think it was that wine she drank. And now what *will* we do, stranded on the lake with no captain?"

Everyone looked at Cherry. She lifted her hands in protest. "Hey, I never said I could pilot a boat, y'all. We could just wait to see if our hostess comes right back."

But nobody thought that was a good idea. After all, Evelyn hadn't *said* she was planning on coming back and rescuing them at all.

"I could call the police," suggested Peggy Sue. "I think they have a boat patrol out here."

"And how excited would they be to rescue a bunch of middle-aged ladies from a picnic?" said Jeanne.

Lulu said, "Cherry, I think you're our only hope. Think you can give it a go?"

Cherry puffed out a breath in consternation and put on her helmet. "Okay." She turned the key gingerly, pulled a lever, and turned a wheel, and sure enough they were moving through the water. Everyone groaned with relief. At least, they did until Cherry said, "Anybody remember where Evelyn's lake house is? All these coves look alike!"

Actually, no one had taken any notice at all of how they'd arrived at their picnic spot. After all, they weren't anticipating being stranded there without their captain.

And so began an hour of cruising through different nooks and crannies of Pickwick Lake. Although it was a very picturesque cruise, to be sure, it was one marked by Cherry's quick confidence behind the boat's wheel—and her rapid transition to speedy piloting, which made Lulu more than a little seasick.

Finally, Flo caught sight of Evelyn's house. "There! There it is!" she cried, standing up in her excitement before quickly falling down on the deck as the boat crested some waves from another watercraft.

"All right, girls, I'm steerin' her in. Somebody jump out when we get near the dock and rope her up, okay?"

"I'll try to," said Jeanne in a trembling voice.

Cherry fired the motor and steered the boat toward the dock. She tried to cut the motor and idle the boat to the dock. But something happened and the motor revved instead of idled. And Evelyn's dock would never be quite the same again.

The next few minutes were a blur to Lulu. The Graces whooped and hollered, the dock fell apart, and Tommie ran down the stairs to the boat, cussing Evelyn out and trying to direct them in. They ended up dropping anchor and giving up on docking the boat to anything at all.

You'd have thought that the afternoon, like the dock, couldn't have been salvaged. But Tommie became the world's best hostess in the absence of their original hostess. They swam in the heated saltwater swimming pool and had the most succulent supper of shrimp and grits that you could possibly imagine. Cherry suggested they play canasta, which Tommie was a whiz at, and they stayed up much later than they'd planned, laughing, dealing the cards, and delving thoroughly into Evelyn's extensive wine collection.

The next day dawned hot and humid. Evelyn had come in pretty late the night before and seemed not at all concerned by the wrecked dock on her property. The breakfast the next morning was mouthwatering—a quiche lorraine, bacon, and poached eggs on toast. By the time Lulu had eaten all that food, she decided to have a second cup of coffee so she wouldn't turn around and head straight back for the bed.

Evelyn had decided to stay on at Pickwick Lake for another day. The gossip in the car was lively as they considered her motives behind this extended stay. "I just know it's because of that boy," said Cherry.

"That boy is her son's age!" said Jeanne. "He must be in his midtwenties." But she wasn't all that shocked, by the sound of it.

"All the better!" said Flo. And the others were just glad Flo was still in an upbeat mood.

Lulu was delighted to see Big Ben, Morty, and Buddy at the restaurant when she arrived. "Good to see

y'all here. I wanted to let you know that Ben called me last
night and said the place was jam-packed with folks. I'm
absolutely convinced it's because of y'all. They're all still
talking about the music you played."

Morty tried and failed to look modest. "Well, we do
have a good time playing it. I guess people are bound to
have a good time when they listen to it, too."

"It sure brought me out of the doldrums," said Lulu.
"And it brought the balance sheet out of the red. Y'all have
a seat and enjoy yourselves. I'll bring you a pitcher of sweet
tea."

"That's the kind of welcome I like," said Buddy.

"What's happening?" bellowed Big Ben.

"Sweet tea," yelled Buddy back. "Can't you put your
ears in? I'm tired of hollering at you!"

Big Ben glared at Buddy but obediently took the hearing aid case out of his pocket. "Interfering friends," he
muttered.

They settled into the rockers on the screen porch and
rocked until the wooden floorboards creaked. Morty un-
furled the newspaper and handed Big Ben the local section,
Buddy the sports and comics, and reserved the A section
for himself. Big Ben flapped open the local section with a
flourish. Buddy peered over at it.

"What kind of nonsensical headline is that?" he asked.

Big Ben was still miffed. He looked at Buddy down his
nose. "What are you griping about now?"

"The headline there. Who wrote such a thing? 'Ninety-
one-year-old Found Dead.'" Buddy snorted.

Morty raised his eyebrows. "What kind of a story is
that? Was it a slow news day?"

Big Ben said with great dignity, "I think there's more to
the story than that. Otherwise, it would hardly be newswor-
thy." He disappeared pointedly behind the paper. Morty

and Buddy exchanged glances. When Big Ben got in a snit, it took a while to jolly him out of it.

Lulu came out on the porch with a big pitcher of sweet tea and some glasses full of ice cubes. A waitress behind her put down a plate of hot corn bread on a table.

Lulu sat down in a rocker. "Is it too hot to sit out here this morning?"

Morty said, "It's hot, but with the fans and the tea, I think we'll be okay. I like to sit here and look at all the people going by on Beale." He looked thoughtfully at the waitress as she went back into the dining room. "Where's Sara? I haven't seen her around lately." Lulu frowned, and he added quickly, "No complaints about the service, Lulu. I was only wondering where she was. She's not been down in the dumps about that scout, has she?"

Lulu mentally kicked herself. She'd been so busy focusing on trying to investigate this murder that she wasn't paying enough attention to her family. "I hope not, Morty. I'm afraid Sara has dropped off my radar. I went to Pickwick Lake with the Graces for a getaway. But I'm hoping Sara wasn't too upset about Miss Adrian. After all, the woman was a food scout. She wasn't any kind of an art expert."

"Or," Buddy added, "a literature expert. Poor Mildred. Have you seen her around at all?"

"Actually, she was here the other night. I was glad to see her. It sounded like she'd decided not to take Miss Adrian's opinion too seriously." She rocked silently for a minute. "Come to think of it, Sara hasn't been coming in to work at the normal times lately. Maybe I better find out what's going on." She looked up as the screen door opened and Seb came in.

"Seb!" It was good to see him and see him looking like *Seb* again. He was clean and shaven and wore clean, pressed clothes. Big Ben lowered his paper briefly to smile at Seb, who always made small talk with him. It was a lot easier to talk to Seb now that he'd ditched those wild herringbone shirts. They'd given him vertigo.

Seb carried a laptop bag and looked ready to work. "Don't look so surprised to see me, Mother," he drawled. "I did tell you I'd come in to work today. It sounds like the office is well on its way to imploding without my guiding hand."

"No, if my memory serves me, you were supposed to come into work a couple of days ago. Except I was conveniently out of the restaurant that day, and you decided not to come in. Besides, Derrick has done a fine job keeping us on track." Not bad at all, thought Lulu. Seb might find himself replaced if he didn't start on the path toward redemption. Seb didn't seem at all concerned by his mother's reprimand. He just nodded a greeting to the guys on the porch and headed to the office.

Lulu drummed her fingers against the rocker arm, and tried to return to her original train of thought. "Now I'm all worried about Sara."

Morty said, "Now, now, Lulu, don't jump to any conclusions. Maybe her allergies have been bugging her. You know how rough the pollen is this time of year. Or maybe she's feeling a little overworked and wants to take a break from the barbeque."

"Or a break from Ben?" suggested Buddy. "Can't be easy to live and work with somebody, day in and day out. You're with them at home, putting up with their bad habits. Then you're sleeping with them at night. And then you don't even escape them the next day because they're right there beside you at work." They quietly reflected on this notion.

"Those poor children," said Lulu. "Think of it—caught between their dueling parents." Her eyes grew moist and she pulled out a neatly folded tissue from her sleeve. "It must be horrible for them."

Big Ben put his paper down again. "Lulu," he said severely, "your imagination is running away with you. You know what the best solution for that problem is?"

Lulu wiped her eyes and shook her head.

"Talking to Ben and Sara about it." Big Ben delivered this pronouncement then disappeared again into the depths of the local section.

"That's what I need to do," she said. "Sorry for the waterworks. I think this case is just getting to me." She walked quickly into the dining room.

"Case?" said Buddy to Morty. "Did she call this a 'case'?"

"That she did."

"Lord have mercy. Is she playing detective, then?"

"I do believe she is," said Morty.

"Well then, God be with her," Buddy said solemnly. "She's gonna need a little guardian angel to keep her from harm."

Lulu strode into the kitchen where Ben was mixing together another batch of dry rub for the barbeque. Ben raised his eyebrows at the sight of his mother with her hands on her hips. "What are you *thinking*?" she demanded.

Ben said, "I'm thinking you've had a small stroke."

Lulu shook her head impatiently. "I mean, why aren't you taking better care of Sara? Why is there this big rift between you right now?"

Ben sank down on a stool. "What? Do you know something I don't know, Mother? Did Sara talk to you?"

"*Should* she have? What's going on?"

"*Nothing* is going on! I have no idea what kind of nonsense you're spewing right now. As far as I'm aware, Sara's had a bad week, but things between the two of us have never been better. I'd like to know why you're thinking otherwise."

Lulu deflated like a balloon that's been introduced to a knitting needle. "Oh. Oh, nothing. Sorry. You can get back to your sauce making now."

"Just hold on there a minute, Sparky. This conversation isn't over yet," gritted Ben.

Lulu pinkened. "It's nothing. I was talking out on the porch with Big Ben, Buddy, and Morty. They mentioned that they hadn't seen Sara waitressing for a while. Then I got to thinking that I hadn't, either. I felt bad that I haven't been on top of things enough to know what's going on with my own family. Derrick had problems, Seb was a wreck, then there was Sara . . ."

Ben said, "And you thought it had something to do with Sara and me? Even with a murder investigation going on and her being laughed at by some know-it-all who actually knew nothing? Thanks a lot." Lulu winced, and Ben said more gently, "She's fine. Go talk to her yourself. She needed a break, that's all. We had full coverage with the waitresses so I told her to go home and relax for a while. And that's all there was," he said firmly.

"Well, now, that *is* a relief," said Lulu. She was now ready to escape Ben's eagle eye. "I'll leave you to the cooking, now."

"Actually, Mother, why don't you go and check on Sara for yourself?"

"I really don't think that's necessary. You've relieved my mind," said Lulu. She continued toward the door.

"No, really. Maybe you're having some sort of divine revelation that you need to go look out for her and make sure she's okay."

"I don't believe in signs," said Lulu, but not in the scornful voice she usually did. In the back of her mind, she wondered if that bad day with Rebecca Adrian would ever have happened if she'd paid attention to all the signs. "But," she added, "I will go out and check on her. Maybe a little company would do her good."

Sara didn't immediately open her front door when Lulu rang the doorbell. In fact, Lulu was about to whip out her copy of their house key, break into the house, and make sure that the mother of her grandchildren was alive and kicking. It's funny, thought Lulu, how irrational anxiety can make you.

Fortunately, Sara opened the door herself after a few minutes. Fortunate, because Lulu was sure she wouldn't have taken kindly to Lulu barging into the house without first being invited.

Sara had practically a whole palette of paint covering her, and they didn't look like colors that she'd be painting a wall. "Oh!" said Lulu. "You're painting again. I'm so *glad.*"

Sara nodded and motioned Lulu inside. "Sorry I haven't been at the restaurant lately." She looked searchingly at Lulu's face. Lulu smiled benignly. "I'm thinking that's why you're here?"

"Ben will probably tell you anyway, so I might as well confess. I'd concocted this horrible scenario in my head about trouble between you and Ben."

Now Sara really looked surprised. "Why would you think something like that?"

Lulu was ready to pass the buck. "I was talking to Morty, Buddy, and Big Ben, and they were wondering out loud where you were. And how it would be tough to live and work with your spouse."

"Well, some days are tougher than others, but I don't

stay home because of it." Sara looked agitated, and Lulu eagerly changed the subject.

"Oh, look! It's Babette." The little dog glared suspiciously at Lulu. On some doggy level she knew that Lulu was hardly her biggest fan. "And she has the most precious outfit on! Who'd have thought to make a cheerleading outfit for a dog?"

Sara rolled her eyes. "Well, Ben does dote on that dog. Of course, to hear him talk about it, B.B. and Elvis are his closest buddies. Guess having Labs as man's best friend goes over better with the guys than a toy dog."

There was an uncomfortable pause during which Lulu made quite a show of lavishing attention on little Babette. The dog seemed to be seriously considering biting her. It curled its lips back in a snarl.

Finally Lulu broke the silence. "How is your art going? I was afraid that you were going to be discouraged by that woman, and put aside the painting and sculpting for a while."

Sara ruffled a hand through her riotous red curls. "Maybe I did at first. But then I remembered what Susan said about Rebecca: she didn't know beans about art. And it's true. She was a food critic, not an art critic. And she wasn't a book critic. Mildred and I projected our own dreams onto her. We put our futures in her hands, and they didn't belong there. Now I'm trying to use the whole experience as inspiration. Let me see how I can prove she was wrong. I'm ready to take the next step."

Lulu nodded. "You're absolutely right. I'm just glad the whole episode didn't get you down."

"What got me down was Derrick," she said. "I hate that he's even considered a suspect at all with this case. I feel like I should have been there for him more. My sister didn't send him down here to be mixed up in a murder. She sent him here because she thought he'd be safe."

"*I* think," said Lulu caustically, "that she sent him down here to get him out of her hair. You've got nothing to feel bad about."

"Still," said Sara. She sighed. "I hope I've heard his whole story, that's all."

Lulu looked closely at Sara. She reminded her of a mother bear protecting a cub. Lulu wondered how far Sara's desire to protect Derrick might go.

Sara registered Lulu's worry. "Now you've checked on me, and you've seen for yourself that everything is just fine. Why not head on back to Aunt Pat's? I'm going to get some work done in the studio before the girls get home from school."

Lulu gave a smile that looked more convincing than she felt. She couldn't shake her sense of foreboding.

Chapter

10

"Graceland was *hell* today," moaned Evelyn. "Who *were* those people? What rocks did they crawl out from under?" Apparently, Evelyn had crashed back to earth again after her extra day of romance at the lake house.

"It must have been bad for you to complain about Graceland. What on earth happened?" asked Lulu.

Evelyn took a big bite of her baked beans, chewed, and said, "I've been there for years and have never seen such wildly behaved people in my life."

Jeanne tried to take a more loving, Christian approach to the wayward tourists. "They were excited, that's all. It was their first time to really *experience* Graceland. They were overwhelmed." Evelyn raised a disbelieving eyebrow. "Well, they were," said Jeanne. "Besides, they couldn't be expected to know the rules."

Peggy Sue said, "Good Lordy, Jeanne. It's not like they're not obvious. When you see a roped-off staircase, most people would assume they're not supposed to go up there."

Jeanne was stubborn. "Maybe that lady was looking for the powder room."

"So when she went up the blocked off stairs and acted like a crazy lady when the guard dragged her kicking and screaming off the stairs, she was just upset about not finding the bathroom? I don't think so. And at her age, too! She must have been seventy-five if she was a day," scoffed Peggy Sue.

"Imagine," said Evelyn, "being that excited about Elvis in your seventies."

"Either that or she was senile," said Peggy Sue.

Lulu noticed that Cherry listlessly pushing baked beans and slaw around on her barbeque plate. Ordinarily, if some questionably sane woman had stormed the upstairs of Graceland, violating Elvis's private quarters, Cherry would have been full of righteous indignation. But Cherry hadn't even gone to Graceland today, citing a headache. And she didn't even seem to be listening to the grizzly tale of the horrific happenings there. What's more, she was wearing a dumpy sweat suit instead of her usual colorful, snazzy attire.

"What happened then?" asked Lulu, still keeping an eye on Cherry.

"Well, the little old lady had a huge fit. She hissed and spat and accused the security guard of brutality. She refused to leave the grounds of Graceland. Said this was her Mecca and she was, by-golly, going to stay there until she got to see Elvis's grave at the end of the tour. She dug her heels into the pile carpet and wouldn't budge."

"Why didn't the guard simply pick her up and carry her out? Especially since she was elderly. She couldn't have been all that heavy," said Lulu.

"I think the security guard was scared that she was going to sue his pants off. Because that's what she kept saying—'I'm gonna sue your britches off!' And she was covered in jewelry from head to toe . . . expensive stuff. And designer clothes. She really meant it. She looked like she had a whole stable of lawyers at her beck and call."

"How did y'all ever get rid of her?" asked Lulu.

"We ended up having to call out the Memphis police. As if they don't have enough going on with real crime. They had to come out and drag her out of there. She wasn't going to be suing *them*. Or they didn't care if she did, anyway."

Flo said, "And that wasn't the end of the problems. There was somebody determined to take flash photography because he couldn't figure out how to turn his flash off. And *he* was belligerent, too! And then there was that kooky woman who was howling crying the whole time during the tour."

"Was there a full moon last night?" asked Lulu.

"Maybe. That might explain it. Although you'd think those folks would have been exhausted enough from howling at it all night to skip coming to Graceland," said Flo. Lulu was glad to see that the good effects from Evelyn's house party were still in evidence.

Evelyn gave a satisfied sigh. "I'm all done, how about y'all? I need to get back home and put my feet up for a while. And maybe have myself a big glass of chardonnay. Today just knocked the stuffing out of me. Everybody ready to head out?"

All the Graces but Cherry said they were ready to go. Peggy Sue looked over at Cherry. "What is eating you today, honey? You're pushing that food all around on your plate. And this is *Aunt Pat's* food. Are you feeling puny today? I thought you said your headache was better."

Cherry shrugged. "I'm just kind of poky, that's all. Y'all go ahead and leave. It'll take me forever to finish up."

"But how are you going to get home?" asked Peggy Sue. "I dragged you out here, remember? You don't have your motorcycle or helmet with you."

Lulu said quickly, "I'm happy to drop her by her house. I'll be ready for a break, anyway. No problem at all."

So the Graces took off, and Cherry stayed behind with Lulu. Lulu took a long swallow of iced tea and watched as Cherry met her gaze and then looked away. Cherry knew that Lulu had a way of pulling information out of people.

"What's going on, Cherry?" asked Lulu in a gentle but firm voice. "You're not acting like yourself. Not going to Graceland, not joining in some lively conversation, picking at your food."

Cherry nodded. "Well, I do have some problems, Lulu. You'd . . . well, you'd just be amazed at some of the problems that I have."

Lulu lifted her eyebrows. "I'm so sorry to hear that, Cherry. Can you fill me in? I'd like to help you any way I can."

Cherry considered this. Lulu wondered whether she was trying to decide about confiding in Lulu or if she was trying to make up a story to tell her.

"I've got the blues, Lulu. No, really! I've been grousing around the last couple of days like you wouldn't believe. Dead bodies popping up, friends acting weird, no success romancing Tony. No, I've got a case of the mopes, all right."

"This is serious, then," said Lulu. "We're gonna have to take some drastic action."

They exchanged a look.

"Something fattening?" asked Cherry. "I think I need something truly outrageous to eat, Lulu. To get through my slump."

"Sweetie, you've come to the right place. Now our usual menu is pretty fattening all on its own, you know. But today the baking bug bit me."

Cherry's eyes opened wide up.

"I've got your taste buds a little treat. But we've got to

keep this quiet. Or else there might be a run on your table and I only made two pies."

"Pies?"

"Fried apple pie, hon. I think we might need to adjourn to the kitchen for this one. Don't want to upset the other guests."

"If I could figure out how to make my own fried apple pie, I'd be one happy camper, Lulu. I tried it twice and almost burned the house down. You wouldn't have believed the smoke! The smoke detector went off, the dog went hysterical—total fiasco."

"That sounds like your oil was too hot, sweetie. I keep it at medium heat." Lulu opened up the kitchen door to get the pie and Cherry waved to Ben, who dusted off his hands on his long black apron and waved back.

"I love this kitchen," sighed Cherry. "It feels happy and safe here."

"It truly is the heart of the restaurant, you know. And one of my favorite places on this earth. I can't tell you how many hours I spent in this very room growing up. I'd sit on a stool and watch Aunt Pat singing as she cooked."

"It's so tidy and organized in here, too," said Cherry. "My kitchen is a raging disaster area, and I don't even cook all that much." She waved a hand to include the big pegboard on one wall with pots, pans, and skillets hanging on it like works of art.

"Oh well, Aunt Pat got the idea from Julia Child. She found out that's how Julia organized her cookware, and anything that Julia did was good enough for Aunt Pat. She even traced around pots as they hung there to create an outline and make sure the right pot went to the correct spot."

Pots hung from the ceiling, too, some of them copper pots that always invoked memories for Lulu of Aunt Pat at the stove, stirring away with her wooden spoons. There was lots of counter space for cutting and mixing, and an impressive array of gleaming knives. The pit was set into a brick wall with steel doors holding in the heat.

"Here," said Lulu, grabbing one of the pies, a pie server, and some plates, "Let's head to the office where we can have a little chat."

"The aroma is divine," breathed Cherry. "Cinnamon and apples and grease—this will cure what ails me right away. You even dusted it with powdered sugar. I don't see how you have the time, Lulu."

"Oh, cooking relaxes me, Cherry. Keeps me from having a coronary after all the stress going on around the restaurant lately. I made my pastry, but you could have almost the same results by getting some of that flaky, refrigerated biscuit dough."

They ate in silence for a minute.

Then Lulu said, "You were going to fill me in on some of your problems? See if I could help you out in any way."

Finally Cherry said, "Well, I'm worried about my bike. It was . . . uh . . . making a funny sputtering *put-put-put* noise the other day. And, you know, that's the way I get around."

"Mmmhmm," said Lulu. She didn't believe a word of this. Cherry would be able to easily identify the problem with her motorcycle. "Sputtering *put-put-put* noises" would not be the way she'd describe a mechanical problem.

Cherry could tell Lulu wasn't buying it. "And then Johnny has been acting funny lately. You know—he's not been acting like himself."

"Mmmhmm," said Lulu. This, again, was quite unbelievable. Johnny was not a great specimen of husbandom at any time. Johnny was ignorant, hardheaded, and argumentative. Any change in Johnny's everyday, ordinary behavior would have to be considered a change for the better.

Cherry dropped her gaze again under Lulu's skeptical look. "And my dog, Trisha? She's been having all kinds of digestive distress. I mean, there's no telling what I might be going home to this evening. Might be floor-to-ceiling poop."

"Honey, I've got some industrial strength cleaner in the kitchen that you are more than welcome to. It'll take spots off a heifer, and you don't even have to rub," said Lulu helpfully.

Now Cherry looked totally deflated. "Okay, so you want to know the deal."

"I do. I do want to know the deal. Because the longer this case goes on, the worse things get. People are acting like little middle-of-the-day shadows of themselves, and I can't stand it," said Lulu.

Cherry looked all around her, guardedly, as if someone had rigged a mike up to listen in on her conversation. She opened her mouth, and then snapped it shut again and rubbed her eyes. "I don't like to tell other people's secrets."

"Cherry, if this is about poor Flo, I already know all about it, remember? Is there something else to the story that Flo isn't telling us?"

"No, it's not Flo. It's Mildred Cameron."

Lulu sat back in her chair with a whump. "*Mildred?*"

Cherry nodded and pushed her pie around with her fork some more. If she moved it around any more, it was going to become mush. "You know how she and I have always been friendly? She's not like one of the Graces, of course. But we're nice to each other."

Lulu said, "Sure." Mildred didn't have many people who called her a friend . . . maybe a few of the regulars at her bookstore could be considered friends. Cherry had always greeted her, asked questions about her book, never pointed out the book hadn't seemed to progress at all, and smiled admiringly at all the right times. Mildred felt like she belonged to the group at Aunt Pat's. And she did.

"Well, last night I was sound asleep, sawing logs. And

my doorbell rang." Just the recounting of the story made Cherry look as startled as she must have looked when it actually happened. "You know that's not a natural sound at two o'clock in the morning."

Lulu's blue eyes widened. "It would've scared me to death. What did Johnny think?"

Cherry rolled her eyes. "I'm sure he'd have been mad as a sopping wet hen if he'd *been* there. But he was off gallivanting with his friend Eric. It was poker night, and they play and drink and play and drink until they fall asleep with their faces on the table. Lots of fun, you know. He usually doesn't drag his butt home until nearly dawn."

"Sounds like quite a party."

"So anyway, there I was in my soft curlers and my nightie and a frying pan in my hand. I put on my helmet in case somebody tried to bop *me* on the head." Lulu peered at Cherry's head. "Oh, the helmet fits right over the curlers, Lulu. Anyway, I look out the window, and who do I see but Mildred standing there." Cherry finally pushed away her plate. "And," said Cherry under her breath, "she was in quite a state, let me tell you. Quite a state."

Lulu could imagine. With her thin arms and neck and her propensity to flap her arms around when she was worked up about something, Mildred had always resembled a fledgling bird trying unsuccessfully to take off.

"She had this baggy sweat suit on, kind of like what I'm wearing now. And she kept looking behind her like the boogey man was going to leap out of my azalea bushes and drag her off into the sewer."

"Had she been drinking?" asked Lulu.

"No. She was her normal, neurotic self," said Cherry. "Only worse. I invited her inside, heated up some water, and made us some Sleepytime tea. I poured some milk in it and a dab of bourbon. I couldn't handle her in the state she was in. She was a good girl and slugged it right on down.

"I asked her what the dickens was going on. She didn't even look concerned at paying a visit at two A.M. She said that she couldn't sleep for being so scared, and she didn't know where else to go.

"I told her to slow down. She took a little breath and said she'd been at the Peabody that afternoon Rebecca Adrian died. But I was like, no, you were at Aunt Pat's being upset. I hadn't realized that she'd left as early as she did. I guess I was thinking more about Flo and Sara that afternoon than Mildred.

"She said she always thinks of comebacks well after the person has left. It drives her crazy. You know, like in high school when someone puts you down and your mouth is flapping like 'uh, uh, uh' and they leave. Then ten minutes later you think of the perfect thing to have said back to them. Well, Mildred is still like that. Except she wasn't happy to let it go. No, sir. She was by-gum going to go to the Peabody, deliver her comeback in person, and then run like the devil out of there before Rebecca could come up with some other insult that it would take another hour to respond to.

"So she finds Miss Adrian at the Peabody. There she is, sassy as anything, drinking a cocktail or something right there in the lobby. She frowns at Mildred as she comes up. In my mind's eye, I see Mildred strutting up, arms flapping, like a chicken. Then she gives whatever put-down it was that she thought up. Probably something that doesn't even make any sense or something that Miss Adrian wouldn't even consider all that insulting. Anyway, she's *right there*. Right by her beverage. And she's mad. So it's the perfect time to poison her."

Lulu remembered to breathe again. "Did she? Is that what she did?"

"Not according to Mildred. She says Rebecca ignored her and just stalked off to the elevators. I guess she wasn't in any mood to chat with her. So Mildred apparently felt like mission accomplished, right? And then she sees someone she knows there. Somebody she's not expecting."

"Who?" asked Lulu eagerly.

"That's what she wouldn't say," said Cherry. "But she looked really . . . haunted. It's been worrying her to death. And they saw *her*, too."

Lulu knit her brows. "Now, it wasn't Derrick that she saw, was it? Because, you know, he was out there slashing Miss Adrian's tires. A really bad, bad thing to do, but he wasn't poisoning anybody."

Cherry said, "I don't know, Lulu. She wouldn't say who it was. Maybe she did see Derrick. But she was just really upset."

"Maybe it's someone that she thinks of as a friend, and then she wasn't sure how to process what she'd seen?"

"I definitely got the impression it was someone she knew and liked. And that wasn't the end of it," said Cherry.

"No?"

Now Cherry was leaning forward across the booth and pinning Lulu with her eyes. "She ended up getting this typed letter. A threatening one telling her that all sorts of awful things were going to happen to her if she didn't keep her trap shut."

"What? So this just happened? She was fine when I saw her the other day—she was blabbing on about research for her new book. She needs to call the police!"

"That's what I was trying to tell her last night. But she said that she burned it up, so there's nothing to show them. And she couldn't even remember what all was in the letter." Cherry shrugged. "But I'll be honest with you; it gave me the heebie-jeebies. I kept wondering if maybe somebody had followed her over to my house or something." She muttered, "It's that crazy old Lurleen probably. Trying to cover up for the fact she killed Rebecca in a jealous rage."

"Are you still stuck on that idea?" asked Lulu.

"Why not? Anybody fool enough to go dancing around in this heat in a fuchsia pig suit has got to be nuts. Besides, she won't serve tap water at her restaurant. She's crazy, I tell you."

Lulu tried to return to the original conversation. "Maybe. But her and Seb's relationship was over before it even really got going. If she's jealous, then she's delusional—it's over. As for Mildred, if she *does* have information about somebody at the scene of the crime—not Derrick, but someone else—then she should share it with the police. Not only for her own protection, but to bring the killer to justice. And maybe prevent another crime."

Cherry smiled a bit of her old smile. "Aren't you the crime fighter all of a sudden? I certainly shared my thoughts on that, too. I even considered going to the police about it myself. But she was *adamant* that the police not get involved. Said that was one of the things that was listed in the letter not to do."

"Since when do poison pen letters make us do anything?" demanded Lulu. "I'm going to round Mildred up, revive her with an especially sugary batch of sweet tea, and march her right over to the authorities. If I need to organize a marathon sleepover at her house with the Graces, Sara, and I taking turns as guards, then so be it. We look after our own here." Lulu thought uneasily about the fact that Mildred had been looking for Seb yesterday. Then she gave herself a shake. Surely Seb didn't have anything to do with the murder. He just couldn't.

Cherry grinned. "I was worried sick. She pledged me to secrecy you know, but I was afraid something would happen to her. Or that something would happen to both of us for withholding information from the police. Now that you're the one coming up with the game plan, I feel much better about it. In fact . . . I think I'm ready for another plate of barbeque."

"What *I* want is to find out if you've found a good excuse to open that delicious bottle of wine, Buddy. I sure am looking forward to its uncorking." Big Ben trumpeted this inquiry in a booming tone that carried to the far reaches of the restaurant.

Buddy answered in just as loud of a voice. "No, I sure haven't, Big Ben. Besides, it might interest you to know that I'm putting my drinking days behind me. I'm no longer going to allow alcohol to sully these lips." He leaned forward and yelled, "And turn your ears on. You're louder than a freight train this morning."

Big Ben's mouth dropped open. He quickly turned up the volume on his hearing aids. After opening and shutting his mouth several more times, he said "Not going to drink anymore? Is that what you said? Have you suffered a stroke?"

Buddy shot him an offended look. "I certainly have not. But it's hard to reconcile my religious beliefs with my indulgence in alcohol. I've given up drinking for God."

Big Ben struggled to recover. "In that case," he said slowly, scratching the side of his face with a long finger, "I think you'd better relieve yourself of temptation. I'll be happy to take your entire collection of alcohol-based beverages from your pantry."

Buddy glared at him. Morty was chuckling beside them both. He said, "Hey, she's gone, Buddy. You can drop the charade now."

Buddy hissed at Big Ben, "I am certainly *not* going to divest myself of my wine collection. You get that thought out of your head right now."

"Well, then, I'm confused. I'd appreciate it if somebody would fill me in," said Big Ben with great dignity. "There's obviously been a romantic development that I'm not privy to."

Buddy ignored him; instead, he motioned Lulu to the booth. "Lulu, what can you tell me about Leticia Swinger?"

Lulu seemed to be fumbling around in her memory. "Well, now, let's see. I've sat down and talked with her quite a few times. Very nice, pretty black lady, in her late seventies. Widowed. I do believe someone mentioned to me that she's the star soloist at . . ." she frowned, trying to remember the name.

"The Eternal Crown of Our Blessed Savior of Memphis," finished Buddy in a gloomy voice.

Lulu nodded, thoughtfully. "Not a church with a big reputation for enjoying alcohol."

"Oh, I see," said Big Ben, crowing. "You've got yourself a new lady friend. And she's a gospel singer, at that! Now you'll be toeing the line from now on. Surrender those bottles."

"Hey, I want in on that, too," protested Morty. "I even promise to keep them closed and give them back to you after you've wooed her enough so that consumption of alcohol doesn't matter anymore." He reconsidered. "Well, most of it I'd keep uncorked. I should get a little something for my trouble, though."

"She's awfully pretty," said Lulu. "And I've seen her walking to church on Sunday mornings wearing the most beautiful hats. And," she added in a confidential tone, "she certainly has been in here a whole lot more than usual. She must have discovered that this was your hangout, Buddy."

A flush spread over Buddy's face as Big Ben and Morty gave whooping laughs. "All right, that's enough of that. We'll see. I do like the lady a lot. Maybe I can squirrel away a couple of bottles to keep at home and outsource some others to y'all's tender care. I'm just working up to asking her out."

"Lulu, she's not seeing anyone, as far as you know?"

"Not as far as I know. What kind of date are you planning?"

"Something nice and quiet. Maybe I'll cook a simple meal at home, and we can sit out on the porch and eat."

"Sure would be a lot nicer," mulled Big Ben, "with a chilled bottle of wine."

Although it took longer than Lulu planned, she was finally able to pull away from Aunt Pat's and go check on Mildred. First she drove over to the bookshop, knowing that sometimes Mildred stayed there late to work on her book or to read for a while. Lulu often wondered if Mildred just didn't completely lose track of time. She didn't have anybody waiting for her at home, so she became completely absorbed in life at Mildred's Secondhand Book Shoppe. Lulu was no fan of putting a "pe" at the end of "shop" but had so far been able to refrain from sharing that bit of information with Mildred.

The bookstore looked dark as she drove by, so Lulu went to Mildred's house. Lulu raised her eyebrows. The house was dark, too. Now Lulu entertained fanciful visions of a depressed and frightened Mildred alone in the dark. Lulu pulled into her driveway and marched to the front door. She rang the doorbell. And again. No answer. Lulu rapped loudly on the front door. No answer.

Lulu tried the doorknob and to her surprise, it turned. Lulu clucked. Wasn't Mildred supposed to be a poisoned-pen-letter recipient? Locking her door would certainly help prevent unwelcome company. Lulu ignored the thought that maybe *she* was unwelcome company. Lulu called, "Hello? Yoo-hoo! Are you in here? It's Lulu."

No answer except from the birds that said, "Hi there! Hi there!"

Lulu could smell something she assumed was Mildred's supper cooking. She walked into the kitchen. Sure enough, the Crock-Pot was burbling away. Lulu peered at it. Why would she have put the Crock-Pot on high if she wasn't going to be home any earlier than this? Lulu lifted the lid off the Crock-Pot. Eww. Whatever sauce she'd put in there had clearly not been enough. The chicken, at least that's what Lulu assumed it was, had completely dried up along with whatever sauce was in there. Lulu made a mental note not to stay for supper if Mildred asked her. She turned the pot off.

"Mildred?" She did a quick search around the house but didn't see her anywhere. Her little house was perfectly tidy, not a frill out of place. But no Mildred to be seen.

So it was back to the dark bookstore. Again, the thought of a frightened Mildred worried Lulu. This time she parked on a side street and walked inside the store.

The bookstore had always felt sad to Lulu. There were lots of yellowing books that had grown musty through the years, and Mildred was sort of a musty person herself. She definitely had regular customers who spent hours perusing the stacks of books, so the store always survived. And there were books everywhere—the shelves were floor to ceiling, and there were rolling stepstools on every aisle. There were also books in baskets, books on the sales counter, and books in every available space. Mildred sometimes greeted customers but sometimes not—depending on how wrapped up she was in the book she was reading or writing at the time.

"Hello?" called Lulu. She had to be there—the door was unlocked. And Mildred was more likely to forget to lock her house up than the bookstore. The bookstore held all of her most prized possessions.

Again there was no answer. The darkened bookstore had an ominous aura. Shelves of teetering books loomed over her. Swallowing down her fear, Lulu looked for the light switch. The store was getting dimmer with the setting sun. There was a switch by the door, but it didn't seem to work. Then Lulu noticed that Mildred apparently preferred lamps for lighting. She turned on a small desk lamp. Lulu noticed other lamps farther into the store and walked down a dark, book-lined aisle to turn them on. Suddenly two hands grabbed her roughly from behind and slammed her to the floor. Before she could even cry out, something hard hit the back of her head, and she pitched into blackness.

Lulu slowly came to. Her head throbbed, and waves of nausea wafted over her as she carefully sat up. She scrambled to collect her thoughts over her pounding headache. Was she still in danger?

She managed to push herself off the floor, which wasn't easy since she was lying on her face and unused to push-ups. She didn't immediately see her pocketbook, so she looked around frantically for a moment. Then she saw that her purse was right under her knees and remembered that it had been hooked around her arm as she'd walked into the bookstore. She opened it and rifled through. Her phone, car keys, and cash were still in there. Lulu frowned. She hadn't been mugged.

Had Mildred done this to her? Maybe she'd thought that Lulu was the person who'd written her the threatening letter. It had been dark in the store. Perhaps she'd been terrified and, acting in irrational terror, had clubbed Lulu over the head in self-defense. And, knowing Mildred, she was totally horrified. Lulu bet that was probably what had happened.

What *had* she been clubbed with? Lulu looked around her and saw a huge, leather-bound copy of *The Sound and the Fury*. Great. Taken out by Faulkner. Well, she supposed she should consider it an honor. If it had been a graphic novel or something, then she really would have felt insulted.

Finally Lulu felt strong enough to get to her feet. She pulled herself up with the help of the bookshelves and managed to stand. After taking a couple of steps, she felt her knees giving way. She stopped and held tight to the bookcases again to regain her strength.

She listened carefully to see if she could hear the old wooden floors creaking as someone else's weight bore down on it. But she really had the feeling that she was the only person in the store. Lulu wasn't sure how much time had passed while she'd been unconscious. It couldn't have been too long, though, because it wasn't much darker in the bookshop than it had been.

"Mildred?" she called. There didn't seem any point in being quiet since the bad guy clearly knew where she was, anyway. It's not like she'd gotten very far. "It's Lulu," she added, on the off chance it was Mildred who'd walloped her. She had no desire to be mistaken for an intruder again. "Are you here? Listen, it's no big deal if you accidentally knocked me out." Like hell, thought Lulu. But they could discuss that part later, after Lulu was feeling better and was more like her old self again. "I just came over to check on you and make sure you were okay."

No answer.

Lulu walked slowly toward the back of the store. She turned on a lamp along the way, which had such an old and dusty bulb that it didn't really shed any additional light. She remembered there were two little rooms in the back of the store: a restroom and a small storage room. The restroom door was wide open, and Lulu didn't see anyone in there at all. She pushed open the storage room. She saw a table stacked high with books. She almost didn't notice the ballet-style flats poking out underneath the table.

"Mildred!" she cried out and hurried over to the motionless body before stopping short. Mildred was clearly dead. There was no need to take a pulse. She had been strangled with her own scarf.

This time Lulu was more used to the drill as Detective Bryce arrived at the bookstore to interview her. Maybe he was getting worried about her heart after walking in on two dead bodies, but he seemed especially gentle this time when talking with her. This time he had a sergeant offer her a cup of coffee before he questioned her about what she'd seen. They had a paramedic to come in and take a look at her head, but it was decided that there was no concussion, so the paramedic provided an ice pack and some ibuprofen.

"First of all," said Detective Bryce, "why were you here to begin with? Were you in to do some shopping? It's after-hours, isn't it?" His blue eyes were innocently wide.

Lulu guessed there wasn't any reason not to tell him why she'd come. Mildred was dead now, after all, and whatever her secret had been, it had died with her. She doubted Cherry would get into any trouble simply because she knew Mildred was worried about a threatening note and something she'd seen.

"I was here because I was worried about Mildred. She'd told Cherry Hayes that she'd followed Rebecca Adrian to the Peabody Hotel the afternoon she was killed. Mildred delivered this comeback that she had thought up long after Rebecca had left Aunt Pat's. But she apparently saw somebody when she was leaving—somebody who shouldn't have been there. She was very concerned about it. I guess it was someone she knew."

Detective Bryce nodded encouragingly while his sergeant jotted down notes.

"Then Cherry said that Mildred had gotten a threatening letter. She must have been worried sick or scared to death or both. I thought it might be a good idea to run by and check on her . . . and persuade her to go to the police. She wasn't at home, so I came by the shop. And, well, you know the rest."

"Did Cherry have any idea who Mildred Cameron had seen that afternoon?"

"She didn't seem to. She was worried for Mildred's safety and also worried about her own, I think."

Bryce looked thoughtfully at Lulu without saying anything. This kind of tactic drove Lulu up the wall because she didn't ordinarily have awkward pauses in her conversations. If there *was* an awkward pause, she always filled it with more conversation. She had a feeling Bryce knew this and was waiting for her to prattle on again.

"I *was* going to get Mildred to call you," she said. "I can't believe what's happened to her. The last time I saw her, she was really excited about starting a new manuscript. It was going to be a mystery, and she was planning on doing a bunch of research. I guess she didn't realize the importance of what she'd seen at the Peabody until she started poking around and somebody didn't like it."

"Did you have any idea who might have knocked you out? Their size or gender? Did you smell aftershave or perfume?"

Lulu shook her head sadly. "No. I wish I had. The first I knew that anyone was behind me was when they grabbed me and pushed me to the floor and bopped me on the head. I wish to goodness I knew more than that. And I didn't even pay attention to the cars that were parked out in the street."

"What time was it when you entered the store?"

Lulu had to think. "Well, let's see. When I left, it was probably seven thirty. The lights were out in the bookstore, so I stopped by Mildred's house first, figuring that she'd closed the shop for the night and gone home. I didn't spend too long at her house, since she wasn't there. It was probably eight o'clock when I went back to the bookstore. It was pretty dark by then." Lulu looked grim. "I guess the murderer was still in the bookstore right after killing Mildred. That's why you want to know what time it was."

Detective Bryce's face was inscrutable. "The medical examiner will narrow down the time of death, too. But, yes, we can assume that you arrived on the scene right after Miss Cameron was murdered. You clearly surprised the killer by your appearance there."

Lulu frowned. "What I don't understand . . . well, I don't understand much about any of this. But one thing I really don't understand is why the store was dark when I drove by. Was the killer in with her at seven thirty? Or earlier? She meant to come home earlier than she did, I'm sure of it."

Detective Bryce asked, "What makes you so sure, Mrs. Taylor? Did you talk with her about her intentions today?"

"No. But her chicken didn't have enough sauce in the Crock-Pot."

Detective Bryce's sandy eyebrows shot up questioningly.

"When I went to her house, I found her door was unlocked. So I went inside," said Lulu. She felt a little bit like Goldilocks. "I walked in the kitchen because there was kind of a funny smell. I know Mildred wasn't a great cook—not by *any* stretch of the imagination—but she was a real penny-pincher. She would never have deliberately ruined two chicken breasts by drying them out beyond recognition. There wasn't enough sauce in the Crock-Pot," repeated Lulu. "She meant to come back earlier in the evening to eat her supper."

Detective Bryce looked like he wasn't all that convinced about the validity of Crock-Pot sauce as evidence of intent. But he nodded politely.

"Why would the murderer still have been at her shop when I got there? Why wouldn't he have left the scene right away?

"That's one of the things we'll be looking at," said Detective Bryce in a soothing tone.

Lulu abruptly felt completely wiped out. Detective Bryce said quickly, "I think that's enough for tonight, Mrs. Taylor. Why don't you go home and try to sleep? It's getting late."

Lulu looked at her watch. Sure enough, it was eleven o'clock. "Will you talk to Cherry tonight?" she asked.

"No, I don't think so. We'll probably leave that until tomorrow. You really should turn in, Mrs. Taylor."

"Oh, I know. And I will." Right after I break the news to Cherry, thought Lulu. She shouldn't have to hear about her friend's death from the police first thing tomorrow morning.

When Lulu saw Cherry's porch lights on, she pulled into the driveway. But she would have pulled in, regardless. Johnny was probably out amusing himself, and it wasn't even midnight yet.

Lulu rang the doorbell, and she saw the curtain in the front room rustle as a suspicious-looking Cherry peered out the window. Her eyes widened as she saw Lulu, and she hurried to unlock the door. Lulu also heard her slide a bolt out. That didn't bode well for Cherry's marriage if she was bolting Johnny out.

Cherry pulled the door open and gaped at Lulu. Lulu returned the gape at the sight of Cherry's red hair completely engulfed by soft pink rollers. Cherry also had some green oatmeal beauty treatment on her face. Cherry grinned at Lulu's expression. "You know, it's a lot of work to look this beautiful." Then she turned serious. "But tell me, honey, what are you doing out here this time of night? And all by your lonesome?"

Lulu patted Cherry's arm. "These late-night visits by friends are starting to become a regular occurrence, aren't they? Can I trouble you for some water? Then we'll sit down, and I'll tell you the story."

The ice water turned into vodka tonic by the time Lulu had finished her story. Cherry had shaken her head and *oh-no*ed through the entire story. When Lulu got to the part where she'd been knocked out, Cherry got up to hug her. And her hot pink–tipped fingers gripped the arms of her chair when Lulu described finding Mildred.

Lulu was positive that Cherry's face would have been pasty pale if it hadn't been caked with green goo. And that's when Cherry poured them both a vodka tonic.

Cherry shot hers down quickly and poured more. "I think," she stated, "that it's all because of that damned book Mildred was writing."

Lulu nodded.

"There she was, telling everybody she was going to write a mystery. She was poking her nose in where she shouldn't have. She started asking questions for research and made somebody worried. It was a bad idea," said

Cherry, taking another big swig from her drink. "A *real* bad idea."

Lulu said, "Is there anything else you remember that she said to you? I know she told you she'd followed Rebecca to the Peabody to deliver her comeback. And that Mildred had seen somebody there she hadn't expected to. And she got a threatening letter that she burned. Was there anything else?"

Cherry slammed down some more vodka tonic, which Lulu was sorry to see. She didn't think it was going to help with Cherry's cognitive process at all.

But apparently Cherry needed the booze for other reasons. "Actually," said Cherry after she discretely burped into a napkin, "there was. She didn't exactly mention anyone by name. I told you the truth about that. But she hinted really strong about who she *had* seen."

Lulu felt more apprehensive than she had the whole rest of the evening. And, considering the night she'd had, that was really saying something.

"She said something about how she was surprised she wasn't waiting tables." Cherry sighed unhappily as Lulu winced. "And then she said she thought someone else would want to stay away from the Peabody, since they'd been miserable there the day before."

"Sara and Flo," said Lulu unhappily. She took a sip from her drink and was surprised to find she'd already drained it. Wordlessly, Cherry refilled it with vodka and tonic.

Cherry also refilled her own glass. Her hand was a lot more unsteady this time, though. "If it makes you feel better, Lulu," said Cherry, "Mildred wasn't making a helluva lot of sense. I think she was making some things up. She made it into this big caper. Her whole life had been boring, and now something exciting was finally happening to her."

Lulu tried to absorb this thought as the alcohol buzzed through her system. "Mildred was a drama seeker?" This didn't seem to jive with the image Lulu had of a middle-aged bookseller with a penchant for Victorian frills.

Cherry nodded solemnly. "She was talking like she was a few bushels short of a full load. Stuff about pink being tacky and remember to put in something about mixed drinks, and then all about pigs: 'I'll call a pig a pig. It's fitting. Maybe pigs like to visit each other.' Something like that. I was just ill over Flo and Sara. But like I say, I felt like she was also getting carried away."

Lulu decided she'd heard quite enough for the night. Cherry obviously didn't have any more information and Lulu was sick at heart over the information she *did* share. "It's time for me to be heading home, Cherry." She hiccupped loudly and clapped a hand over her mouth. "Goodness gracious. And I'll need a ride back. I'm sorry, Cherry."

Cherry said, "No apology needed, Lulu. You've had a gosh-awful night. Beaned on the head, had a nasty shock—or two or three—and now you're tired and the vodka tonics have sunk in. I totally get it. But you know, I can't drive, either. We could walk." Then she changed her mind. "No, we couldn't. Too far. Okay, I'm calling Ben. You're never too old to have to parent your child." Which, thought Lulu, would have made perfect sense except that *Lulu* was the parent and *Ben* was the child. Good thing that Cherry *wasn't* driving the car.

Cherry called Ben and Sara's house. The phone must have rung a lot because it was a while before anyone picked up. Cherry said, "Ben? Hi there. It's Cherry. I'm sorry to call you so late. No, no, everything is fine, nothing to worry about. It's just that your mama and I drank some, and we're not fit to drive your mama home." She listened for a minute. "Okay, we'll see you then."

Cherry rung off and laughed. "I don't think Ben ever thought he'd get a phone call like that. Hoo-boy!"

"You didn't want to tell him about everything else?"

Cherry shook her head. "Too much to process at one o'clock in the morning. Hard enough to absorb the fact his mama is out drinking in the middle of the night."

Chapter

12

The next morning, Lulu was so exhausted by her previous day's adventures that she didn't respond to her alarm. The sun's ascent infused her bedroom with a bright light that she slept right through. And the rapping at her front door and the insistent ringing of the doorbell didn't even cause her to roll over.

Only the feel of a rough, wet tongue against her face, snuffling in her ear, and a yippy bark brought her to a startled awareness. "What the *hell*?" she croaked as she blearily gazed into the small, determined face of Babette and the more distant faces of Ben and Sara.

"Sorry, Mother. I used my key since you didn't answer the door. Babette is just *so* excited to see you."

Lulu shoved her pillows in a ball and leaned against them as she sat up. "Ben? Sara? Isn't it awfully early to make social calls? Or break into folks' houses?" Or foist yappy rodents on unsuspecting sleepers?

"Well, after Cherry filled us in on everything that happened to you yesterday, we thought it best to make sure you were doing okay."

"*Cherry* was up?" Lulu groaned. "She must be made of steel."

"She's probably more used to tossing down vodka tonics than you are, Mother. But I'm still trying to figure out why you think eleven thirty is early."

"*What?*" Lulu pulled back the comforter that had blocked the view of her clock. "Lord have mercy. I have *never* slept so late in my life." Babette stared disapprovingly at her. "Who's at the restaurant? If you're here," said Lulu, struggling up in bed, "then who is on the pit? Good Lord, Ben, you didn't put Seb on there, did you? He might be pouring sauce on the ribs instead of dry rub." Lulu put her hands over her mouth in horror at the thought of how Seb might destroy Aunt Pat's sterling reputation.

"It's Sunday, Mother. We don't open until five thirty tonight, remember?" Ben now frowned at her. He leaned forward, the better to look at her head. "How do you feel?"

Lulu abruptly realized that her head was throbbing. She felt underneath her hair and made a face. "There's a big knot there."

Sara was already moving toward the kitchen. "I'll get you a glass of water and ibuprofen, Lulu."

Ben sat down on the end of Lulu's bed, and Babette jumped into his lap. He patted her absently. "What I don't understand is why you were at the bookstore to begin with."

"I was checking on Mildred; she hasn't been acting like herself lately. Cherry said that Mildred had gotten an anonymous threatening letter after she started trying to write that murder mystery. I wanted to make sure she was all right. Which, clearly, she wasn't." Lulu had a horrifying urge to start crying. She angrily blinked back tears.

Ben became very absorbed in Babette to give Lulu time

to recover. "You were good to check on her, Mother. But couldn't you have called her store phone?"

"I did, but no one answered."

"No one answered where?" Sara came back in and handed Lulu the ibuprofen and glass.

"Mildred's shop. Mildred didn't answer her phone yesterday. I drove over to her house, thinking she'd already gone home for the day. Her door was unlocked, so I walked right on inside. After a couple of minutes, I could see that she wasn't there, so I drove back to the store. I had this awful feeling that maybe she needed some help. I didn't think anyone was really trying to murder her—I just wondered if she was doing okay."

Sara sat down in the armchair across from Lulu's bed. "You know, I was there yesterday. At her shop."

Ben swung his head around to look at her. "I thought you were in the studio all day yesterday. Are you *sure* you went to the bookstore? Yesterday? Maybe you're thinking about a couple of days ago."

Sara said, "I was in the studio a lot yesterday. Then Mildred called me and asked me to come by the store—she said that she wanted to talk to me."

Ben looked unhappy with the direction of the story.

Lulu knit her brows. "I don't understand, Sara. Why would Mildred want to talk to you?"

Sara rubbed her eyes tiredly. "She accused me of killing Rebecca Adrian."

"*What?*" chorused Lulu and Ben.

"Oh, she saw me at the Peabody that day Rebecca was killed. She thought I was acting shady, so she confronted me about it."

Ben frowned. "I didn't know you were even *at* the Peabody that afternoon." He tried to recreate the day in his head. "You were at Southern Accents in the morning, then you waited tables."

"And you drove Tony and me over to the Peabody," added Lulu, confused.

"Right. But I knew Derrick was upset that day from being humiliated the day before. And I knew exactly how he felt. I had a bad feeling that he hadn't gone to school that morning. When I called the house, he didn't answer. Then I called his cell phone and he acted very strange. He admitted he was at the Peabody."

"I thought you just told him on the phone to come home when you realized what he was up to. But you actually went over there," finished Lulu.

"I was only gone for fifteen minutes," said Sara. "I drove the block or so over there, asked Derrick what in the blazes he was doing over there, ordered him to drive back to the house, and then I was back at the restaurant."

"You didn't say anything about it to us," said Ben reproachfully.

Sara shook her head. "I didn't want either of you to worry. Besides, you'd both had bad days already, what with the tasting and the scene with Mildred. I couldn't figure out what I wanted to do—if I should approach Tony or Rebecca about the tires privately and offer to pay for them, or if I should let that be the final straw and call the police and let them handle it."

"Didn't you feel uncomfortable in the car with Tony as we went to the Peabody?" asked Lulu.

"Not so much. I mainly wanted to make sure that Derrick's car wasn't back over at the hotel. I was worried he might somehow have gone back and was up to more devilment. Then . . . we found Rebecca's body."

They paused and considered the implications of that for a minute. "So, you were worried," said Lulu, "that Derrick was somehow involved."

"That was a deep-down fear," said Sara. "I just needed to talk with him first and convince myself that he had absolutely nothing to do with it."

"But," said Ben, "as far as the police are concerned, you had a raging argument with Rebecca Adrian the day she was killed."

"Right," acknowledged Sara.

"And your feelings were horribly hurt and you were very angry with her."

"Right," said Sara.

"And now we know you were at the scene of the crime around the time of the murder," said Ben.

"Sort of," said Sara. "But Derrick knows I stayed in the parking lot." She had a funny look on her face, though.

"Was he with you the entire time?" asked Lulu.

"Sure. Well . . ."

"What?" asked Ben.

"Except for when he went inside the Peabody to use the restroom. He was covered with oil and grease from the van, and I didn't want it all over the seats of the car."

"So," concluded Lulu, "During the time Derrick was inside the Peabody, he could have poisoned Rebecca."

Sara nodded reluctantly.

"And *you* could have gone in and poisoned Miss Adrian."

"I *could* have. I *wanted* to. But I *didn't*." Sara rubbed her eyes. "But I guess the police won't see it that way."

"Did Mildred see it that way?" asked Lulu.

"She was in quite a mood, yesterday, let me tell you. Nervously excited—almost exhilarated. She'd look at her notebook like she was reminding herself what questions to ask. Then she'd ask me something and write it down."

Ben said, "That's what got her killed. Acting like a detective."

"I don't think she was trying to be a detective, Ben. I think she was trying to be an investigative journalist. After all, she was writing a mystery," said Lulu. "I think she went through a whole bunch of emotions last week. She was scared at first that she was going to be arrested for the crime. When that didn't happen, she was excited about the idea of trying something different—writing a mystery instead of a romance. So she acted like an investigator and asked questions of all these different people. Then she ended up being really scared again. That's after someone got worried she was getting too close to the answer and they wrote her a threatening letter."

Sara picked up Babette and patted her a moment. "Well, I'd changed my mind and decided that Mildred had killed Rebecca Adrian. It was better than the alternatives. I guess her murder puts a hole in that theory."

Lulu sighed. "Now the focus of the police is going to shift back to Aunt Pat's and all of us."

Ben said, "Sara and I will let you get back to sleep, Mother. You had one hell of a day yesterday. Just watch your step. Someone around here is getting desperate."

Lulu didn't feel nearly as sore on Monday after spending a quiet day on Sunday. By Monday afternoon, she was feeling like her old self again. Back in the restaurant, she was talking to customers and taking orders just like a normal day. Although she found herself spending a lot more time in the kitchen than usual. The delicious aroma the dry rub lent the pork and Ben's bustling as he manned the pit and kept an eye on the baked beans gave her the comforting feel of the familiar that she clung to.

Morty flagged Lulu down. "Got some bad news," he said to her mournfully.

"Oh heavens. Is it your gallbladder again? I know it acted up like the dickens the last time."

"No, nothing like that. Actually, this time it's Buddy."

"Buddy has a gallbladder problem?" asked Lulu, her eyebrows drawing together.

"Buddy has a girl problem."

"Oh," said Lulu. "Oh dear. So Leticia turned him down?"

Morty nodded.

"Well, maybe she had a conflict, Morty. You know how sensitive Buddy can be. Maybe she already had a commitment for the evening."

"That could have been the case. Except that Buddy left it as an open-ended invitation. He told her that any time she was available, his schedule was wide open and he'd be happy to accommodate her."

"Oh dear," repeated Lulu. They sat quietly. "I guess he's very upset? He seemed to really like her a lot."

"Yes, he really does." Morty added, "I wondered if there was a way that we could help him out. I think Leticia might not want to talk to me about her love life, but do you think there's any way you might sit down with her for a few minutes? Maybe find out what her issue with Buddy could be?"

"I'd be happy to," said Lulu. "I owe all of you for helping draw business back into Aunt Pat's. Besides, maybe it's something small that's keeping her from going out with him."

Morty brightened. "Sure! Maybe she just wishes he'd change his socks more often. Or not slurp his iced tea." His eyes looked dreamy, and Lulu could tell she was in for another rendition of his fanciful reminiscences. "I remember my own dating days when I was a young man. All the girls were so beautiful. When they're young, they're *all* beautiful, of course. And I was playing the blues, and they'd look up at me with those big, doe eyes." He heaved a sigh. "Those were the days."

Morty brought himself back to the present with some difficulty. "Anyway, anything you could do, Lulu, would be really appreciated."

"I'll do my best," promised Lulu. "I hope that she comes back into the restaurant. I haven't seen her in the last few days. I hope she's not avoiding Aunt Pat's because she's worried about seeing Buddy here. I'd hate Buddy to lose out on a relationship, and I'd hate for us to lose out on a good customer."

Lulu smiled when Derrick came into the restaurant after school that afternoon. Derrick's transformation into someone pleasant to be around was amazing. The office purchasing and bookkeeping was going much smoother (especially since Seb's work schedule was still erratic). Derrick's smile was the biggest difference she'd noticed.

Today was a continuation of the same pattern they'd gotten used to. Derrick came in, sat with Lulu on the porch for a while, telling her about his day at school and eating a bowl of red beans and rice.

Lulu said, "Sweetie, I know how much you love fresh peaches. I picked up a basket of them at the farmer's market. I cut up a big bowl full and sprinkled them with some brown sugar and put sour cream and pecans on top." Lulu beamed as Derrick hugged his thanks and headed off to the kitchen to fix himself a helping and get to work on the restaurant's brand-new website. At least, the afternoon started out that way. But it ended abruptly when the Memphis police came in the door. And it didn't look like they were there for a discounted barbeque plate.

Five minutes later, they read Derrick his rights and led him, pale and shaken, out the back door of the restaurant. Lulu immediately called Jed to ask him to meet Derrick at the police station.

Although the police hadn't dragged him out in front of the dining room, everyone seemed to know what had happened. There was whispering and concerned looks, and the normally chatty room was quiet enough to hear a pin drop.

Finally, Big Ben motioned Lulu over. He leaned over as if he were about to murmur sweet nothings in her ear. This attempt at a discrete whisper resulted in something just short of a bellow. "Is it true?" he asked. "Is it true what they're saying? Was Derrick arrested?"

Lulu nodded. "He's on his way to 201 Poplar," said Lulu, giving the well-known address for the Memphis jail.

"Ahh, mercy me," said Big Ben quietly.

Buddy, whose long life included a stint as a preacher, said a quick prayer. They all sat quietly for a minute.

"This too will pass," said Buddy. "I don't believe for a minute that Derrick would have done such a thing. It seems unfair that this is happening right when his life is turning around."

"What's going to happen now?" asked Morty quietly.

"Jed is on his way to the station. And he's an excellent lawyer." Lulu hoped he was even better than she thought he was. After all, with a police record and several run-ins with the law under his belt, Derrick didn't look like Memphis's most upstanding citizen. Especially considering that his last meeting with police involved his confessing to the tire slashing of a murder victim's van.

Sara materialized, red hair wildly untamed. "Sorry,"

she apologized to Buddy, Big Ben, and Morty. Then she hauled Lulu off by the arm to the back office.

"Ben called me," she said. "I was in my studio. What'll we do?"

Lulu was taken aback by Sara's breathless appearance. Her face was ashen, and she looked almost ill.

"Sara, I've called Jed. He's on his way to the station now. Derrick's in good shape."

Sara shook her head. "No, he isn't. You know that as well as I do. This wasn't supposed to happen. When I promised my sister I'd take care of Derrick . . ." She shook her head again.

Sara took her keys out of her purse.

"Where are you going?" asked Lulu

"Down to the station," said Sara grimly.

"I think it's about time for us to leave," said Buddy. "We've hung out here for so long that now I'm hungry again."

"We could always have another order of ribs," suggested Morty.

"Maybe *you* could," said Buddy. "But I've already reached my daily intake limit for salt."

"What?" bellowed Big Ben. Morty impatiently signaled him to turn up his hearing aid. He reached up to both ears and turned them on. They filled him in.

This time Big Ben spoke in a more normal volume. "Let's go out and eat," he said.

"You paying?" asked Morty. "Because I've used up my eating-out money for the day."

"I was thinking," said Big Ben, "that we could go to Costco. Do a little sample dining."

"Only old folks do that," scoffed Buddy.

"And what are we?"

"Only as old as we feel," said Buddy.

"Well, I think I feel like a sample dinner. Anyway, I'm going over there. Anyone want to join me?"

Big Ben said, "Well, I could go. But what'll we do afterwards? This has been a rough day for me. I'm right shocked about young Derrick—right shocked. I might be needing some libations afterward to revive me."

"Such as?"

"Like that gem of a bottle you've been hoarding like a miser."

"The Domaine Vincent Dauvissat Chablis Les Preuses?"

"That's the very one."

Buddy looked at him sadly and shook his head.

"Come on, man. It's needed for medicinal reasons. Can't you make an exception to your rule?" asked Big Ben.

"Eating samples at Costco does not qualify as a special occasion," said Buddy sternly.

"I'm not even mentioning the special occasion! I'm talking about the fact that I need a little something to get over my horrible shock. And I thought I remembered you were interested in drowning your sorrows over Miss Leticia."

"I think a little whiskey would work much better for shock and sorrow drowning," said Buddy.

"Let's go to the warehouse," said Morty. "There's some chicken salad in a teeny cup that's calling my name. Maybe we can even lap Costco twice."

Chapter

14

The rest of the day was a blur for Lulu.

"I did it," Sara had confessed when she arrived at the police station, to the great consternation of the policemen there. She had been immediately detained, and Derrick remained locked up, too.

Lulu had called Jed as soon as she'd heard about Sara's confession. He drove right over to the police station. After what seemed like ages of waiting, Jed called Lulu back on her cell phone.

"It seems," said Jed slowly, "that the police have evidence linking Derrick to Mildred's murder."

"Why on *earth* would Derrick want to kill Mildred Cameron?" asked Lulu. "It simply doesn't make any sense."

"Their theory," said Jed, "is that she knew he'd killed Rebecca Adrian. Then she confronted Derrick about this information, and he murdered her."

"What evidence do they have against Derrick?"

"His jacket was left there at the scene of the crime. And it did have Mildred's DNA on it."

Lulu's eyes widened. "I bet you it's that jacket he's had at Aunt Pat's since March. I've been fussing at him about not taking it home and letting it clutter up the office. And now it's hot as the blazes."

"Anybody who came into the restaurant had access to the jacket," mused Jed.

"And couldn't they have rubbed his jacket on Mildred after they killed her? Planted some incriminating evidence?"

"Sure they could have," said Jed. "Which is exactly the argument I'm going to use."

"This thing about Sara just blows my mind," said Lulu. "She's only confessing because she's trying to protect Derrick."

"Well, I'm going to remind her that she also has a responsibility to her daughters. What kind of mother can she be to Coco and Ella Beth from prison?" said Jed.

"The good news is that the girls don't know anything about this," said Lulu. "And I don't plan on letting them find out."

"More good news," said Jed, "is that they're almost certainly going to end up releasing Sara, confession or no confession. They're going to ask her things that only the killer would know—and I'm pretty sure she won't know the answers."

Jed was right, and Sara was released by the end of the day. Not that she was all that pleased to be out, thought Lulu as she drove her home.

"What on earth were you *thinking*?" asked Lulu, thumping her hand on the steering wheel.

"Well, maybe I *did* do it," said Sara in a petulant voice. "You weren't there, Lulu. I was awfully mad at Rebecca. And I was there at the scene of the crime."

"And Mildred? You expect me to believe you'd actually kill poor Mildred?" asked Lulu.

Sara sat in a stubborn silence for a minute. "I could have killed her, too, Lulu. She asked me to talk to her at the bookstore. She'd seen me at the Peabody. I had motive, after all. And opportunity. And the means was right there around her neck."

The next morning, Sara was back at the jailhouse bright and early. Because Sara was now spending so much time with Derrick, Lulu tried to make things as normal as possible for Ella Beth and Coco, who hadn't yet been told what was going on and were out of school for a teacher inservice day.

Ella Beth seemed determined to try and find out, though. Lulu caught her skulking around the kitchen. "What are you doing, honey?" asked Lulu. Ella Beth jumped.

"Oh, nothing, Granny Lulu. I'm just collecting clues. It's time for this case to be cracked."

Lulu lured her to the office with chocolate chip cookies. "Tell me what you've uncovered."

"Well, for one, I found out that Coco wears makeup at school and then takes it off in the school bathroom before she goes home." Ella Beth handed Lulu an incriminating picture from her pocket. Sure enough, there was Coco with blush, eyeliner, and lipstick on, and a look of complete dismay on her face. Lulu groaned and handed the offending picture back to Ella Beth.

Coco picked this moment to walk in. "What are you looking at?" she asked suspiciously.

"Pictures of you looking like a blond Cleopatra," said Ella Beth. "That's an amazing amount of shadow on your eyes."

Coco stamped across the office and peered over Ella Beth's arm. She gasped. "What are you doing with those? You took pictures of me in the hall at school?" She gave a weak smile at Lulu. "It was Halloween, Granny Lulu. I was dressed up like a model. You know."

"Funny," drawled Lulu, "but you seem to have a tank top on. And it sure wasn't that warm last October. We had that cold snap."

"Like I said," said Ella Beth with a sniff, "These were *recently* snapped photos."

Coco decided it was time to take possession of these pictures. She ripped them out of Ella Beth's hand and tore them into a million pieces. Whirling around, she left the office, slamming the door behind her.

"Good thing I uploaded those pictures online," said Ella Beth. "But then, Coco has always been behind the times."

Lulu couldn't help but chuckle, despite loving Coco to pieces. "It's good of you to look out for Coco at school. We don't want people to think that she's some kind of hoochy-mama. At least, I *suppose* that was your motivation."

Ella Beth smiled sweetly.

"Did you find out any other interesting information during your detecting?"

"I did take some more pictures, Granny Lulu. Because sometimes you need evidence, you know."

"Evidence of what?" asked Lulu. She could only imagine the kind of dirt that Ella Beth was digging up. She wasn't going to be very popular at school if she kept behaving this way.

"Evidence that Uncle Seb and Lurleen Ashton from Hog Heaven have been messing around."

"*What?*" Lulu glanced up to ensure the office door was securely shut. Although, truth be told, the office was probably the most unlikely place to find Seb lately. His work ethic had taken a major nosedive.

"Like I said." Ella Beth looked at Lulu, puzzled. She spoke a little louder, "Uncle Seb and Miz Ashton are messing around. I even told Coco about it a long time ago."

Lulu didn't really want to know the definition of "messing around." "Honey, they *were* seeing each other, but then they stopped just a few days later. Now Miss Ashton is just trying to get ahold of Uncle Seb to get him to come to the high school reunion."

Ella Beth looked dubious.

"That's what I've heard," said Lulu.

"I've come to a different conclusion, Granny Lulu."

"And how exactly did you come to this conclusion?"

"Well, a few days ago, I went off to feed the ducks and fish on the river. Remember? Daddy had a bunch of stale hamburger buns and told me I could take them. So I headed off down the street to the Mississippi River."

Lulu nodded. "Go on."

Ella Beth started to warm up to her story. Lulu wondered if maybe she would do better to consider a career in journalism instead of detecting. "It was a hot day, so I put my hair up in a ponytail. I didn't look a lot like myself, right?"

Ella Beth never did anything with her hair, so Lulu could see where a ponytail would throw almost anyone off.

"I threw the buns in the river, and they were gobbled up in no time. But I wasn't really ready to go back to the restaurant yet."

Now Lulu was thinking that maybe they ought to think about keeping a closer eye on Ella Beth.

"I turn around and who should I see, loving it up on a bench, but Uncle Seb and Lurleen Ashton. It was revolting." Ella Beth looked ill from the memory.

"Are you *sure* that's who it was?" asked Lulu. But she had a sinking feeling that her tomcatting son was a likely match for Lurleen Ashton.

Ella Beth gave a long-suffering sigh. "Like I said, sometimes you need evidence." She pulled out some pictures from her pocket.

Sure enough, it was Seb and Lurleen. And they were so

absorbed in each other that they didn't even notice there was a little girl taking a picture of them! Lurleen, thought Lulu cattily, had way too much makeup on her face and was wearing a too-tight, unflattering dress. Brazen hussy. Except Seb didn't seem to mind it.

"I'll take these if you don't mind, Ella Beth. You haven't told anybody about this except for me?" Ella Beth shook her head. "Then do me a favor and don't. And please stop sneaking around and taking pictures of things. I don't want to see you get into any trouble, honey. There's a real scoundrel on the loose."

Before Lulu could look for Seb and find out what in the dickens was going on with her younger son, she had some unfinished business to attend to.

Coming out of the office, Lulu had noted Leticia Swinger walking warily into the restaurant. She scanned quickly, then seemed satisfied. The hostess seated her at a table for two by the window.

Lulu approached Leticia's table with some trepidation, which she hoped she hid with a big smile. After all, Leticia didn't know she was on a special mission for Buddy. Lulu usually *did* sit down with Leticia for a few minutes and catch up while she was waiting on Leticia's order to come up from the kitchen.

Leticia smiled. "Hi, Lulu! Come to sit down with me for a few minutes? Tell me how things are going."

Lulu filled her in on the rebounding business at Aunt Pat's. She wound up the short summary with, "And really, Morty, Buddy, and Big Ben had a lot to do with all the customers coming back in. They put on this wonderful blues concert the other night, and business has been booming again ever since."

Leticia seemed at a loss for words. Lulu said innocently, "You might not even know about their concert, Leticia. I noticed you haven't been in for a little while."

"Oh," said Leticia, drawing her finger though a circle of water her glass had left on the table, "I was in here after their concert. It's just been the last few days that I guess I haven't. Here's the thing," she said, leaning forward to talk to Lulu. "Maybe you can give me some advice, since you know all the players in the drama. Buddy asked me to go out with him."

"Oh?" asked Lulu, trying to look surprised.

"That's right. The funny thing is that I'd been dying for him to ask me out for the longest time. We seemed like we had a lot in common—he's a musician, I'm a singer. But then . . ." Leticia hesitated.

Lulu leaned forward a little more, waiting for the truth of Leticia's rejection of Buddy.

"I overheard him the last time I was in here. He was talking to his friend—the deaf one? So I could hear him really easily. He was telling them that he didn't want to drink anymore. He sounded like he was such a conservative that I thought maybe I was wrong and we didn't have as much in common as I thought."

Lulu's eyes opened wide. A spontaneous laugh leaped out of her. She apologized to the frowning Leticia. "Honey, I'm sorry. I'm not laughing at *you*. I'm laughing at how funny men are. Even the old ones turn into little boys again when they're trying to impress a lady." She reached out and patted Leticia's hand. "He *was* trying to impress you. He drinks, he cusses, he dances. He thought that you didn't do those things because you sing gospel at the Eternal Crown of Our Blessed Savior. He's a very nice man, but not *that* nice."

Leticia laughed, too. "You're right . . . men don't really have a clue, do they? I would have jumped at the chance to go out with him before I heard him spouting all that nonsense. After all, Jesus himself drank!"

"Want me to put a bug in his ear? Let him know you

might be receptive to the idea of going out with him after all?" asked Lulu.

"Sure. If you'd do that, it would be great. I don't much feel like calling him up and asking him out myself. I'm liberated but not pushy. You know."

Chapter 15

Lulu decided she'd address Seb's wayward love life before playing Cupid for Buddy and Leticia.

Lulu *thought* she knew where Seb was. That is, she *thought* his lazy self was going to be at home in the bed or watching television. She knocked loudly on his door, expecting another glimpse into one of Dante's circles of hell when Seb opened the door. He didn't answer. She tried calling the house to tell him she was on his doorstep, but there was no answer. Then she called his cell phone, but it went right to voice mail.

By this time Lulu was fuming. She hoped to goodness he wasn't where she thought he was. She got back in the car and headed to a parking deck so she could walk down Beale over to Hog Heaven.

Sure enough, there was Seb. Instead of the pitiful, weak, dirty, slothful creature that she's seen after Rebecca Adrian's murder, she saw a spiffy, clean-shaven, nicely dressed man with his arm tight around Lurleen Ashton. He looked flustered when he caught sight of his mother.

Lulu wasn't sure what part of all this upset her the most. But she wasn't a big fan of scenes and certainly didn't want to show Lurleen how upset she was. She spun around on her heel and marched right out the door.

Seb soon caught up with her. He looked worried, but Lulu was convinced that his anxiety was not prompted by a desire to make up with his mother. No, he was likely more concerned about keeping his job.

Seb gave a short, nervous laugh. "What's this all about, Mother? I didn't realize you were so fascinated with my love life. Are you planning on chaperoning my date to the prom?"

"If I do, I'll be sure to give you a drug test before we leave. Because I am absolutely convinced that you're doing drugs again."

"What?"

"You clearly must be. Because I can't see what you see in Lurleen Ashton unless your mind has been insidiously twisted by drugs. Plus, you know she's probably just going out with you to discover our secret sauce recipe."

"What a horrible thing to say to your son, Mother! I'm sure she's more interested in my other attributes."

Lulu didn't want to dwell on what those might be. "I can't imagine why you aren't interested in nice Susan Meredith."

Seb groaned. "Not this again." He put his hand out and stopped Lulu's determined march to the parking deck. "I'm *not* on drugs, Mother. I'm totally clean. See, *this* behavior of yours is why I'm seeing Lurleen behind your back. I knew you'd flip out."

"You told me she was only looking for you because she was setting up your high school reunion! You said that you'd broken up with her after a couple of days. How long exactly have you been seeing her?"

"A few months. Soon after I came back to Memphis.

Like I mentioned, Mother, we went to school together. We weren't exactly strangers."

"I'm starting to think," said Lulu, "that *you're* the one who is the stranger. For all we know, Lurleen Ashton poisoned Rebecca Adrian herself."

Seb's face flushed with anger. "Come on, Mother. That's completely ridiculous."

"What's so ridiculous about it? Seems to me that Lurleen was determined to lure Rebecca Adrian over to Hog Heaven. She was handing her ads out in my own restaurant, for heaven's sake. Maybe"—Lulu frantically grasped at straws—"maybe she thought Rebecca was competing for your affections. That's what Cherry thinks, too."

"And jealousy is a long way from killing somebody. Besides, she would have just found out that Rebecca and I had been involved, and *I* had just found out that Rebecca was here in Memphis. First you thought *I* killed Rebecca, now you've moved on to Lurleen. Nice. Don't you remember, Mother, that Lurleen was coming in after Rebecca was already on her way out? I'm not sure how she would have managed to poison her food after the fact."

This stopped Lulu short. It was true. But that didn't mean she had to admit Seb was right. Maybe it was a good time to change the subject.

"Actually, I'm sure you're aware there's been another murder."

"Yes. I think her name has been changed to 'Poor Mildred' by the good people at Aunt Pat's."

"Now you *know* I'm worried about you, Seb. As a mother. I'm wondering where you were that night that she was killed."

"Where I was," drawled Seb, leaning against Lulu's Cadillac, "was the Memphis police station. Which, I'm sure you'd agree, is a pretty good alibi."

"The police station?"

"Yes, Mother. I was arrested for driving drunk. Ben bailed me out. You really haven't been plugged into the family news stream, have you? Maybe you should try Twitter."

Lulu felt a wave of relief. She really didn't want to think that Seb was capable of killing Mildred. "Well, I never thought I'd get to the point where I was relieved to hear one of my children was in jail. How about your Lurleen? Where was she?"

Seb rolled his eyes like he was a teenager again. "Okay, Mother, let's have it your way. Let's say Lurleen did kill Mildred. Why? Why would she do such a thing? What possible motive would she have had?"

Lulu opened her mouth but then snapped it shut again. She honestly couldn't think of a reason.

"I mean, did Lurleen even *know* Mildred? Why would she? Mildred was a loyal customer. She never would have darkened the door of Hog Heaven. Their paths would never have crossed. And surely you're not suggesting that Lurleen was jealous of Mildred."

This was true, thought Lulu. But if she followed this line of reasoning, she was completely at a loss as to who *did* commit these murders. She thought about Derrick, Sara, and Flo. None of them seemed likely candidates for murderers. Lulu wondered if Memphis had its very own serial killer who was just getting warmed up.

Seb said under his breath, "The way you're acting you'd think Lurleen and I were Romeo and Juliet."

"In no way do you resemble Romeo," said Lulu sourly. "And Lurleen Ashton certainly is no Juliet."

To make matters even worse, Lurleen strode up to them, smirking. Lulu felt all the muscles in her back and neck tense up.

"So, what's the story, Seb? I was thinking your mama was at Hog Heaven to try out some *real* barbeque."

Oh, she was so obnoxious. "That's funny," said Lulu with dignity, "because I was just telling Seb you were dating him to discover our secret sauce recipe."

Lurleen entwined her tanned arm in Seb's and started pulling him back toward Hog Heaven. "Come on, Seb. Your mother has sour grapes because she doesn't want her little boy dating a big, bad woman like me. Who was it again that she was trying to hook you up with?" She looked up, laughing at him through lashes heavily encrusted with mascara.

"Susan Meredith," said Seb with a lazy grin.

"That hippie gallery owner? She couldn't handle you, honey."

"No," said Lulu clearly. "No, I don't want him to hook up with Susan. He's not good enough for her. And now, if you'll excuse me?" Seb stepped aside, and Lulu strode off to the parking deck.

Lulu was decompressing at home when she got a phone call that finally made her smile. Ben had posted Derrick's bail, and he was out free.

"I am so glad you let me know that, Ben. Is he home, then?"

"Yes, Sara's with him. Seems like this whole episode has really scared him straight. Although I thought he was already straightening out just fine before this happened."

"He certainly was!" said Lulu indignantly. "He didn't need an experience like that to make him any straighter."

"At any rate, he's out now, Mother. And Sara's home, too. Thank God. I was starting to think this whole family was falling apart at the seams. Next it might have been Coco getting pulled in for pocketing costume jewelry at the mall. Or Ella Beth for fraud." He gave a hearty sigh of relief as if a heavy burden had been lifted from him.

"You know, Ben, I think I'll drop by there a little later. I need to run by the grocery store and pick up a couple of things first, though. Can you handle the restaurant this afternoon?"

"Sounds good. Feel free to drop by the house—unless you're worried about catching our law-breaking affliction over here. I'm thinking it might be an epidemic."

Lulu was in the produce section, surreptitiously pulling off some grapes from a bunch that was way too big for one old lady, when she saw a very tall woman wearing espadrilles and looking through the Vidalia onions. She wore a huge hat and sunglasses on top of what appeared to be a black wig. Lulu didn't know why, but she had a sneaking suspicion that this odd-looking creature was Flo.

Lulu pushed her cart a little closer and peered at the woman. She seemed completely absorbed in choosing the onions, which Lulu attributed to the dark sunglasses she wore and the difficulty inherent in seeing anything while wearing them. "Flo?" Lulu asked.

The woman shrieked and threw the onion down like it'd bitten her. Lulu shrieked, too, it startled her so badly.

The sunglasses slipped down a little on the woman's nose, and Lulu saw Flo's eyes looking at her in a panic before pushing her sunglasses up again. "How did you know it was me?" she hissed. "I'm in disguise."

"I've no idea," said Lulu, bewildered. "I guess I've known you for so long that there was something about the way you were standing there that seemed really Flo-like. Plus, you love espadrilles. And Vidalia onions."

Flo swung her head from side to side, looking all around her. "Lulu, I don't mean to hurt your feelings, but I can't be seen talking to you," whispered Flo hoarsely. "I'll meet you later . . . at your house. Ten o'clock tonight." Then, like

an international spy (who was trying way too hard), she
was gone.

Lulu hoped her visit with Derrick would be less
lively than her brief conversation with Flo, which she was
still trying to recover from.

She was relieved to see that Derrick actually looked
pretty good, except for the tired circles under his eyes. Lulu
gave him a hug tight enough to make him gasp. Everything in Ben and Sara's house seemed very orderly. Except,
of course, for Babette, who snarled and yipped angrily at
Lulu's heels as she followed Derrick into the house. Lulu
rolled her eyes. Too bad Elvis and B.B. were at the restaurant with Ben. Those were the only Taylor pets that Lulu
found it possible to warm up to.

Derrick explained that Sara had gone out to run a few
errands. This suited Lulu pretty well, since she hoped to
get a little information out of him and she had a feeling that
Sara might jump in and change the subject. But Derrick,
unused to hosting, was beginning to look uncomfortable.
"You know what would really hit the spot right now, Derrick? A glass of iced tea. Your aunt Sara makes some wickedly good iced tea."

Derrick relaxed and gave a relieved smile. "Sure. Should
we go into the kitchen?"

Apparently Sara's recent mindset had not been condu-
cive to iced tea making. Derrick rummaged for a minute in
the refrigerator and came out with a pitcher that had only a
few drops in it. "Is this okay?" he asked doubtfully.

No, Lulu didn't think it probably was okay. Who knew
how long that stuff had been sitting in Sara's fridge? It had
an oily appearance, like nothing that Lulu had ever seen
before.

"Or maybe," said Derrick still digging down deep, "some orange juice?"

The orange juice looked like it was well on its way to meeting the same fate as the java-esque iced tea.

"Water," said Lulu. "Water would be perfect."

As Derrick got out the glasses, Lulu took a seat at the kitchen table. "Honey, I am so glad to see your handsome face. I was worried to death about you."

Derrick brought over the waters. "Me, too," he said in a voice so quiet that Lulu had to strain her old ears to hear it.

This kid wasn't used to opening up to anybody. That was only normal, considering he was usually trying to cover up some misdemeanor. And considering the adults around him hadn't exactly inspired confidence, either.

Lulu suddenly made a big show of looking all around her suspiciously and checking under the kitchen table. She even peered suspiciously into the fake flower arrangement (that needed dusting) in the middle of the table.

Derrick narrowed his eyes as if he were concerned that Lulu had picked this moment to finally crack up.

Lulu finally sat back as if satisfied. "We're safe, Derrick. There are no signs of Ella Beth anywhere. And I don't even think the place is bugged."

Derrick broke up in laughter while Lulu beamed. She was so glad to see this boy relax.

"Did you hear," he said, "that Ella Beth caught me going in to get a tattoo? I can't even wipe my nose now without Ella Beth watching me and taking notes."

"Honey, you couldn't even have gotten a tattoo. You have to be eighteen."

"They wouldn't have cared," insisted Derrick.

"I know she's driving you nuts. She's all set now to be a detective. But I'm glad you didn't get a tattoo. It might look cool at your age, but it sure doesn't by the time you get to be mine."

Impulsively, she reached out a hand and squeezed his arm. "I've gotten so fond of you these last couple of weeks. I would *hate* for anything to happen to you. And I'm so afraid that something might."

Derrick hunched down in his chair, and Lulu hoped that all his old defenses weren't about to go flying up. "Why don't you just tell me what you know? It might not even be anything that's all that important? You'll feel so much better not having to carry the weight of those secrets around."

He shook his head. "The only things I know don't make any sense. They don't have anything to do with anything. There were some things that seemed weird to me."

"Like?"

"Well, you know I was real upset that night before Rebecca was killed. The next day I felt a little better because I'd decided to get her back. It's hard to explain . . ." Derrick hesitated. "It's like, when you finally decide to do something and it's really destructive, it makes you feel *alive*." He flushed as he looked shyly at Lulu.

"There's part of me that can understand that, Derrick. It's like when I get really angry at somebody and I go out in the backyard with my hoe and start whacking weeds."

He nodded. "Exactly like that. Except what I was doing wasn't right."

Lulu didn't want to sound like the sanctimonious adult, so she treaded carefully. "I was hoping that when you were in your aunt Sara's studio that the art was making you feel alive," she said slowly.

"It does, sure. Especially the pottery. Pounding the clay is awesome. And—it's weird, but I feel that way when I'm doing all that boring accounting work in the office." He seemed really surprised by that realization.

"Anyway," he hurried on, not wanting to do too much self-examination. "I'd skipped school, like you know. And I ended up at the Peabody parking deck, ready to do a number on that Cooking Channel van."

He rubbed his eyes for a minute, tiredly. "It was different this time. Usually it's night, and I'm sneaking around in the dark when no one is out. This time, it was the middle of the afternoon. Slashing tires only takes a minute, so it wasn't like I was really worried about getting caught. But then it seemed like everybody I knew was at the Peabody."

Lulu leaned closer.

"For one thing, I heard this motorcycle drive up, and it was Cherry. Anybody who saw me would have known I wasn't supposed to be there—it was a school day and school would still have been in session. So I kind of crouched down. And she was only in there for a few minutes, then she came back out again and left on her bike."

Lulu said, "Sweetie, I had a long conversation with Cherry. She was at the Peabody to see if Tony was there. She just wanted to spend some time with him."

"Okay," said Derrick, but he didn't look convinced.

"So then I hear somebody talking on a phone, and I know it's Seb. I crouch down really low again and wonder what the hell is going on. Seb is saying, 'I'm not going in. I don't care about being blackmailed. It doesn't matter.' I'm listening real close now to hear what else is going on. Then he sounds like he's angry about something. He says, 'Okay, never mind. Fine. Have it your way.' Then he just sat in his car, smoking."

Lulu said, "Well, that actually sounds really good, Derrick. I know that Miss Adrian was trying to blackmail Seb." Derrick raised his eyebrows and Lulu explained, "She'd known him in New York. Apparently, Seb ran into some trouble with the law up there that Miss Adrian thought he might not want us all to know about. But Seb told the police that he didn't care if we found out about his jail time in New York or not. So what you're saying seems like it matches what he was saying. And—if he was talking to her and then stuck around in his car, it sounds like he didn't go in the hotel to kill Rebecca."

Derrick shrugged, and Lulu could tell he wasn't totally convinced. "I've seen enough players to know one when I see one," he said. "No offense," he added hastily.

"Then what happened?" asked Lulu. "Was this when Sara came to check and see what was going on?"

"Yes. She'd found out that I wasn't at school that day. The school sends out an automated phone call when a kid isn't there. So she called my cell phone, and I told her what was going on. By that point, I was just done with it. Aunt Sara zooms up in the car and is really mad about the van tires. I was thinking, 'Great. Aunt Sara's going to call Rebecca and tell her, or maybe even call the cops.' But I'm covered with grease and dirt from the van. I had to dodge behind and under it so many times that it got all over me.

"She didn't want dirt all over the car seat in my car . . . which, of course, is really her and Uncle Ben's car. She sent me into the Peabody to get cleaned up. She followed me into the hotel. I guess she wasn't really sure what kind of stuff I might do. Maybe she thinks I might start tearing up the Peabody lobby. We walk into the hotel and see Rebecca there in the lobby, having a cocktail or something. She's talking on her phone, and she sees me and Aunt Sara. I guess she's thinking we're going to have some kind of a big scene, so she rolls her eyes at us and walks off a little ways, standing there with her back to us and talking on her phone."

Probably when Evelyn overheard Rebecca telling the loan creditor to stop harassing her, thought Lulu.

"I go into the restroom and clean up a little bit and get a bunch of paper towels to kind of spread over the car seat to keep dirt and grease off. But, when I come out of the restroom, I see Aunt Sara shaking something into Rebecca's drink while her back was turned." Derrick looked more than tired . . . now he looked exhausted. "I don't know what it was. And she never saw me, because I ducked into the restroom for a minute, then came back out like it was the first time."

"But at that point, you didn't know that anything was really wrong. Rebecca was still alive and well."

"Sure. And talking on her cell phone. So I thought Aunt Sara had probably done something like put salt in her drink. But then Rebecca ends up dead a couple of hours later." He blew his breath out in a puffy sigh. "The whole day was insane. So . . . we're leaving. Aunt Sara has pulled out of the parking lot and is heading back to the restaurant. I'm leaving, too, and see Mildred Cameron going into the Peabody. And then I see Flo's car pulling in, but she's got her eyes on Mildred, who is going into the lobby. By this time I'm wondering if there was some kind of Aunt Pat's party that was going on at the hotel that I didn't know about."

Lulu was now feeling like she wanted to wrap up this conversation before she discovered that Ella Beth and Coco had been at the Peabody, too. And the news that Sara had actually gone into the Peabody, when she'd said she'd stayed outside gave her a sick feeling in the pit of her stomach. "Well, I'm sorry to hear about all this, Derrick, but I think everything can be really easily explained. Seb obviously was talking to Rebecca on the phone, and then decided he wasn't going to be blackmailed and left. Cherry was trying to make moves on that cameraman, Tony. Aunt Sara might have just emptied the salt shaker into Miss Adrian's drink, like you said. She was plenty mad at her. Mildred was on her way in to deliver the comeback she'd been thinking about. Flo . . . well, I'm not so sure exactly why she was there, but I think I have a pretty good idea.

So don't worry your head anymore, Derrick. Consider it all taken off your shoulders."

She got up from the table to give Derrick a hug. Babette growled ominously at her. Lulu glowered but stopped when Derrick started laughing again. She fussed, "I don't know why that animal despises me so much. I've given it treats, cooed at it. What more does it want?"

Derrick shrugged, still chuckling over it, and Lulu smiled back. "I guess if she's trying to protect you from my hugs then the creature can't be all bad. Anyway, honey, you take care. I love you and don't want to see anything happen to you. Thanks for telling me what happened that day. I promise it's going to work out just fine."

"Thanks, Lulu. It's kind of a relief to talk about it. Don't worry; my tire-slashing days are over."

"Well, thank the Lord for that. I couldn't stand to have any more troubles with you, Derrick. My poor heart couldn't take it."

Chapter

"So," said Lulu with lifted eyebrows, "your invitation to Ms. Swinger went well last night?"

Buddy had come into the restaurant with a spring in his step and now was puffed up like an elderly peacock. "She said she'd *love* to come over to dinner with me. And she thinks it's the sweetest thing that I'm going to cook my special dinner of Cornish game hens. It's regionally famous, you know."

"And," said Lulu, "I found out from Leticia that alcohol is *not* a problem for her. We were all just making assumptions about her because she was a choir member. She likes her wine just fine."

Buddy looked vastly relieved.

But Big Ben looked morose. He apparently had his ears turned on since he spoke in a normal volume. "I guess this means you'll be opening the Domaine Vincent Dauvissat Chablis Les Preuses? If a first date isn't a special occasion, I don't know what is."

"Well, now, I'm thinking that this isn't really the best

time to uncork that particular bottle. Opening a bottle with that degree of magnificence might give a lady the wrong idea. She might worry that I'm hurrying into a significant relationship too fast. It might make her want to put on the brakes."

Big Ben brightened. "That's true. I think it would be much better for those of us at this table to share the bottle. We could celebrate your good fortune in having such a wonderful dinner partner tomorrow night."

Buddy frowned. "A first date isn't a reason for celebration. Putting too much stock in something that could so easily go haywire could set me up for some bad karma. I'll tap into the bottle another time."

"Hope I'm not dead by then," muttered Big Ben. He thought for a minute. "Don't you think serving Cornish game hens might give her the wrong idea, too? That's pretty fancy stuff."

Buddy looked startled. "You know, I didn't think of that. Maybe I should stick with my special meatloaf. I think it'll fit the bill just fine."

Lulu said, "Mmm! That sounds absolutely delicious, Buddy."

"But what," said Buddy thoughtfully, "if the lady doesn't like meatloaf?" They all groaned. "I'm just saying! Sometimes people are funny about meatloaf. It's a different consistency. So I'll ask our resident food guru. Lulu, what do you think might make a special, but not too special, meal for my date?"

This was one of Lulu's favorite kinds of questions. Just the process of mulling over menus was fun—there were so many flavor combinations to go with. "We *know* she likes pork," said Lulu. "After all, she eats it every time she comes into the restaurant."

"That's a fact. But maybe that means she'd like something a little different on her special evening out."

Morty groaned. "I think you're overthinking this, man! I remember my days of wine and roses. All I needed for my dates with the pretty ladies was a great bottle of wine, some flowers for the table, and a serenade I'd provide my own self. Who even cared what we were eating? It was all about the love."

Buddy carefully ignored him. "I do have some black-eyed peas I picked up from the farmers' market yesterday. They'd make a good side."

Lulu nodded. "Mmmhmm. Makes me hungry just thinking about it. Put them in a bowl full of water tonight; refrigerate them overnight so they'll be in good shape tomorrow."

Buddy nodded. "And cook them with? Lots of bacon?"

"Oh, honey, *yes*! Bacon makes everything better. Buy that yummy smoked bacon. Bacon and red onions and garlic."

Big Ben said, "Don't forget a little hot sauce. I do love hot sauce in my black-eyed peas."

"So that's the perfect side. We're all in agreement?" Buddy asked.

They all nodded.

"But then what to go with it?" Buddy had an edge of exasperation to his voice. Lulu figured he must really like that lady.

"Buddy, we've talked about food before! Didn't you tell me you had a great recipe for country fried steak?"

Buddy considered this. "It's absolutely delicious. I make it with a nice gravy and mashed potatoes. And the black-eyed peas on the side." He hesitated. "Will it be too messy, though?"

"I think Leticia will love it. If she doesn't mind the mess of barbeque, I don't think some meat and gravy is going to bother her much," said Lulu. "It sounds like a down-home, tasty meal for someone who isn't trying to show off too much but wants to make something memorable."

◇◇◇◇◇◇◇◇

After a while, being at Aunt Pat's ended up being more of a strain. Lulu usually loved cracking jokes with her customers. And she was a whiz at remembering orders and getting the orders to the right tables. Today, though, she couldn't seem to focus. When one of the tables asked about the coleslaw they didn't get, Lulu realized that her mind wasn't at Aunt Pat's at all. It must be somewhere at the Peabody. She walked back to the kitchen, looking for the missing coleslaw.

Lulu glanced blankly around the kitchen. She couldn't even remember what it was that she'd gone in there for. Was it baked beans? Corn pudding? Lulu frowned. When Ben saw her, he said, "Mother, why don't you go home for a little while? You look completely wiped out."

"Is it that noticeable? I don't know what's come over me—I don't feel all that well today."

"It's probably the stress. I bet you haven't slept all that well since this whole thing started, have you?" Lulu shook her head. "Well, you're not doing yourself or anyone else any favors by staying here. Go home and take a nap. It's slow—the lunch crowd is over, and it's hours before we're busy for supper and the blues band. I'm going to tell Sara to go home in a little while and let her put her feet up, too. I think she feels just as worn out as you do."

Lulu had no intention of actually going to sleep. Instead, she thought she'd putter around the house and get some light housework done. Maybe read her book for a little while. But the dim lighting in her living room made her drowsy. And the plump pillows on her plaid sofa looked so inviting. She decided to lie down for just a few minutes. She covered up her legs with Aunt Pat's old knitted afghan from the back of the sofa.

The next thing she knew, there was a knock on her door. Lulu squinted at the clock and saw that an hour had passed. She struggled up out of the sagging sofa that seemed determined to imprison her.

It was Sara. "Uh-oh—looks like I woke you up. I came by to make sure you were doing okay, that's all. Ben mentioned that you were under the weather when you left."

"That's no problem, honey," said Lulu sleepily. "I appreciate your coming to check on me. I'm feeling better after my nap. Just woke up with a dry mouth is all."

"Why don't you sit back down on the sofa and let me get us something to drink?"

Since Lulu didn't make her usual objections to being waited on, Sara figured she must still be foggy from her nap. She walked to the tiny galley kitchen.

Sara loved Lulu's house almost as much as her restaurant. The wooden floorboards creaked as she walked and the floor dipped down a little in places, but it all combined to give the house a cozy and welcoming feeling. The inside smelled like old wood and the books that filled several glass-fronted cabinets.

A few minutes later, Sara returned with two tall glasses of lemonade. Sara knew that this lemonade wasn't from a mix, but from scratch. She handed Lulu a glass and then settled down in a worn armchair across from her.

"Perfect!" said Lulu. "A glass of lemonade hits the spot."

"Do you just keep a bag of lemons at the ready?" asked Sara.

"I like to keep them around. It's nice to add a little lemon zest sometimes, or some lemon juice to my meats. And my lemonade! Can't live without my lemonade. And you know, I've been squeezing lemons my whole life and didn't know if you microwaved the fruit for fifteen seconds, you get double the juice out."

"I'm going to have to give that a go," said Sara. "I hate

it when the lemons are so hard that they're impossible to juice."

Lulu looked closely at Sara as she started to feel a little less groggy. "Ben sent you home, too. How are you holding up? Have you been sleeping as poorly as I have?"

"Sleep," said Sara wryly. "Define sleep. The last few days I've felt like I can't turn my brain off. Do you ever get that feeling? My mind is whirling around and doesn't shut down. On the upside, things are going great with my art. I get out of bed in the middle of the night and go to my studio. It's amazing what you can get accomplished when insomnia adds three or four extra hours to your day."

Lulu opened her mouth to say something but then hesitated. "Sara, you know I trust you completely. I don't want you to think that I have the slightest bit of suspicion against you. But . . . I did have one question. I was visiting Derrick yesterday, and he told me about the afternoon you'd found out he'd skipped school and was slashing Miss Adrian's tires. He said that when you made him go get cleaned up in the restroom, he saw you put something in Rebecca's glass when he was coming out."

Sara said, "Ohhhh." She thought about it for a minute. "I'm sorry he saw that. Has he been worried the whole time that I murdered Rebecca?" She rubbed her eyes. "Bless him. And he's kept quiet this whole time."

"I know you didn't have anything to do with it, but, well—"

"What *was* I doing?" Sara gave a short laugh. "Acting about as mature as Derrick is what I was doing. I did pour something in her drink. *Not* poison, though."

"So . . . she was in Chez Phillippe?" asked Lulu with a frown, mentioning the restaurant inside the hotel, right behind the lobby and bar.

"No, she was sitting out in the lobby. She'd ordered a

cocktail, and it was sitting right there on her table. She got up and walked away from her table for a minute to talk on her cell phone. I had a couple of packets of salt in my pocket that I'd absentmindedly stuck in there when I'd helped bus one of our tables. It was totally juvenile, but I ripped those packets open and poured them right into her drink. I thought I'd spice up her beverage a little bit. At the time, it seemed harmless enough. I'd just pay her back for her nasty comments about my art. And, of course, I didn't have a clue that she was going to end up dead, or I'd never have done something that stupid."

Lulu relaxed. "I knew it had to be something like that, Sara. But you know why I had to ask you. It's been eating poor Derrick up, thinking you were somehow involved in the murder."

"The only reason I didn't say anything about it is because I thought nobody had seen anything and no harm had been done. I'd put *salt* in her drink, after all. But I felt so immature that I kept quiet about it."

"Maybe you can have a talk with him today and clear everything up," said Lulu in a soothing voice.

"I'm surprised," said Sara, "that Derrick actually opened up to you enough to say anything about it. Usually when I try to talk to him, he clams up completely. I mean, I could be asking him about something totally innocent: 'Derrick? Don't you want a little more to eat?' And he acts like I'm trying to strong-arm his computer password out of him or something."

"I convinced him to tell me what he knew for his own safety. After all, if Mildred Cameron was murdered for what she knew, someone could just as easily decide to take Derrick out, too."

Sara looked quite fierce. "Not if I have anything to say about it. Derrick becoming a real member of the family is about the only good thing that's come out of this whole mess. I guess it was the final straw for him—the turn-around point. Whatever it was, I'm so glad it happened. He's been wonderful with the girls lately, helps Ben in the kitchen and the office, and has some really promising artistic talent. I've been very surprised with what I've seen him create in the studio."

Sara finished her lemonade. "I'd better let you get some more rest, Lulu. Maybe you can go back to sleep now and catch up on some of those lost z's. I'm going to try to do the same thing."

Physically, Lulu felt a lot more refreshed. There was nothing better in this world than a nap. But whenever she thought about Rebecca Adrian's murder, she got a sinking feeling in her stomach that all the mint chocolate chip ice cream in the world couldn't get rid of. But she did give the ice cream a *try*.

Lulu wondered if she'd hallucinated the entire episode with the disguised Flo at the grocery store. After all, stress does funny things to people, and she was feeling poorly today. But then, at ten o'clock that night, there was an odd scratching knock at her kitchen door.

Lulu opened the door and there was Flo. At least, Lulu supposed it was Flo. She still wore the large hat, figure-concealing caftan, gigantic sunglasses, and black wig.

Flo looked nervously behind her, and Lulu ushered her in, quickly. "Sunglasses at night, Flo?"

Flo snatched them off. "Well, I'm not wearing them because of the glare," said Flo snappily. "They're to keep my face covered." She rubbed her eyes and said, "I'm sorry, Lulu. That was so rude of me. I'm too stressed out today, that's all."

"I can see that, honey. I just don't understand *why*. I'm

guessing it must have something to do with your no-good ex-husband."

"You smacked that nail right on the head. Somehow he found out that I was here in Memphis."

"How on earth could he do that?" asked Lulu. "He hasn't found you for the past ten years."

Flo shrugged. "Who knows? Maybe his private eye finally tracked me down. Or . . . remember the day Rebecca was murdered? The news was filming nonstop around Aunt Pat's and the Peabody—inside and out. I even saw myself on CNN that night. He could have watched the story in Mississippi. That's when I really started getting freaked out. Most times I can just go about my daily life and not even think about Virgil at all. But when I saw myself on TV, I wondered if I'd ever really feel safe again. So . . . well, I guess I started acting kind of weird." Lulu thought that "weird" was one way to describe Flo's messy appearance and drunken episode at the mall.

Flo waved her hands in the air. "I don't care exactly *how* he got here. I just need for him not to find me now that he's here. I mean, *clearly* he knows I'm in Memphis. But if I wear a disguise and don't go to the places I usually go, maybe he won't find me. And then he'll go off to whatever town in Mississippi he terrorizes."

Lulu peered close at this unfamiliar Flo. "You look so pale, Flo!"

Flo nodded. "I stopped tanning. 'Cause I don't look like myself when I'm all pale and white."

"I'll say you don't. Mercy!" Flo was a regular at the Copacabana Tanning Beds. And Lulu could see why. "How did you know he was here?"

"Well, I'd just left B.B. King's on Beale, and I saw Virgil walking down the street. Of course, I did this huge double take, thinking I was having some kind of optical illusion nightmare. Then I saw I *wasn't*, so I popped into B.B.'s again real quick." She made a face. "I could see him looking to the right and the left—searching, you know. He doesn't know the name I'm using, so he can't look me up online or in the phone book."

"And you got a disguise to stay under cover," said Lulu.

"I figure that he doesn't know exactly where I am, but he knows I've been to Aunt Pat's. And Beale Street is the area he was looking in. I thought if he saw me talking to you at the grocery store, and you'd been on TV, too, that he would see through my getup and know who I was," said Flo. "I'm on borrowed time, though. He must have been pretty sure of what he saw. But what he saw on TV was a blond, tanned woman," said Flo, looking hopeful. "Now I'm different."

"What did he *do* to you?" asked Lulu.

"Made my life a living hell," said Flo quietly. "It was his fault I went to jail to begin with . . . because I was determined to kill him. Unfortunately, I'm a bad shot. They locked me away for attempted murder. I was lucky to be released early for good behavior and get out of Mississippi before he knew I'd left. He was never going to let me have a life. That man is so jealous and controlling that he'd never let me escape from him."

"The only thing . . ." Lulu paused. "Well, honey, your disguise is really over the top, that's all. It might even draw attention to you instead of making you fade into the background."

"I know. But Virgil isn't the sharpest tool in the shed. He doesn't know that *I* know he's here. So he would be looking for a tanned blonde, not a pale brunette. He might look at me, but then I don't think he'd look any closer than that."

"Maybe that's so," said Lulu. "I hope you know what you're doing. You've had such a rough couple of weeks."

"Rough for this very reason," said Flo. "The reason I was so upset with Rebecca Adrian wasn't because I didn't want Memphis to know my past. It was because I was worried if she aired something on the Graces and my past, that Virgil would watch the Cooking Channel and find out. I'm just so tired of worrying about him." There were big, smudgy circles under Flo's eyes.

"Flo," said Lulu slowly, "I did want to ask you about something. Derrick says he saw you at the Peabody the afternoon that Miss Adrian was killed. It worried him to death, so I told him I'd ask you about it. I know there's probably a good reason why you were there."

"Not really," admitted Flo. "I was there to threaten Rebecca. I was determined to warn her off the story one way or another. Problem was, Mildred Cameron was already stomping into the Peabody, and I surely didn't want her to see me there. So I hung out and waited a little bit until she left. But—she did see my car, even though I was in the parking deck. I guess writers must really pay attention to little details.

"She even had me meet her later at the bookstore and ask me about being at the Peabody. I told her I'd parked my car at the deck there and walked to Aunt Pat's because Beale Street was so busy right then. But she knew that wasn't the truth. So I told her that I needed the exercise, too. I don't think she bought it, though. I got the feeling she was treating the whole thing almost as a game. Playing detective. At first she acted so upset about the murder. But then I guess she realized the police weren't hauling her off to jail. Then she started thinking that maybe she could write a book about it all. And she changed."

Lulu said thoughtfully, "Mildred made some pointed accusations to nearly everyone she knew. No wonder the poor thing ended up dead. She was playing a very dangerous game."

"She sure was," agreed Flo. "Because there was no way in hell I was going back to jail because of a crime I didn't commit. I didn't kill her, but somebody felt just as strongly as I did and followed through."

Lulu hesitated. "Flo, I know the police are working as hard as they can, but they don't have the personal reasons that I have to solve it quickly. Everybody who's close to me is a suspect. Can you think of *any*thing you saw that afternoon that Rebecca was killed? Even something that doesn't seem important."

Flo furrowed her brow. "I saw Mildred coming and going. Like I mentioned, she noticed my car. When I went into the hotel, I looked around for Rebecca in the bar area, but I didn't see her. I figured she'd gone up to her room. Lurleen was at the front desk . . ."

"*What?*" asked Lulu. "Lurleen Ashton was at the Peabody?"

Flo looked at Lulu with surprise. "Well, sure. Oh, listen, she was just there to meet her sister who'd come into town. It wasn't anything."

Lulu blinked. "Pickle is in town?"

"She's named *Pickle?*"

"Well, she's not really *named* Pickle, but everybody calls her that. She was all the time getting herself into pickles—you know, trouble."

"I don't guess *she* killed Rebecca?" asked Flo hopefully. "It certainly would make things easier on the rest of us."

"That's for sure. But, for the life of me, I can't see why Pickle Ashton would come into town and murder a Cooking Channel scout."

"I guess you're right," said Flo. "Too bad. But really, that's all I know, Lulu. I talked to Lurleen for less than a minute . . . she asked me for the time. Then Lurleen said, 'Oh, okay. I guess maybe she hasn't gotten here yet. That's okay—it'll give me time to dash off and do a couple of errands.' She left pretty fast. I got Rebecca's room number from the front desk and went up the elevator to her room."

Flo thought for a minute. "I knocked and Rebecca didn't answer the door, so I really started pounding on it. Then I yelled at the door, calling her. I thought maybe she was trying to avoid me. I guess she must have already been dead," said Flo slowly.

Lulu shivered at the thought. "What happened when you met with Mildred? Did you see or hear anybody then?"

"Oh, that wasn't even the same day she died, so I didn't see a thing that would help. Sorry. You know I want this case wrapped up, too."

Lulu stifled a yawn, and Flo picked up her sunglasses. "I'd better go. I'm sorry you won't see me around as much at the restaurant. I'm laying low and not going to my usual hangouts. Thanks for talking with me tonight. I only wish I had given you something useful."

But Lulu thought that maybe Flo *had* given her something. She just needed to figure out what it was.

Chapter

17

Lulu spent a restless night dreaming about Sara killing Rebecca with poisoned pickles and Derrick slashing all the tires in the Peabody parking deck. She woke up early the next morning and left her bed behind quickly, eager to interrupt those dream sequences.

Since Lulu couldn't shake her worrying, she avoided contact with her customers, not in the mood to visit and not wanting to pass along her bad mood.

Around lunch, though, Morty, Buddy, and Big Ben came in and Lulu decided to make an exception to her non-visiting rule.

"Tell me something good," urged Lulu. "*Any*thing good. I need to hear something happy."

Morty cleared his throat. "Actually, I *do* have some good news to report," he said. "After five years of really horrible luck, my fortunes seem finally to have changed."

Lulu leaned in. "Really? What's happened, Morty? Won the lottery?"

Buddy gave a sputtering laugh. "Hardly!"

Now Morty looked at them all with affronted dignity. "If you're going to be that way, Buddy, I don't think I'm going to tell the story at all."

"Please?" wheedled Lulu, shaking her head at Buddy.

Morty looked coldly at Buddy. "It so happens that I won bingo today at the Seniors' Community Center."

Lulu could see why Buddy wasn't so impressed with this story. "Why—that's wonderful, Morty! Congratulations. What did you win?"

"A roll of stamps," said Morty in a happy voice. There was a sudden roar of laughter from Big Ben and Buddy. "What on God's green earth is so damned funny?" he demanded. "This was a *big* roll of stamps, I'll have you know. And they're the *Forever* stamps—the ones you can use forever, even when the price of stamps goes up." The uproar turned into snickering, and Morty said, "What? Forever stamps aren't a big deal?"

"I thought you were emailing everybody, Morty. And that you'd switched to online banking to pay your bills. So what are you going to use your Forever stamps for?"

"They might end up being a collector's item, man," said Morty defensively. "By the time Ella Beth and Coco are grown-ups, they might not even know what postage stamps look like! Besides, I don't see you two winning anything. I think you're just jealous."

"Actually," said Buddy, "I did win something lately. There was one of those wedding trade show things last weekend. I went to it and won a door prize."

Now Big Ben and Morty gaped at Buddy. Big Ben turned up his hearing aid a little higher, thinking that maybe it was malfunctioning. Lulu could hear it making all kinds of screechy sounds. "I'll go ahead and ask, Buddy," said Lulu. "*Why* exactly were you at a wedding trade show? Is there something we should know about? Are things moving along quickly between you and Leticia?"

Buddy said calmly, "I think wedding trade shows are something *everybody* should know about. It's like a big party. You get a plastic bag full of freebies and coupons. The food vendors have samples out and the wine vendors have tastings. There's music playing from every type of band you could think of. I ate ten different kinds of wedding cake. It's air conditioned, and I got a door prize. What more could you ask for?"

"What was the door prize?" asked Morty.

Buddy looked at them with great dignity. "What I won is not the point. The point *is* that I win things, too. You're not the only one, Morty."

They all just looked at him, waiting. Finally Buddy realized he was not going to get away with a policy of nondisclosure. "I won," he said gravely, "a beautiful lace garter. To throw away to the single fellas at the wedding, you know. I'm the wrong gender, but maybe my great-niece might like it. She's engaged."

Amazingly, no one laughed or teased Buddy. But Big Ben spoke in a halting voice that sounded suspiciously like he might be holding back laughter. "I'm pretty *sure*, Buddy, that this is a cause for celebration. You've won something *very pretty*." Buddy looked hard at Big Ben, but Big Ben retained his composure. "I think . . . this is the right occasion to open that special wine you've been telling us about."

"The Domaine Vincent Dauvissat Chablis Les Preuses?"

Big Ben nodded, and the others held their breaths.

"Winning a lovely lace garter at a wedding trade show is very *nice*," said Buddy. "But it's *not* a special occasion."

Lulu laughed. "Well, I hope the special occasion comes quickly because I'm getting old enough that I might miss it if we have to wait too much longer."

◇◇◇◇◇◇◇◇◇

Lulu's unhappy episode with Seb wasn't sitting right with her. She hated being on the outs with Seb and wasn't really pleased by her behavior. After all, he was a grown man and Lurleen was a grown harpy, and they could date whomever they wished to. Besides . . . in the past, whenever Lulu had officially sanctioned one of Seb's relationships, it meant that relationship's days were numbered. Lulu wondered sometimes if Seb's taste in women was intended by design just to irk her.

Lulu was surprised and pleased to see Seb already at work in the office when she opened the door and peeked in. And Seb was surprised and pleased that his mother was talking to him.

"Seb," said Lulu sweetly, "I'm sorry we had words yesterday. I could hardly sleep last night for thinking about it. I know you're a grown man and you can see who you want. I guess I was just surprised and a little hurt that you didn't tell me that you were dating Lurleen."

Seb smiled back. "Well, I'm sorry that I jumped down your throat about it. I should've told you that I was dating her when we started seeing each other."

"And actually," said Lulu, smiling determinedly, "she's a much nicer girl than I thought. After all, her family is really lovely. Just lovely people. And she's such a pretty girl. I think I can hear wedding bells ringing already." Seb looked completely stunned. "And maybe some more grandbabies for me? You know how I love my grandbabies. Maybe a little boy or two . . . like you and Ben." With these words, carefully chosen to strike terror in Seb's heart, Lulu sailed out of the office, smiling as she left.

Seb worked in the office all morning, took a break for lunch, then came back and continued working. Lulu guessed he was trying to make absolutely sure he still had his job. He knew that his mother meant it when she said she'd fire him. Lulu was working hard, too, because the dining room was at full capacity for lunch. The local fire station's firemen had all come over for some ribs, and Lulu and Sara were serving them as fast as they could in case the firemen got called to leave.

Lulu noticed Ella Beth peeking over the back of a booth. "Mercy! Is it already two thirty? Where has the day gone?"

"School's been out for a while, Granny Lulu. Coco is still doing her homework out on the porch with B.B. and Elvis, but I finished early."

"Where does the time go?" Lulu sighed. She noticed Ella Beth had something in her hand. "Whatcha got there?"

"My camera," said Ella Beth airily. "You know how it helped me find out about Uncle Seb and Miss Ashton. You never know when a camera is going to come in handy when you're a detective."

Lulu got an idea. It had nothing to do with cameras, but since Ella Beth was just *dying* to do some detecting . . . "How about if I retain your services for a few minutes? A real detective gig. Do you think you could handle that?"

"For real?" Ella Beth's eyes shone behind her glasses. "Sure thing!"

"Okay," said Lulu. "Here's what I need you to do."

Seb was still pushing papers around on the desk in the office when Ella Beth joined him. "What's up, sweetie?" asked Seb absently. "You need to do some homework on the computer?"

"Nope. I got it already taken care of," said Ella Beth. "I thought I'd come in and talk to you for a minute, Uncle Seb."

Seb pushed his chair away from the desk and looked at

Ella Beth with surprise. Usually he wasn't the go-to guy for conversations with kids. "Sure. Anything on your mind?"

"Nothing too much, I guess. But some kids at school were kind of giving me a hard time about my name."

Seb frowned. "They were giving you a hard time over 'Ella Beth'? That's not a weird name."

"Well, I didn't think so either, but the kids have been calling me 'Smella Beth.'"

"What kind of kids *are* these that you're going to school with?" Seb rolled his eyes. "There's nothing at all wrong with your name, honey, so don't worry about it."

"That's what Granny Lulu was telling me. She said that you had some trouble in school with your name, too. That's what I wanted to talk to you about." Ella Beth pushed her glasses up on her nose and looked seriously at Seb.

"I sure did. That's why I go by Seb and not Sebastian. The kids at school thought it was the weirdest name ever. Lots of kids had even weirder names, though."

"Like who, Uncle Seb?"

"Well, there was a boy named Poppy and a girl named Pickle, for instance."

Lulu busily came into the office with a pile of papers and started shuffling them around in a corner of the room.

"Pickle? Really?" asked Ella Beth innocently.

"Yep. Now *that's* a funny name. Not like Ella Beth."

Lulu turned around from her paper pushing. "Whatever happened to Pickle, Seb? I'm sure you probably know, since you're dating her sister. Is she here in town?"

"Lord, Mama, Pickle joined the Peace Corps. She's off in some remote Tanzanian village showing farmers how to increase their crop production or something. I don't think she's ever coming back to join us mere mortals again."

"That does surprise me," said Lulu. "Pickle didn't strike me as the volunteering type."

"No, she was always in some sort of a jam. I guess at some point she must've gotten her act together."

"So is she coming here for a visit anytime soon?"

Seb snorted. "No way. She and Lurleen aren't even talking to each other. Lurleen thought she was a nut to go over to Africa, so she gave her a real hard time over it. And their parents are dead. Besides, Memphis and Tanzania aren't exactly close to each other on the map."

"Poor Lurleen and Pickle. Losing both parents like that," said Lulu absently.

Her thoughts were interrupted by Ben, who popped into the office from the kitchen. "Say, Seb, want to go hunting this weekend?"

Lurleen lied to Flo at the Peabody. She wasn't waiting for her sister at all. But why was she lying? Because she had just murdered Rebecca Adrian? Lulu was completely prepared to jump to that conclusion but knew the police wouldn't handle the information the same way. After all, Lurleen could have been lying because she was meeting a married man at the hotel and didn't want anyone to know about it. Besides, why would Lurleen kill Rebecca Adrian?

The dinnertime crowd was starting to come in. Lulu walked around and chatted with some of the customers. Then Big Ben, Morty, and Buddy sat down at their favorite booth. "We thought we'd eat a little earlier tonight," said Big Ben loudly. He turned up his hearing aid when Morty gestured to his ear. "All three of us had a really early start this morning."

"Went fishing?" asked Lulu.

"No, just the old age schedule. You know—get up at five o'clock. Eat breakfast. By the time two o'clock rolls around, it's time for supper, and you can go to a restaurant and get the early-bird special. Then it's time for bed at eight o'clock. You're not doing that yet?"

Lulu was old, but Buddy, Morty, and Big Ben had her beat by twenty years. "Not yet, but I'm sure it's coming. Early bird specials sure would be nice."

Lulu was on her way to the kitchen to see if they were getting backed up and needed help when Cherry tore inside, red curls bobbing around, and no helmet in sight. She spotted Lulu and pulled her off to an empty booth.

"Cherry, what's wrong?" asked Lulu. "And where's your helmet?" It must be something really bad for Cherry to be helmetless. "You didn't ride on your motorcycle like that?"

"Yes, indeed I did," said Cherry. "And thank God nobody stopped me. That would have been the last straw after the afternoon that I've had. Listen, we've got to find a place for Flo to sleep tonight. Have you got any ideas?"

Lulu's eyes widened. "What happened? Was it her ex-husband? He found her?"

"He certainly did. Right in the middle of a tour at Graceland."

Lulu gasped.

"We were doing our regular tour. Flo had her disguise on and everything. Graceland was really understanding about it all. We just love them there. Anyway, I guess either Virgil wanted to see Graceland himself as a tourist, or maybe he remembered how crazy Flo was about Elvis. Either way. . . . he ended up on a tour."

"Flo didn't see him in enough time to go hide?"

"She'd gone off to use the restroom and came back, and he was there waiting with the tour group. Well, he saw her right away, through the disguise and everything. And he went *wild*." Cherry looked shaken at the memory.

"What happened?"

"Oh, he grabbed her by the arm and twisted it around

her back and started yelling at her right in her face. Did she
think she could really get away from him? Did she think he
was stupid? That kind of stuff."

Lulu grimaced. "What about Flo?"

"She couldn't get away from him, not the way he was
holding her arm. But she was putting up a real fight, trying
to kick him and all. She's got plenty of spunk, you know.
And the rest of the Graces and I all jumped on him, yelling
and kicking. I don't know if we were so good at kicking on
target—I got some bumps and bruises myself. But then security stepped in, and *they* got his butt out of there. And no
refund for him, either." Cherry bobbed her head in angry
satisfaction.

"But he didn't find out where she lived or what her name
was, right?" Lulu asked anxiously.

"No, Graceland wasn't about to release any personal
information on their docents. Somebody in the office did
tell us that a man called in a little later, trying to ever so
politely ask for information on the black-haired docent. But
they'd have nothing to do with it."

"But you're still worried he might be able to find out
where she lives."

Cherry nodded. "I think it's only a matter of time. Now
he knows she volunteers at Graceland and eats at Aunt
Pat's. He knows the places where she spends her time. And
it's miserable for Flo to have to live like this and not do any
of the things she usually does. I hate the idea of her sleeping there by herself. At least if she's with one of us and he
finds her, then we can help her to beat him off or can call
the police or something."

"Good idea. She's welcome to stay with me, you know,"
said Lulu.

"She knew you'd offer, Lulu, and thought that was so
sweet. But Virgil already knows you spend time with Flo

because of Aunt Pat's. I think your house might be one of the places he'd look for her."

Lulu thought again. "How about Pickwick Lake? I'm sure Evelyn wouldn't mind—she doesn't even live there during the week at all."

Cherry snapped her fingers. "That sounds like just the thing! I'll give Evelyn a call and see if she'd mind."

"Will it be okay for Flo to be there? I mean, Evelyn won't be there entertaining her Jet Skiing friend, will she?"

"Oh, that relationship is *so* day before yesterday, Lulu," said Cherry with a dismissive wave of her hand. "The only problem with the Pickwick Lake setup is that I don't know how long this is going to go on."

"Surely Virgil has another life he's got to get back to in Mississippi," said Lulu. "He should have a job, if nothing else. He shouldn't be able to afford to go hunting for Flo forever."

"That's true. But maybe he has more money saved up than we think. If it looks like Flo needs to hide out for a while longer, we can always move her around from house to house."

"Sounds like the witness protection program." Lulu clucked. "The poor thing. I hope life starts looking up for her soon."

"Maybe," said Cherry in a hopeful voice, "he'll do something really bad and end up getting locked up. Nothing to *Flo* of course. But maybe he can commit some little felony or something while he's in town. At least then Flo would know where he was."

Lulu frowned. "What about Dammit?"

"Oh, Lordy, I forgot about Dammit. And I can't take him because Johnny is allergic to cats, he *says*."

"I could take him, Cherry. Flo's got to be worried about him. And if the cat doesn't warm to me, I can always have

Derrick come over and keep him company after school. Weird animals seem to like Derrick," said Lulu, picturing Babette's slavish devotion to him.

"By the way," said Lulu, "Derrick saw you at the Peabody the afternoon Rebecca was killed. I explained that you'd gone to see Tony and that was it. You weren't over at the Peabody murdering Rebecca."

Cherry hooted. "Darn right I didn't murder Rebecca! But I left my phone number with the reception desk at the Peabody for Tony. Just in case he got a little lonely." She heaved a sigh. "I guess that was right when all hell broke loose at the hotel." She flushed a little, looking at Lulu. "I wouldn't have actually done anything, Lulu. I do still love Johnny, slug though he is. But it would have been nice to have a drink with Tony and flirt a little and feel special again." She looked across the restaurant and brightened. "Hey, there's Pink Rogers! Maybe he could give us some advice about Flo."

The huge policeman had come in for his half-price plate of ribs, slaw, and red beans and rice. When Cherry motioned to him, he came right over.

"Hey, Pink." Cherry subconsciously flirted with every man who talked to her. "How are things going with the crime-fighting life?"

"Oh, I can't complain. I surely can't complain."

"We had a question for you. Flo is really being badgered right now by this guy . . . her ex-husband, you know." Cherry gave an exaggerated roll of her eyes.

Pink raised his eyebrows. "I didn't even know that Flo had ever been married!"

Lulu thought that there were a lot of things the policeman didn't know about Flo. And Flo would probably like to keep it that way.

"See, the thing is that she's terrified. And he's somehow found out she's here in town, and now he's canvassing the neighborhood looking for her. So she's been wearing a disguise, and now we have to find another place for her to stay until he stops looking for her . . ." Cherry trailed off, sighing melodramatically.

"That's a tough one, Cherry," said Pink thoughtfully. "Has he made any specific threats? Was there any bodily injury?"

"No, thank goodness. But not for lack of trying! He attacked Flo at Graceland," said Cherry. "But she was okay. I mean, he didn't break anything, and she didn't have to go to the hospital."

"Unfortunately, he has every right to be in the city as long as he's not breaking any laws. And Graceland is a public place, so he wasn't trespassing—although he did use violence there. If Flo wants to come in and file a restraining order, I'd definitely encourage her to go ahead and do that. Particularly since he's already tried to attack her once."

"Thanks, Pink. I'll let her know."

Lulu said, "By the way, Pink, how are things going on the case?" Pink made a face like he didn't want to really talk. "I mean, don't tell me anything you can't tell me, but I was just wondering."

"There are definitely things that we're trying to work on," said Pink. "It's not directly my case, you know, but I'm hearing a lot of talk about it. This is all unofficial, and you're not hearing it from me, understand."

Lulu nodded. "I simply can't think what Mildred would have known to get herself killed. I mean, you knew Mildred, Pink. She was just this little mousy thing."

Pink said, "She certainly was that, but then she got interested in stuff she shouldn't have stuck her nose into. As far as we could tell, she was researching a new book. That was a surprise to me since I didn't know they had murders in romance novels. I mean, I've seen her working on that same book since I was a young man, and I never knew her to be interested in murder before."

"This was a new book, Pink. She was done with her romance novel. Rebecca Adrian had made fun of it, you know, and I think it put a bad taste in Mildred's mouth. How did you know she was doing research? Were there notes?" asked Lulu.

"There were notebooks full of different notes," said Pink. "Some of them were a lot more helpful than others. As far as I could tell, she took notes on almost everything . . . weather, people who were nice, interesting names. But it only got helpful for us when we read all her thoughts about Rebecca Adrian's murder. She made notes of who she thought might be involved and why. And, of course, you know she was interviewing people and trying to find out more information that way."

Lulu nodded. "But—there wasn't any information on the killer?"

Pink looked around and said in a low voice, "I think there might have been. I'm pretty sure there was something in that notebook that her killer didn't want anyone else to find out about. Because those pages were ripped right out."

The more Lulu mulled it over, the more she became convinced that Lurleen was up to her neck in this
murder. And since Seb was apparently Lurleen's love slave,
she was willing to bet that he was somehow involved in
the mess.

If Lurleen had assigned Seb the task of hiding evidence, that meant that Lulu should go straight over to W.C.
Handy Park right down the street on Beale. If Seb, God
forbid, were in charge of concealing evidence, he would
most likely revert to his childhood hiding place. Ben and
Seb had spent so many summer days playing "buried treasure" there while blues bands played in the background . . .
and Lulu didn't think Seb was creative enough to think of
something different.

She stuck her head in the kitchen and told Ben she was
going for a walk. Then she headed out the door to the
park.

◇◇◇◇◇◇◇◇◇

The more Big Ben mulled it over, the more he became convinced. He should buy his own damned bottle of wine. He and Buddy clearly ascribed to different wine-drinking philosophies: to Big Ben, *every* day was a cause of celebration. He was eighty-six, after all.

He called the wine shop right off Beale to see if they had a bottle in stock.

Lulu parked the car and scanned the park. It had changed a lot in the years since Seb had been little, of course. Now the park had a stage for music venues, a concession stand to the side, and folks sitting on benches while kids ran up to the stage.

Was the tree still *there* even? There weren't so many trees in W.C. Handy Park, anyway. At first, Lulu wasn't sure she could remember where it was. She walked into the park a little ways, looking around her. More people were filing into the park around her, drawn by the crooning blues musician on the stage.

And then she saw it—just as gnarled as it ever had been, but still alive and thriving. Sure enough, there was the hollowed-out spot. Ben and Seb had had to climb up the tree to put things in it when they were kids, but Lulu was able to stand up on her toes and reach high over her head to feel inside it.

Lulu's fingers brushed against paper, and her heart sank. She carefully lifted out the papers and leaned against the tree for support. She saw the bench nearby was empty and quickly sat down so she could read.

Lulu recognized Mildred's prim handwriting and girlish, giggly schoolgirl observations, sprinkled with a liberal number of exclamation points. Her words were damning:

> *Today I really know for sure who killed Rebecca Adrian! This tells me that my instincts were right—*

I'm going to make a wonderful mystery writer! If I can solve crimes for real, it will be even easier to solve them on paper.

It's clear to me now that Seb and Lurleen have set their caps for each other! Really, they must be in love. He looks at her so tenderly that it sets my heart to beating! It's too bad, though—since he's mixed up in murder.

How did I figure this all out? It was easy! I heard Rebecca's cell phone ring, and then she got up from her table. She walked really, really close to where I was standing in the Peabody—but I wasn't ready for her to see me! I still wanted to give her my comeback but not with anybody else around—I'd had enough of big scenes in front of a crowd of people. Rebecca mentioned Seb's name when she was talking, so I knew she was talking to him.

I was still waiting for her to get off the phone, and I saw Lurleen Ashton come in. I thought that was really weird! Why would Lurleen be at the Peabody? But then I noticed her looking over to where Rebecca was and then hurrying in front of her table. Her back was facing me, but now I know she was shaking something into her drink! Of course, I didn't understand this at the time, but soon this would all be clear to me.

Rebecca finished her phone call and sat back at her table. She took a big gulp of her cocktail, then she made a face and stopped drinking it. Lurleen had gone off a ways and was sitting down, kind of watching from a distance. She wasn't close enough to hear, though. I went right up to Rebecca's table and gave my comeback—and didn't her face turn red! I was giddy, I was so happy.

So then I turned to walk out the door with my head held high. I saw Lurleen at the front desk, which I thought was weird. And then, when I left, I saw Flo's car there. Then I saw Seb's car. Why was everybody there? When I got in my car, I saw Lurleen hurry out and get in Seb's car. Ahhhhh, I thought! He looked at her so lovingly but she scarcely even looked at him—just seemed like she was fussing at him as he started up the car and left.

When I found out later that Rebecca was murdered, I wasn't too sorry. After all, she'd been a mean, hateful thing. But I was worried at first. Really worried. What if the police thought that I had done it? I didn't need to go to jail. It was too bad there had been that awful scene at Aunt Pat's. And what if someone had seen me at the Peabody? After a while, though, I decided the police really weren't going to arrest me. And I got a great idea—start writing mysteries. I was so excited to be a detective and solve my first case! And I knew who the suspects were, of course.

Lulu had tried to make me feel better by telling me that Rebecca Adrian was rude to everybody. That Tony was telling the Graces and Seb that you could be having a conversation with her and she'd spin around and walk off to take a phone call.

So Seb knew that. And I think he called Rebecca so that Lurleen could have a chance to poison her drink. Wait until I tell Detective Bryce! This will be great publicity for my book.

An icy voice from behind her said, "Seb, you fool. When I told you to destroy the journal, I meant for you to burn it or flush it or put it in the river. What the *hell* were you thinking to hide it at a public park?"

Lulu froze. Lurleen Ashton had a cold blankness in her eyes as she sat down next to her on the bench. The gun she poked into Lulu's leg was very, very real.

Seb quickly sat next to Lurleen on the bench. "Lurleen, what the hell? This is my mother."

"I know who she is," snapped Lurleen. "And don't play innocent with me. You don't want to be caught, either. Did you *enjoy* your time in jail? No? Then shut up while I figure out what I need to do."

Lulu cleared her throat to speak, since Seb didn't seem inclined to. "This was all a mistake wasn't it, Lurleen? I'm sure your mama didn't raise a killer. But you've always wanted to win, haven't you? I remembered the other day how you'd had a private coach so you could make the varsity squad. You just meant for Rebecca Adrian to get a little sick, right? Then she'd make a derogatory report on our restaurant and be a lot more receptive to the barbeque at Hog Heaven."

"Sure. We could use more business. Our barbeque is a ton better than Aunt Pat's, but you've been around for so long that nobody even thinks about the quality of the food anymore. All they're thinking is, 'Oh, we're hungry for barbeque. What's that place we always go to? Aunt Pat's.' But if there was some kind of food scare, like salmonella or something, then maybe they'd start looking for someplace else to go. And Hog Heaven is right there waiting for them to wake up."

"But something happened, didn't it? A kink in your plan."

"What happened is that I had no idea the woman had some kind of underlying health issue. I mean, God, look at her—she was in her twenties and looked strong as a horse." The thought that Rebecca had a weak immune system seemed to irritate Lurleen even more—like Rebecca was guilty of false advertising.

"And your darling Seb was going to be the one to go through with it. We had a plan for him to slip the poison into the food at Aunt Pat's. But for whatever reason, he chickened out at the last moment. Apparently, he's more into drugs and fraud than inflicting bodily harm."

Lurleen curled her lip at Seb's criminal shortcomings.

"So then you were forced to take matters into your own hands, right? Over at the Peabody."

"She'd left, but I figured there was still plenty of time to slip her something. After all, I didn't want her to *die*. The police were never supposed to be involved in this. She was only going to get really sick and think: 'Oh. Aunt Pat's barbeque must have done it.' Then we'd be in business."

"But nothing really went according to plan, did it?" asked Lulu. "You went in there and were able to mess with Rebecca's drink pretty easily. But then you saw Mildred there."

"No, I never did notice her. *She* saw *me* there, though."

"She made some kind of a comment to Cherry about pigs visiting pigs. I wondered if she'd meant the fuchsia pig you used for drawing customers over to Hog Heaven. I guess she wasn't a fan of yours. I know what she thought of Rebecca," said Lulu.

Lurleen made a face. "I didn't even know the woman. But I guess she was part of that rabid pack of Aunt Pat's fans who believe I commune with the devil under every full moon or something."

"And you also saw Flo there, right? At the front desk."

"Yes, she was there, planning to see Rebecca Adrian. I'd already slipped Rebecca the poison in her cocktail. She took a big chug of it before she could taste how bad it was. She looked like she had an upset stomach right away, so she headed right off to the elevator as soon as Mildred finished talking to her. I was getting out of there when I saw Flo coming in, and I had to make an excuse fast as to why I was there. So I acted like I was checking at the front desk to see if my sister was there. Then I left with Seb."

Seb looked surprised, then frowned. "Oh, I see. So that's

why you were suddenly so interested in Pickle, Mother. You were trying to catch Lurleen out in a lie."

"Great. Just great. So you fouled that up, too," said Lurleen. "No wonder your mother figured out I was involved."

Lurleen was getting more agitated, so Lulu cut into the conversation. "What happened with Mildred exactly?"

"Well," drawled Lurleen. "She was murdered."

Lulu tried hard not to let Lurleen's shocking lack of feeling rile her up. "Yes, but how did it come about? She set up one of her meetings with you, right?"

"She did. I guess she was trying to play detective, so she was ready to ask all kinds of questions about what I'd been doing at the Peabody. Apparently, she'd seen me leaning over Rebecca's drink, although my back was facing her, so she wasn't positive I'd put something in there or not. But no one else knew I was on the scene except for Flo, and she didn't even think twice about the explanation I'd given her."

"So you strangled Mildred," said Lulu with a shiver.

"I didn't *want* to," said Lurleen, rolling her eyes. "For heaven's sake, you'd think I was some sort of crazy killer. The whole Rebecca thing was an accident—basically a prank gone wrong. I didn't deserve to go to *jail* for something like that. But Mildred was one of those snoops who was determined to make trouble. She was acting like she was a detective, trying to solve the case. Nosy. I tried just to *warn* her off. I sent her that letter. But she was still interviewing suspects at her bookstore. Then she seemed convinced it was me. She was going to expose me, and I was going to end up in jail. I had to stop her. Just like I have to stop you," said Lurleen calmly.

Seb gave Lurleen a stony stare. Lulu was most disturbed by the way her son seemed to have already accepted that Lurleen was going to shoot and kill his mother and then dump her body somewhere. He was going to be seriously piqued over it, but that was his only reaction. "What was Seb's involvement in all this? How did it come about?"

Seb looked at his mother balefully. "Simple. I came back to Memphis, started dating Lurleen, and got mixed up in her crazy plan and cover up."

"Not *that* simple, Seb. Your drug addiction had a little something to do with it, too, you know. The fact that I have some connections that can keep you in your drug of choice for a while. Although I didn't realize how weak you were. I thought you would actually be able to slip out of the office and put a little something in the woman's food. After all, you wanted to get back at her for the blackmailing attempt just as much as I wanted to get her sick to get bad publicity for Aunt Pat's." Lurleen looked disgusted.

"It wasn't that easy for me," groaned Seb. "I told you that already. That's why I decided not to go into work that day. I told you on the phone that morning that I didn't want any part of it."

"Well, because you knew about the plan and everything, you're as guilty as I am, Seb. I hope you know that. You're an accessory. And you'll be named an accessory in the bookstore woman's death, too. You knew what the plan was ahead of time. You even took the kid's jacket so we could plant some evidence against him."

Lulu's heart skipped a beat. She had not wanted to believe that Seb would have anything to do with poor Mildred's death. "Tell me you didn't have anything to do with that."

Seb didn't say anything.

Lurleen said, "Your baby boy had plenty to do with it, and don't let him tell you otherwise. He knew that Mildred seen not only me at the Peabody, but Seb in the park-
. You see, after I found out that Seb had chickened
e restaurant, I asked him to go ahead and try again

at the Peabody. I figured it would be much easier for *him* to make an excuse to see Rebecca. After all, they'd dated each other. Or Seb could say something to her about the blackmailing again. But he chickened out of that, too."

Lulu said, "So when Derrick heard you talking on the phone in the parking lot, you were actually talking to Lurleen; telling her that you weren't going to go in. That you didn't care about the blackmailing."

"Which meant that I had to come over to the Peabody on some trumped up reason. Rebecca looked like she was in such a black mood that I don't think she ever even noticed that I was there. But I saw Flo there and had to give her an excuse, so it was just as well that I'd come prepared with a story. When I told Seb that I was going to try to sneak something into her drink, he said the cameraman had mentioned that she always wandered away to take her cell phone calls. Finally I got him to help me out. He called Rebecca from the parking lot so she'd leave the table for a minute."

"And Mildred saw both of you at the Peabody. Which wouldn't have been significant at all, except for the fact that Rebecca was murdered. So she wanted to talk to both of you."

"She wanted to talk to both of us. First Seb went, the day before Mildred died. He was trying to figure out what exactly she knew. That way, if it really wasn't anything important, we could let it slide. But he found out, by chatting the crazy thing up a little bit, that she knew about *me* being there. And she knew that I had been leaning over Rebecca's drink. So it was clear that we were going to have to take care of that. I didn't even know she was at the Peabody when I was there. Seb knew the plan, but he had the stupidity to go drink and drive right before we were going to go through with it. But he'd have been right there on the scene if he hadn't been at 201 Poplar."

Now Seb could no longer meet his mother's eyes.

"So I had to do the job myself. And then you came in, Lulu. You just couldn't stop nosing around, could you? I had to clock you. I looked around real quick to make sure I'd planted Derrick's jacket that Seb had gotten for me and that I hadn't left anything else behind. Then I got the hell out of there.

"And now," said Lurleen, "we've got you on our hands again. I've stopped believing that Seb can be any help at all to me. Obviously I'm going to have to take care of this myself."

Seb said in a quiet voice, "Lurleen, let Mother go. She's not going to tell anybody about this. Are you, Mama?"

"I absolutely am," said Lulu in a deadly serious voice. "As soon as I get away from you, I'm calling the police. I can't believe the two of you and all the misery you've caused. It's time for it to be over."

"Yes. It's time for it to be over—for you," said Lurleen. She pressed the gun into Lulu's leg. "Come on, let's get out of here. And don't make a sound or I'll shoot you right here in the park."

"You're going to have to shoot me in the park, then, Lurleen. I'm not going off to some remote location with you," said Lulu.

"Okay, have it your way. As long as nobody knows who I am, I can still get away with it. I'll get ready to run." Lurleen put on a huge pair of sunglasses as the sun shone down on her glossy black hair. Seb put his arm around Lurleen.

"Can't we talk about this honey? Just for a minute?"

Just then, a man shot out from the trees behind them. "Aaaaaaaahhhhhh!" he yelled as he tackled Lurleen and Seb at one time and whaled on them with both fists.

Seb and Lurleen were so taken by surprise that they were easily overcome by the attack. In the scuffle, Lurleen's gun went flying—a yard from Lulu's feet. Lulu scooped it up and pointed it, shaking, toward the three on the ground, not sure if her savior was as bad as the rest of them. There was screaming around them in the park and the music stopped playing.

An angel, reflected Lulu later, in the form of Big Ben had appeared suddenly on the scene. He'd decided that he was a grown man and could get his very own bottle of Domaine Vincent Dauvissat Chablis Les Preuses. He was just picking it up from the wine store off Beale when he saw Lulu holding a gun on three people. He drew in his breath, dropped the bottle to the ground, and started a stiff, arthritic run to the policeman he'd passed in the street seconds before.

Chapter

19

The sweet tea was very refreshing. But Lulu had the feeling she was soon going to need something completely different: and alcohol based.

Detective Bryce had, by now, gotten every little bit of information that she knew out of her. Lulu could tell he wasn't too pleased. He kept pressing his lips together when she mentioned piecing the clues together. Well, at least he should be happy she solved his case for him. Lulu only wished she had something to celebrate herself. Despite having grown apart from her son, Seb was still her baby. And the fact he would surely be on his way to prison felt like a knife stabbing her right in the heart. She'd already called Jed, their lawyer. She felt it was the least she could do, considering she blamed herself somehow for Seb's fall into crime.

She wearily said, "Are we about done, Detective Bryce? I feel really weary and still need to thank my hero, Big Ben, for calling the police. I don't know how long I'd have been able to hold that gun on those three, and things at the park were getting crazy. They might have jumped me to take it back, or I might have accidentally fired off a shot and hurt them or an innocent bystander. Or one of the people at the blues concert might have decided that *I* was the dangerous one and wrestled the gun away from me while Lurleen went free."

Detective Bryce said gently, "I have full confidence that you would have been able to do anything necessary to get safely out of the situation. And you would have been well within your rights."

He stood up to leave. "You know, though, the identity of the real hero is complicated. I think most people would think it was Virgil. After all, he's the one who knocked the gun out of Lurleen Ashton's hands. He's the one who stopped you from being moved from one location to another. Maybe he's the hero."

Lulu looked at him with surprise. "Well, I didn't think of that. He's an antihero, isn't he? It was just a series of fortunate events for me. Or maybe, it was my guardian angel looking out for me. What are the chances that Virgil would be convinced that dark-haired Lurleen Ashton was Flo in a wig? What are the chances that he'd even be passing the park at that time?"

"I believe he knew that you and Flo spent time together, so maybe when Virgil saw *you*, he decided you must be with Flo. And Lurleen's hair is so black it's almost unnatural. Plus, her sunglasses apparently matched Flo's, too."

"And," mulled Lulu, "when he saw Flo in the presence of a nice-looking man who was putting his arm around her, he went absolutely wild. Thank goodness."

There was a soft rap on the office door, and Detective Bryce left through the door past Big Ben, who smiled in at Lulu. "Are you okay?" he asked (softly, since he'd turned up his hearing aid).

"Thanks to you I am," said Lulu, giving him a big hug.

"I simply can't thank you enough. You sure were at the right place at the right time."

"You were already taking care of yourself pretty well when I got there," said Big Ben, as he took a seat in the office. "You looked like Annie Oakley standing there."

"Yes, but if they'd jumped on me to take the gun away, I wouldn't have shot them," said Lulu. "It's just not something I could have done. So grabbing that policeman made all the difference in the world."

There was a deep, harrumphing cough behind them, and they turned to see Buddy and Morty at the office door. "Mind if we come in?" asked Buddy.

"We were so glad to hear you were okay," said Morty, giving Lulu a tight hug.

"When we heard the story from Big Ben, we couldn't believe it," said Buddy. "And we are so sorry about Seb. We know you've got to be sick over it, Lulu."

Lulu sighed. "I really am. But I'm coming around to the way of thinking that Seb was an adult who made his own choices, bad and good. He clearly is in no shape to be out in society right now. I'd like to think that deep down, Seb *is* a good man who made some awful decisions because of drugs. Maybe this will be a wake-up call for him. Or maybe he can get the help he really needs there."

Buddy lifted up an arm to show he carried a canvas tote bag. He said hesitantly, "I thought it might be best, Lulu, if we could somehow focus on some of the good things about today. I knew what a blow Seb's arrest is for you. So I started thinking about some of the good things that happened today."

Lulu smiled. "I'm liking the way you think, Buddy. I'll start and make mine about Seb. He's still young enough to turn his life around. And Jed says the charges won't be as severe as Lurleen's, since he was an accessory after the fact, or something."

Morty said, "And that wicked Virgil is off the streets and won't be bothering Flo anymore. They've locked him up good."

Lulu brightened. "That's true. And Detective Bryce said that he was wanted in Mississippi for a whole slew of things. It sounds like he's going to be in the slammer for quite a while."

Big Ben chimed in. "And everybody can breathe easier now that they're not under suspicion of murder anymore."

"And the murders have been avenged," said Lulu. "And"—she got up to hug Big Ben again—"my dear friend, with his quick thinking, averted a major crisis at the park, possibly saving my life or others' lives."

Buddy put a tote bag on the desk. He said, "Keeping these good things in mind, and, considering the need for a little something alcoholic under such circumstances, I hope my friends will join me in a drink."

Big Ben said in a breathless voice, "Is that what I think it is?"

"If you're thinking it's the Domaine Vincent Dauvissat Chablis Les Preuses, then you're right. Because," added Buddy, "it's not every day that I get to celebrate one friend saving the life of another."

He reached into the tote bag again and pulled out another bottle of the same label. "This one is for you, Big Ben. Your allowing that bottle of wine to bust on the asphalt to run to take care of Lulu kind of put it all into perspective for me."

Buddy uncorked one of the bottles and poured them all a glass. Lulu closed her eyes a moment as the soothing warmth of the delicious beverage coursed through her. Then she said, "Know what would make this moment even better? A big plate of lip-smacking barbeque."

Recipes
Put Some South in Your Mouth

Lulu's Famous Red Beans and Rice

This red beans and rice recipe is an homage to the dish I tasted in Memphis—the Louisiana-style Creole version is very different and would omit the tomatoes.

3 15- or 16-ounce cans kidney beans, drained and rinsed
2 14½-ounce cans low-salt chicken broth
1 14½-ounce can diced tomatoes in juice
1 pound smoked beef sausage, fully cooked and diced
2 cups sliced mushrooms
1½ cups white and wild rice blend (not the quick-cooking kind)
1 cup chopped onion
1 cup chopped green bell pepper
½ cup sliced jalapenos from jar, drained and chopped
¼ cup steak sauce
2 tablespoons Worcestershire sauce
3 garlic cloves, chopped

Dash of Tabasco
Salt and pepper to taste

Mix all ingredients in heavy large pot. Bring to simmer over high heat.

Reduce heat to medium-low, cover, and simmer until rice is tender, stirring occasionally, about 35 minutes. Season to taste with salt and pepper.

◇◇◇◇◇◇◇◇◇◇

Tommie's Southern Potato Salad

3 pounds red potatoes
4 hard-boiled eggs, finely chopped
½ cup mayonnaise
¾ cup sour cream
2 tablespoons chopped onion
2 tablespoons sweet pickle relish
1 tablespoon prepared mustard
1 teaspoon salt
½ teaspoon pepper
½ pound bacon, cooked and crumbled

Boil potatoes until soft. Cut into cubes.

Sir potatoes and eggs together.

Stir all other ingredients together if serving immediately. If chilling before serving, sprinkle bacon on last.

◇◇◇◇◇◇◇◇◇◇

Tommie's Breakfast Casserole

1 16-ounce package of hash browns (thawed if they are
   frozen)
8 eggs
2 cups milk
3 cups shredded cheddar cheese
¼ cup diced onion
1 pound bacon, cooked and crumbled
¼ cup diced green bell pepper

Preheat oven to 400 degrees. Spray a 7-x-11-inch casserole dish.

Line the bottom of the dish with the hash browns and bake them for 15 minutes until the edges brown slightly.

While the hash browns are cooking, beat the eggs and milk together in a big bowl. Mix in your cheese, onion, cooked bacon, and green pepper. Pour the egg mixture on top of the cooked hash browns.

Reduce oven heat to 350 degrees. Bake uncovered for 35 minutes, then cover with foil and cook another 10 minutes.

If you refrigerate the mixture first, your cooking time will be significantly increased.

◇◇◇◇◇◇◇◇◇

Pulled Pork Barbeque and Sauce

DRY RUB FOR THE PORK:

3 tablespoons paprika
1 tablespoon garlic powder
1 tablespoon brown sugar
1 tablespoon dry mustard
1 tablespoon salt
1 (5- to 7-pound) pork roast, preferably shoulder or
    Boston butt

Mix all the ingredients (except the pork) in a bowl and rub the mixture on the pork. Refrigerate for an hour or overnight.

Preheat the oven to 300 degrees. Roast the pork in a roasting pan for 6 hours (until it's 170 degrees Fahrenheit), or until it falls apart.

When the pork is cooked, remove it from the oven and let it cool for 10 minutes. While it's still warm, pull the pork with a fork. Serve on hamburger buns with sauce.

AND NOW FOR THE SAUCE:

2 cups ketchup
2 cups tomato sauce
1¼ cups brown sugar
1¼ cups red wine vinegar
½ cup unsulfured molasses
4 teaspoons hickory-flavored liquid smoke
2 tablespoons garlic powder
½ teaspoon butter
½ teaspoon chili powder
¼ teaspoon onion powder

1 teaspoon paprika
¼ teaspoon ground cinnamon
½ teaspoon cayenne pepper
1 teaspoon salt
1 teaspoon coarsely ground black pepper

Over medium heat, mix the ingredients in a large saucepan until it bubbles.

Reduce heat to low and simmer for up to 20 minutes.

◇◇◇◇◇◇◇◇◇

Aunt Pat's Spicy Corn Muffins

2 eggs
⅓ cup shortening, melted
1 cup self-rising cornmeal
1 cup sour cream (not low fat)
1 8-ounce can creamed corn
¾ cup picante sauce
1 tablespoon finely chopped jalapeno
1 cup grated extra-sharp cheddar

Preheat oven to 400 degrees.

Grease a 12-cup muffin pan.

Beat the eggs into the melted shortening (after it has cooled somewhat)

Stir cornmeal into egg-shortening mixture. Add sour cream, creamed corn, picante sauce, and jalapeno. Beat well.

Spoon half the batter into muffin cups. Sprinkle with cheese. Cover with remaining batter.

Bake for 30 minutes or until done.

Buddy's Country-Fried Steaks

    1 cup flour
    1 teaspoon salt
    1 teaspoon pepper
    ½ teaspoon garlic powder
    1 package of cube steaks
    Cooking oil
    1 diced onion
    1 cup water

Mix together dry ingredients and put them in a plastic zip bag. Put cube steaks in the bag and shake until they are well covered.

Heat oil in a heavy pan until hot (about 2 minutes). Add the cubed steak and fry over medium-high heat for half a minute, then flip to cook for another half minute. Continue cooking and flipping frequently until the meat is brown and the inside isn't pink (about 4 minutes.)

Remove steak from heat and drain on paper towels. Leave 3 teaspoons of grease in the pan, then add onions and 5 tablespoons of the leftover flour mixture from the plastic zip bag. Cook over medium heat, stirring constantly as the flour browns and the onions cook.

Add one cup of cool water, whisking gravy until all the lumps are gone. Add more water if you want a thinner consistency.

Add the steaks to soak in the gravy, simmering for 10 minutes.

◇◇◇◇◇◇◇◇◇◇

Lulu's Early Morning Gingerbread Treat

½ cup granulated sugar
¼ cup softened butter
½ cup orange juice
⅓ cup molasses
1 egg and 1 egg white
1½ cups all-purpose flour
2 teaspoons ground ginger
½ teaspoon baking powder
½ teaspoon baking soda
½ teaspoon ground cinnamon
¼ teaspoon salt
¼ teaspoon ground nutmeg
1 teaspoon powdered sugar

Beat sugar and butter at medium speed until well blended. Add juice, molasses, and eggs. Beat well and set aside. Lightly spoon flour into dry measuring cup. Level with knife. Combine flour, ginger, baking powder, baking soda, cinnamon, salt, and nutmeg in a small bowl. Gradually add flour mixture to molasses mixture, stirring until well blended. Pour batter into an 8-inch square pan coated with cooking spray. Bake at 350 degrees for 30 minutes or until a wooden pick inserted in the center comes out clean. Cool gingerbread in pan on a wire rack. Sift powdered sugar over cooled gingerbread.

**THE FIRST IN THE NATIONAL BESTSELLING
CANDY HOLLIDAY MURDER MYSTERIES**

TOWN IN A

Blueberry Jam

B. B. HAYWOOD

In the seaside village of Cape Willington, Maine, Candy Holliday has an idyllic life tending to the Blueberry Acres farm she runs with her father. But when an aging playboy and the newly crowned Blueberry Queen are killed, Candy investigates to clear the name of a local handyman. And as she sorts through the town's juicy secrets, things start to get sticky indeed . . .

penguin.com

M772T0910